WITCHING FOR GRACE

PREMONITION POINTE, BOOK 1

DEANNA CHASE

ABOUT THIS BOOK

Welcome to Premonition Pointe, where witches take care of their own.

Grace Valentine had the perfect marriage and a great career managing her husband's real estate office. Or so she thought until three months ago when she was served with divorce papers. Thanks to her philandering ex, not only is she out of a husband, she's out of a job, too.

At the age of forty-five with the help of her coven, Grace is ready to pick up the pieces and move on. But her only job prospect is at the rival real estate office, and it's only for a trial run. She'll need to prove that she can sell the haunted properties of Premonition Pointe before she's hired permanently.

But who has time to deal with haunted houses when she's testing out every anti-perspirant on the market to combat her escalating hot flashes, trying not to succumb to the advances of the hot thirty-four-year-old in her office, and ignoring the urges to hex her ex with erectile disfunction? Okay, maybe she doesn't ignore the urges. She might be a witch, but she's only human. Can Grace prove to herself and her new boss she has the magical touch to sell the impossible and find the courage get her groove back... even if her new love interest is a decade younger?

CHAPTER ONE

"$\mathcal{E}$rectile dysfunction!" Joy exclaimed as she stood and raised her wine glass toward the churning ocean. Her long blond hair flowed out behind her, lifting gently on the breeze as if she were in some sort of shampoo commercial. "That's it. That's the curse we're going to inflict on that no-good, two-timing jackhole."

Grace eyed her normally even-tempered friend. She loved this new diabolical side of her and forced herself to shake off the tiny stab of jealousy that tried and failed to creep in. Joy Lansing was youthful-looking with her tall, model-thin physique and luxurious golden locks. Even at the age of forty-eight, most people guessed her to be in her early thirties. Lucky bitch. Grace on the other hand, who was five feet seven, twenty-five pounds over her goal weight, and in desperate need of coloring her silver roots to match her auburn-dyed hair, was only forty-five and had recently been given the senior citizen discount at the local dry cleaners. When she'd scoffed, the cashier just shrugged and said there were advantages to aging gracefully. Grace had instantly made a note to schedule an appointment at the spa for every treatment available to de-hag her appearance. So far she hadn't gotten around to it.

"I don't think Grace needs the karma that would come along with that sort of hex," Hope said, brushing her black curls out of her dark eyes. She was the short one of the group but full of self-confidence, and she had an air about her that just made people listen when she spoke. It was part of why she was such a great event planner. Hope smirked at Joy and raised her wine glass in solidarity as she added, "But I like your style."

Grace eyed her two closest friends, taking in their windswept appearances and glinting eyes, and decided they were brilliant. She didn't need an ungrateful husband who'd already moved on to a woman half his age. Good luck to him when his new fiancée had no idea how to run his office. The place had to have erupted into chaos on her first day. Grace was sure of it, since she'd been the one running his office for the past twenty years. But he definitely deserved some sort of other retaliation for walking out on her three months ago and moving right in with her replacement.

He hadn't even been gone a week before he'd asked her to sign divorce papers. After getting the settlement she wanted, two weeks later, they'd both signed. Everything was done on their end, only now they were in the six month waiting period for the state to finalize things. She couldn't wait for the day her divorce certificate showed up in the mail so that she would finally be free of the bastard. Twenty years was a lot of wasted time on someone who just dumped her for the next best thing. She straightened her shoulders, determined to wreak some havoc on her ex, and said, "Nope. That's the curse we're doing. That... jackhole? Is that what you called him, Joy?"

"Yep. Jackhole. Douchecanoe. Poopstain. Take your pick." The tall, willowy blonde downed the rest of her wine before adding, "I hope his girlfriend gives him genital warts. That would serve him right."

"Poopstain?" Grace choked out a laugh, wondering just how much wine Joy had sucked down. Normally her friend was the stoic voice of reason. Of the three of them, she was the only one with children and often played the role of den mother of their little coven. "Genital warts? Who are you right now?"

"It's been a rough week, okay?" Joy poured another glass of wine, filling it almost to the rim, and sat next to Grace. "Hunter got into a fender bender, Britt started dating that biker guy from Hollow Hills, and I walked in on Kyle when he was... uh, having a private moment while watching free porn on the internet. And you know where Paul was for all of this?"

Grace shook her head, but she'd already guessed that Paul had been at work, too busy to help Joy deal with anything on the home front.

"At the office... pretending he's important?" Hope asked as if the answer would ever be anything different. She sat cross-legged in front of them on the grassy cliff and wrapped a shawl around her curvy frame.

Grace snorted at Hope's question. Hope Anderson was always the one to tell it like is. But she was also never short on optimism, while being the fiercest and most loyal person alive. It sometimes amazed Grace that Hope had never gotten married or had children. Not because Grace thought there was anything wrong with that choice. In fact, in light of

Grace's impending divorce, she was starting to think she should've followed in Hope's footsteps. No, she was amazed because when Hope loved someone, she stuck. She was even godmother to the children of two of her former boyfriends.

Joy sighed and rubbed her temple with two fingers. "Of course he was at the office. And it's not even tax season. If it wasn't for his fear of STDs, I'd suspect he was having an affair."

Grace bit down on her tongue. Hard. Three months ago, she'd have sworn her husband wasn't having an affair either. There hadn't been one sign. Not even a slowdown in their love life. They'd been making love once a week, just like clockwork, on Tuesdays after a night out for dinner at their favorite sushi restaurant. She hadn't even minded that the variety was gone or that Bill often had trouble keeping it up unless she was giving him a blow job. He'd always taken care of her needs, and that was enough, right?

No. Not right.

It turned out that he'd had trouble keeping it up because he was dipping his pecker in the office blonde. Grace let out a low growl as an image of the perky younger woman flashed in her mind. She sneered and wished them both an acute case of the genital warts Joy had mentioned. Her hand tightened around the wine glass as she jerked it back up to her lips.

"Um, Grace?" Joy said, lightly placing her hand on Grace's arm. "You might not want to drink that."

Grace froze and eyed the glass. She blinked and then frowned at the now putrid-smelling green liquid. "What the hell?"

"Looks like you turned your wine into some sort of

potion." Joy eyed the liquid. "A really nasty one. What the heck were you thinking about?"

"Ohmigod!" Grace jumped up and ran over to the edge of the cliff and flung the putrid potion into the ocean. The saltwater would neutralize it.

"That bad, huh?" Hope asked from right behind her, laughing.

"STD bad," Grace confirmed. She closed her eyes and sucked in a deep breath. "Genital warts."

"Holy shit, Grace." Joy snorted. "It's a damned good thing I stopped you."

An entire body shudder shook Grace to the core. "Good goddess. I can't believe I just did that."

"I can." Joy swept her long hair out of her eyes and smiled gently at Grace. "You've been hurt. Wounded and—"

"Joy," Grace said with a heavy sigh. She didn't want to think about how devastated she'd been for the first few weeks after her husband replaced her. It had been a dark time, and she was just now starting to feel like she was ready to move on. "Do we need to do this now?"

"Yes," Joy said, her eyes glinting in the moonlight. "It's time to reclaim your self-confidence."

"I have self-confidence," Grace insisted, looking around for the bottle of wine. If she'd ever needed another drink, now was the time.

"Of course, you do. That's why I said reclaim it. Now is the time to acknowledge what happened and what you went through so you can completely let it go." She produced the wine bottle she'd apparently been holding behind her back. "Hope and I are your witnesses."

"Exactly." Hope stepped up to form a small three-person

circle and held out a box wrapped in silver paper. "These are for you and your interview tomorrow."

"What? You didn't have to get me anything." Grace stared at the box and felt her heart swell. Who needed a no-good husband when she had friends like Hope and Joy?

"We didn't have to, but we wanted to. It's just a little something for your interview tomorrow." Hope took the bottle of wine from Grace and placed it and the box in the middle of their circle. "Now, repeat after me."

Grace snorted. "We're doing a ritual without candles?"

"I have candles," Joy said, flicking her wrist and pointing at the shoulder bag she'd left on the ground. Three large white pillar candles slipped out of the canvas and floated through the air until they stopped right in the middle of their small circle. With another flick of her wrist, the candles came to life, their flames flickering in the wind.

"Well, you two did come prepared," Grace said.

"Of course we did." Hope raised her hands toward the sky and again said, "Repeat after me."

Smiling, Grace joined her friends and raised her hands toward the night sky.

Hope nodded to Grace and said, "I, Grace Valentine, am a new woman."

Without hesitation, Grace repeated the words.

"Tonight, I shed any remaining ties to that bastard Bill Munch and invite love, opportunity, and adventure into my life."

"Love?" Grace narrowed her eyes at Hope. "I don't think so. Been there. Done that. Got the divorce to prove it."

"Yes, love," Hope insisted, staring Grace in the eye. "This is about moving forward and not letting that jackass affect your future, whatever that may be."

"I'm not dating again," Grace said, lowering her arms. She was deadly serious as she added, "I'm done with men."

"Fine." Hope smiled serenely at her. "Perhaps a sexy woman will pop up and buy you a drink then."

Joy laughed, and the sound was ethereal in the wind.

"You think you're being funny, but at this point, if she were fun and attractive, then why not?" Grace grinned, though she didn't really mean it. She'd never been attracted to women, but she often thought her life would've been easier if she had been.

"Why not indeed?" Hope asked, grinning at her. "Did I tell you about the blind date I had last week?"

"What?" Joy dropped her arms and rounded on her. "You were holding out on us."

"Not intentionally." Hope chuckled. "It just slipped my mind. Imagine me, sitting at Claire's nursing a margarita, when Chris walks in, orders me another, and places her hand on my knee."

"*Her* hand?" Grace asked.

"Yes. Her." Hope nodded. "Macey, the caterer I've been recommending to my clients lately, set us up. She just assumed I was a lesbian because I'm over forty and have never been married." She rolled her eyes. "But let me tell you… if I did play for the other team, I'd probably still be in bed with Chris. Not only is she smart, she's hot as hell. I mean, talk about the full package. So, Grace, if you do decide to give it a go, I'll set you up."

"Nah. I'm good, but we should set her up with my neighbor Kristen. Her ex blew out of town a couple of months ago, and she deserves some fun."

"We'll do that. Now, back to this ritual." Hope raised her hands again and nodded for Grace and Joy to join her.

"Repeat the words, Grace. Tonight, I shed any remaining ties to that bastard Bill Munch and invite love, opportunity, and adventure into my life."

Grace considered arguing again but knew she'd never win that fight. Hope and Joy just wanted the best for her, and she knew that. After sucking in a deep breath, she echoed Hope's words, putting some of her magic behind them as they faded into the night.

The candles burned brighter, and the flames shot up into the air just before they disappeared, leaving the three witches bathed only in moonlight.

"Well?" Hope asked. "Did it work?"

Grace straightened her shoulders and shifted her gaze to the sky. A lightness filtered through her as if an invisible weight had been lifted off her, and a small smile played at her lips before she grinned at her friends. "You know, I think it did. I feel... weightless and free in a way I haven't in years."

"Perfect." Joy kneeled down and grabbed the box. "Here. Open it."

"You guys really didn't need to get me anything," she said as she lifted the lid off the box. "Hanging out with you, performing rituals and—" She let out a gasp as she stared down at the gorgeous blue high heels with the stunning gold accents. Grace ran a light finger over one of the shoes and chuckled when a ripple of magic sparked over her skin. "They're spelled?"

Joy nodded, looking pleased with herself. "It's just a little self-confidence spell. Wear these tomorrow for your interview. The spell can't hurt, and at the very least you'll be the most fashionable real estate agent Kevin Landers has ever laid eyes on."

"These are too much," Grace said, unable to tear her eyes

away from the shoes she'd been drooling over since she'd spotted them in Miss Kelly's shop window three months ago.

"Nope. Not too much," Joy insisted.

"She's right," Hope added. "And don't even think about refusing them. We won't take no for an answer."

Grace glanced at her two friends, one tall and willowy, the other shorter and full of fire. Grinning, she shook her head. "No way I'm refusing them. These babies were meant to adorn my feet." After quickly shucking her ballet flats, she shoved her feet into the most comfortable heels she'd ever encountered and then flung her arms around her two friends. "I love you both, you know that?"

They both hugged her back. Joy kissed her on the cheek while Hope whispered in her ear, "Of course we do. Now, you walk into that office tomorrow and make Kevin believe he can't go another day without hiring you."

"Count on it," Grace said, squeezing her eyes shut and praying she landed the job at Landers Realty. "If not... well, I might as well embroider my name on an apron, because the only other place hiring is the local diner."

Hope cackled. "You can't be a waitress. You'd dump a milkshake on the first person who ordered one."

Joy laughed too and shook her head. "Or she'd take a bite out of the sundae before serving it. You know how she can't resist chocolate fudge."

"Okay, enough," Grace ordered, but she couldn't help laughing. They were right. She'd be a terrible waitress. But there was one thing she'd been doing for twenty years, and that was selling houses while her soon-to-be ex-husband took all the credit. There was nothing she wanted more than to be hired at the competing firm so she could outsell his cheating ass. She'd already gotten her license, now she just needed contacts. And since all of hers technically belonged to her ex's real estate office, they were off limits. "I'm obviously not going to be a waitress. I just need to convince Kevin Landers to hire me."

"That won't be a problem," Hope said with finality as if it were already a done deal.

But Grace knew better. Kevin Landers wasn't exactly her biggest fan after she'd helped her husband out negotiate him and his clients for years. "I doubt it will be easy to convince him," she said. "But I'll get there. Because if there's one thing I know how to do, it's selling houses."

"Here, here!" her friends chanted, producing their wine glasses and raising them in the air. "To Grace and her new job at Landers Realty."

Grace clinked her glass to theirs, glanced at her shimmering shoes, and then downed her wine. The world seemed to slow for just a moment before suddenly, a sense of calm washed over her and she knew deep in her bones that everything was going to turn out exactly how it should.

CHAPTER TWO

Grace slipped out of her front door and walked the half mile to the short path that led to the bluff overlooking the ocean. The wind was calm for once, and the sun was just peeking over the horizon, turning the sky a mix of pale orange and purple. She wrapped her sweater tighter around her body and quickened her pace.

Once she exited the high grass of the pathway, she noted the remnants of their coven meeting off to the left. Damn. She must've had more wine than she'd thought since she never left debris behind. That was sacrilege. But she ignored the litter for the moment and stepped right up to the edge of the cliff.

It was at that spot, at the edge of the Pacific Ocean with the waves crashing on the rocks below, that she felt most at peace. It was where she often went to center herself at the start of the day ahead. And today was important. She needed to be ready for her job interview. If she didn't land the position at Landers Realty, she was going to either need to start an agency herself—which was more risk than she was willing to take—or commute inland to the valley an hour each way to work every day. She had a friend who'd already offered her a position if she didn't get hired in Premonition Pointe.

"Please, Eos, goddess of the dawn," Grace whispered into the morning air, "send me your strength and your blessings for these new beginnings."

A slight breeze kicked up, ruffling her long locks and forcing gooseflesh to appear on her arms.

Grace smiled. "You heard me."

The wind stilled and the morning took on a slightly eerie silence, despite the waves still churning below. The first time she'd experienced the phenomenon, she'd been a little freaked out. The sound of the waves shouldn't just disappear. They were still battering the rocks. But she'd learned this magical time happened every morning. It was what calmed her, helped her focus, and fueled her for her day ahead.

Grace raised her arms out to the sides, took in a deep breath, tasting the sea salt on her tongue, and felt all the tension drain from her body. This was her happy place. The small beachside town in Northern California, populated with a high density of witches like her, had become her home over twenty years ago. It was where she wanted to live and work for the rest of her life. And she'd be damned if she'd let Bill ruin it for her.

He's waiting for you.

The words seemed to float in from the sea, barely a whisper.

"What?" Grace asked the universe as she frowned. "Who's waiting for me?"

New possibilities await you. Open your heart and your mind. He's waiting.

Grace sucked in a sharp breath. The words had been stronger that time, making her squint out at the ocean as if she might see whoever it was that had spoken. That was absurd. Of course she wouldn't see anyone.

The words weren't from Eos or any other goddess. They were from the magical energy that churned within the very heart of her adopted town—Premonition Pointe.

She'd heard of the "voice of Premonition Pointe" before. But it was the first time she'd ever heard it speak to her. Miss Francie, the town baker, heard the voice after her husband of forty years passed. And Penelope heard it after her husband ran off with a woman thirty years younger than her four years ago. Of course, not everyone had lost a husband. Some had illnesses to overcome. Others were just at a crossroads in their lives regarding their careers or relationships.

Grace had come to think of the voice as a guiding oracle of sorts. What had it told her? *He's waiting. Open your heart and mind. New possibilities await.*

Sure, she thought. New possibilities sounded right up her alley. The only question was who exactly was waiting for her? Kevin Landers? She doubted it. In fact, she was certain he'd be happier if she ditched her appointment with him. But no way. It was too important to her.

Grace was determined to be open to new possibilities... whatever they were.

With her head held high, she turned, walked across the bluff, cleaned up the debris left from the night before, and hurried back to her cottage. She had an interview she needed to crush.

GRACE STRODE into Landers Realty with her head held high and exuding confidence. Selling real estate was practically in her DNA at that point in her life. Doing the job wouldn't be an issue. She just had to convince Kevin that he needed her.

"Good morning," a waif of a woman, who couldn't have been older than twenty-one, said pleasantly. "How can we help you with your real estate needs?"

Real estate needs? Grace almost smirked at the overly formal greeting but kept herself in check. She needed this job, and she wasn't going to score any points by suggesting a more personal welcome. Peering briefly at the nameplate on the desk, Grace said, "Hi, Nina. I'm here to meet with Mr. Landers. Can you tell him Grace Valentine is here?"

"Oh, right. Grace," the dark-haired woman said, her pleasant facade shifting quickly to something close to contempt as she stood on her slim six-inch heels. "I'll see if Mr. Landers is free."

"Thank you," Grace said, giving Nina a wide smile. She was going to kill them all with kindness even if it did make her want to vomit. Moving over to the window, Grace stared at her reflection. She'd pulled her hair up into an elegant bun in an effort to hide her silver roots, but that had been wishful thinking. Nothing short of a scarf was going to hide her neglected dye job. Otherwise, she thought she cleaned up relatively nicely. Smiling to herself, she took in her black ankle-length trousers and the romantic blue blouse that matched the fabulous shoes her friends had given her the night before, and decided her outfit and shoes made her look better than she had in weeks.

When footsteps sounded behind her, she turned, feeling as if she could take on the world.

"Grace Valentine," a vaguely familiar and incredibly

handsome man said, giving her a warm smile as he held his hand out. "It's nice to see you again."

Grace felt a flutter in her gut as she took his hand automatically. The man had to be at least ten years younger than her, but there was no denying he was the most beautiful specimen she'd ever seen in real life. It was a miracle she wasn't drooling. "I'm sorry. I'm having trouble placing you. Where have we met before?"

He chuckled. "I was the agent for the buyer on the Friendly Drive property that has that devastating view of the ocean."

"Right." She'd shown that property just a few hours before Bill had dropped the bomb on her that their marriage was over. The beautiful man shaking her hand had been representing buyers from a town inland, and she was pretty sure that's where he was based, too. "Owen, was it?"

"That's right." His lips were curved into a sexy half smile as he swept his gaze over her, making no effort to hide the fact that he was checking her out.

Well, hell. That made her feel good, even if he was way too young for her. It felt awesome to be appreciated. She was warm with pleasure as she asked, "Are you here negotiating a deal?"

"Nope. I just moved to Premonition Pointe and started working here last week. Kevin liked that I have connections to buyers from the city. A lot of them want beach property."

What the actual hell? If Kevin just hired this guy, he certainly wasn't going to be in the market to hire Grace. Why did he even have her come in? To humiliate her? That was likely, but she damned well wasn't going to go down without a fight. She suppressed a frustrated groan and forced a tight smile. "That sounds like a good arrangement for both of you."

Owen's smile slipped, and his brow furrowed as he studied her. "Is everything all right, Grace? You seem—"

"Mr. Landers will see you now, Ms. Valentine," Nina said from behind them, cutting Owen off.

She whirled around. "Great. Thank you." With a polite nod to Owen, she followed the young woman back to Kevin Landers' oversized office.

"Grace," the older man who was built like a linebacker said, pushing himself to his feet. He wore a camel colored suit that was already wrinkled and… Was that a jelly stain on his light blue tie? He held out his hand. "It was good of you to come in."

She took his hand and shook it. "Thanks for meeting with me."

"Of course. Anything for the wife—ahem—woman behind Munch's operation." He smirked and waved to one of the plastic chairs in front of his desk.

As Grace took a seat, Nina bustled back into the office and placed a mug on Kevin's desk. She took a small step back and gazed adoringly up at her boss. "Is there anything else I can get for you, Mr. Landers?"

"Only if Ms. Valentine would like something to drink," he said, narrowing his eyes at his assistant.

"Oh. Yes. Ms. Valentine, can I get you anything? Coffee? Tea? Water? A donut?" She glanced at the open door and then snapped her fingers. "But you'd probably prefer a piece of fruit, right? We have bananas and apples for those who are trying to watch their weight."

Oh, no she didn't. Grace gave the child receptionist a glare that could melt steel and said, "No thank you, Norma. I'm fine."

"It's Nina," she said.

"Oh. Is it? My mistake." Grace smirked at her and then turned back to Kevin and raised one eyebrow. "I think your receptionist might need better training."

Kevin let out a bark of laughter and nodded to his assistant. "Shut the door on your way out, Nina."

"She's interesting," Grace said once the receptionist was gone.

"Nina thinks sucking up to the boss will get her a raise." He leaned back in his chair and crossed his arms over his chest as he eyed Grace.

"And being rude to a potential agent is sucking up to her boss?" Grace asked conversationally. The last thing she wanted was for Kevin Landers to think this situation was getting under her skin.

He shrugged. "She knows there's no love lost between me and your husband."

"Ex-husband," Grace corrected. "Whatever issues you have with Bill, I hope you realize that they don't have anything to do with me."

"But weren't you the brains behind the operation over there?" he asked, his expression unreadable.

He was trying to find a reason to not hire her. That much was clear. If she claimed she was instrumental in closing a majority of their sales over the years, he'd have every reason to hold a grudge against her. But if she didn't, then her experience wouldn't be enough to land her the job. Grace cleared her throat and leaned forward, staring Kevin Landers in the eye. "I am good at what I do. I know how to list and show a property so that it moves, and I know how to find buyers to match even the most challenging of properties. And I do it with integrity by creating trust between me and my clients."

"Integrity?" he asked, staring back at her. "Is that right? Is that why On Pointe Realty has been trying to poach my clients for the past ten years?"

Grace knew she'd need an answer for this question. Years ago, Bill and Kevin had gotten into it over a difficult whale of a client who'd fired Kevin and hired Bill. In the end, Grace had been the one to find him his perfect vacation home. Ever since, there'd been bad blood between the two of them with both of them trying to woo each other's clients. "I dealt with the contracts at On Pointe, Mr. Landers. Trust me when I say I have never knowingly signed a client when they were still under contract with another Realtor. Besides, that's not my style. After you work with me for a few weeks, you'll see exactly who had the integrity over at On Pointe."

Landers didn't say a word as he continued to eye her. Then suddenly he threw his head back and laughed.

Grace waited him out, wondering what she'd said that had him so amused.

After taking a long swig of his coffee, Kevin opened a side drawer and pulled out a folder. He set it in front of him and said, "I like how you called out your ex without actually spelling out what a douche he is. And because of that, I'm willing to give you a trial run."

"Really?" Excitement mixed with relief washed over Grace. "Thank you. I promise you won't be disappointed."

"I hope not." He passed her the folder. "Here are three properties that have proven to be tough sales. If you can move at least one of them in the next three months, I'll consider hiring you full time. If you move all three, the job is yours, no questions asked."

Grace knew the real estate market in the small coastal town of Premonition Pointe had been fairly robust. If a property hadn't moved, it was likely either overpriced or needed a lot of work.

No matter. Either way, she had confidence that she could convince the sellers to make the changes that would make them marketable. Before she even took a look at the properties in the folder, she said, "Sounds fair enough. I assume you're fine with me picking up new clients while I work on them?"

"As long as they're sold under the Landers Realty umbrella, then that's perfectly fine with me," he said, sitting back in his chair once more, looking way too self-satisfied. "See Nina about the agency agreement. Once it's filled out, feel free to get to work. I'm certain Mr. Saint will want a meeting as soon as possible."

"Good." She grabbed the folder and started to stride toward the door. But as soon as Mr. Saint registered in her mind, she froze and then groaned. "Mr. Saint?"

"Yes. He owns all three properties." His lips were curved into a nasty little smirk, telegraphing the fact that he fully expected her to fail.

And why wouldn't he? Mr. Saint owned three large homes that had been on and off the market for three years.

They were haunted.

CHAPTER THREE

*I*nstead of heading to her car, Grace made a beeline for the independently owned café a few doors down from the real estate office. She'd been too nervous to really eat much before the interview, and suddenly she desperately needed a slice of coffee cake and a latte.

After chatting with the owner, Vanessa, while she waited for her order, she took a seat near one of the windows. There was a peek of the ocean off in the distance, and just the blueness of the Pacific calmed her. There was something about the water that soothed her soul, and that was why she hadn't been able to comprehend living or working anywhere else.

Grace took a long sip of her latte and opened the file Kevin had given her. After a quick scan of the details, she frowned. The Saint residences were the worst possible listings for any agent, much less one who had something to prove. Moving haunted property was tricky at best, but these three had everything stacked against them already. They were all overpriced and had been on the market for far too long for her to suddenly find buyers for them in just three months.

"Not your ideal first day?" a familiar male voice said, startling her out of her thoughts.

"Owen?" She jerked her head up and stared into the impossibly warm dark eyes of her new colleague. "What are you doing here?"

His lips curved into a smile as he lifted the cup and white paper bag in his hands. "Late breakfast before I meet with a potential buyer. Mind if I sit with you for a minute?"

She glanced around the busy café, noting all the other tables were occupied. Grace wasn't in the mood to make small talk with a guy she'd just met, but she couldn't exactly say no without being completely rude. "Sure. Of course."

"Thanks." He sat across from her and pulled a croissant from the paper bag. After eyeing the folder still sitting on the table, he added, "He gave you the Saint properties, didn't he?"

Owen was a new hire to Landers Realty, and it irked Grace to no end that this guy hadn't had to prove himself by selling impossible properties. "How did you know that?"

"Landers tried to pass them off on me, but I was more than willing to take a job with On Pointe if it came to that." He grimaced. "It looks like I'm the reason you're stuck with them."

She blew out a breath and shook her head, knowing he wasn't to blame. "It's not your fault. Kevin has a grudge against Bill, my ex, at On Pointe. He was never going to hire me without making it painful. Unfortunately for me, my options are limited."

"If you want any help, I'm willing," he said, flashing a smile that brought out one dimple.

"Why?" It was an honest question. They'd just met, and with another agent around that meant more competition for commissions.

"What can I say? I'm a sucker for a smart, beautiful woman in heels." He glanced at her shoes and then winked.

Grace's entire body heated, and she had to refrain from fanning herself, though she wasn't sure if she was having a hot flash or a surge of pure lust for the man. He was gorgeous. And flirting with her. How long had it been since a man had shown interest in her? Or at least interest that she'd noticed? Grace hadn't had a wandering eye during her marriage, and any guy who'd flirted with her had been brushed off. She'd loved Bill and had thought they had a good life together. Too bad he'd blown it all up by not only sleeping with their receptionist but falling for her as well.

She continued to gaze at Owen and then took a long sip of her coffee. That only made her insides burn hotter, and she lost the battle and started fanning herself. "Is it hot in here?"

Owen chuckled. "I hadn't noticed, but you do look a little flushed. You're not coming down with anything are you?"

Just a case of complete mortification. Was she really lusting after a man who was at least ten years younger than herself? *Snap out of it, Grace,* she thought. *You're not a silly teenager. You're a grown-ass woman who needs to stop drooling over this man.* "I'm fine. Really." She averted her gaze to get herself under control. "I just need to come up with a plan of attack for these homes."

"How about we discuss it over dinner tomorrow night?"

Her gaze snapped back to him. "Are you asking me out on a date?"

A wavy lock of his dark hair fell over his glinting eyes. "If I say yes, will you let me pick you up at six?"

"No. That's really—" she started.

"Too early? You'll probably need some time after work. Seven then?"

She sputtered out a laugh. "You're not going to take no for an answer, are you?"

"If the answer's no, then sure." He leaned in, holding her gaze. "But I'd really like to take you to dinner, celebrate your new job, and get to know you a little bit. Is it so terrible for two coworkers to have a friendly dinner?"

"Just friends?" she asked, dying to say yes. She knew she shouldn't. He was too young for her. They were going to be working together. And yet, she liked him. What wasn't there to like? He was tall with broad shoulders, a trim waist, handsome face, and an easygoing, friendly personality. If only he was a bit older, she'd have felt like she'd hit the jackpot.

"Definitely. Friends." But he placed a hand over hers and caressed her palm in a very more-than-friendly manner.

Gods, that feels good, Grace thought. Resisting the urge to close her eyes and revel in his touch, she forced out a laugh. "Owen," she said as she pulled her hand away, regretting the broken connection instantly. "Stop. Friends, remember?"

He placed his hands face down in front of himself and grinned. "Friends. Definitely. Seven then?"

Saying yes would be a mistake. There was no doubt in her mind. She opened her mouth to suggest lunch later in the week instead, but all that came out was, "Sure. Seven."

* * *

GRACE WALKED along the stone pathway, through the overgrown foliage, and onto the porch of the Victorian at 5 Seaside Drive. The old dingy yellow paint was peeling, and she noted rot around the front door right away.

"Oh, man," she said to no one. It was obvious just by the little she'd seen that the place needed a lot of work. She wouldn't be surprised to find out the roof needed to be replaced along with electric, some plumbing, and the HVAC. Those were the big four and if any one of them was on the fritz, it could be a deal breaker. All four? It would take a miracle to find a buyer unless the price was attractive enough. But she already knew that wasn't the case. She'd either need to convince Mr. Saint to lower the asking price or spend some money to get it into better shape.

Grace punched the numbers into the lockbox, retrieved the key, and steeled herself as she entered the large home. After a quick glance around, she let out a huge sigh of relief. The inside was infinitely better than the outside. The place had gorgeous wood floors. They weren't in perfect condition, but they had enough character that the right buyer would likely fall in love with them. The den to the left had vintage built-ins, and everything appeared freshly painted. Even the kitchen had been updated at some point.

"I can work with this," she said, peering into the downstairs bathroom and nodding at the subway tiles and raised glass sink. Maybe the big four weren't as bad as she'd thought. Someone had put some money into the place at some point. After she toured the home, she made a couple of notes about a crack in a bedroom wall, a running toilet, and a window that needed a new pane of glass. She also made a note to ask the seller about the electrical, plumbing, HVAC, and the roof. Just because the inside was pretty, that didn't mean they hadn't neglected the unsexy parts of the house.

She'd just finished taking new pictures for the listing when she heard a knocking sound coming from upstairs. Frowning, she followed the sound up to the master bedroom, which was completely empty.

Ghosts? Probably. The place was known to be haunted.

"Do you do this every time someone views the property?" she asked, inviting the spirit to communicate with her. As a witch, she didn't have the power to see ghosts, but she could get them to talk sometimes.

The knocking sound vanished and there was complete silence.

"Are you trying to scare off buyers?" she asked.

The knocking started back up immediately, only this time it was twice as loud.

"Whoa! Stop with the crazy noise. I got the message, okay? This is your house, right?"

The lights flashed on and off.

"Understood. But if you don't let someone else move in here, then the place is going to start falling down around itself and your house will cease to exist when the city demolishes it. Do you want that?" Her threat wasn't a lie. She'd watched it happen to another property when a ghost wouldn't stop harassing people.

The lights flickered again, and there was a zap and a sizzle as smoke puffed out of a nearby outlet.

Grace cursed. "Perfect. You just shorted out the wiring."

Grumbling to herself, Grace made a note to have Mr. Saint call an electrician and left the upstairs, knowing there was nothing she could do about the ghost without supplies.

She'd need a dozen smudge sticks and the help of her coven to deal with the haunting.

After locking up, Grace visited the second house. It was a large white cottage overlooking the ocean on the opposite end of town. Everything about the place was sunny and perfect except for the ominous feeling that overtook her the moment she stepped into the place. There was a darkness that settled over her, making her chilled to the bone.

Evil lurked in that house, making Grace shudder. It didn't take long for her to run back out of the house and jump into her compact SUV. No wonder it hadn't sold.

The third house was a on the hillside, nestled in the trees with a cleared lot for organic gardening. The two-story craftsman was in decent shape. The only areas she'd recommend putting money into were the floors. They looked newer, but the scratches in them were a deal breaker for most buyers. They were so deep Grace wasn't even sure they could be refinished. But at least the house felt welcoming. If someone had asked her, she wouldn't even have guessed that the place was haunted. That didn't mean it wasn't; it just meant the spirits were silent that day and didn't have an evil presence.

Grace did her tour, took more notes and photos, and then jumped into her SUV and headed home. She needed to figure out what to say to Mr. Saint to convince him to make some adjustments and then call him first thing in the morning.

CHAPTER FOUR

"Hello?" Grace called as she walked into her small two-bedroom beach house. The lights were on and her niece's Jeep was parked in her driveway.

"In here." Lex's voice sounded gruff as it floated from the back of the house.

Grace made her way to the kitchen and stood in the doorway, watching Lex angrily chop an onion. She wore leggings and an oversized sweatshirt that hung off one shoulder. Grace chuckled, thinking all she needed was a hair scrunchie and she'd look like she walked right out of the eighties.

"It smells fantastic," Grace said. A pot of water was on the stove along with another one full of red sauce. The package of manicotti pasta on the counter told her everything she needed to know. Her niece was making Grace her favorite meal. "What did I do to deserve this lovely visit?"

Lex glanced at her aunt and sniffled, wiping her weepy eyes with the sleeve of her sweatshirt.

"Whoa, sweetie. What's wrong?" she asked as she moved

quickly to her favorite person in the entire world, pulled Lex into her arms, and hugged her. When she pulled back, she pressed one hand to Lex's flushed cheek and said, "What happened? Did you and Bronwyn break up?"

Her red eyes went wide with unbridled horror. "Gods, no."

Relief rushed through Grace, and she blew out a breath. "Oh, thank goodness." Grace took another step back and grabbed Lex's hand, squeezing gently. "Then what is it?"

"Not a what. A who." Lex tightened her fingers around Grace's and then let go and went back to chopping onions. Only this time her strokes were measured and deliberate instead of angry and haphazard.

Grace leaned her backside against the counter and studied her niece. Her face was flushed, and her short blond curls were messier than usual, as if she'd been running her fingers through her hair. There was also a tinge of sadness in her eyes mixed in with her pure frustration. Usually Lex Marian had an easy laugh and was easy to love. Whoever had put her in this mood had just become Grace's least favorite person. "I'm here if you want to talk about it."

"It's mom," she blurted. Tears pooled in her pale blue eyes as she blew out a breath, shaking her head. "I guess I shouldn't be too surprised. She hasn't really gotten over the fact that I'm never going to marry Jackson Dixon." A tiny shudder ran through Lex, and she visibly shook it off. "She still can't stop talking about how cute our kids would've been."

Grace blinked. "What? Surely she knows that you two never actually dated, right?"

"Of course she knows," Lex spat, angry tears spilling

down her cheeks. "Apparently that doesn't stop her from wishing her daughter was straight."

Jackson Dixon was one of Lex's best friends. They'd met in grade school and had been practically inseparable up until graduation when they'd gone off to different colleges. Now they had both moved back to town and were rekindling their friendship. But there was absolutely no reason to believe they'd ever be a couple considering they were both same-sex oriented. "Did your mom actually say that?"

"She didn't have to." Lex dropped the knife and tossed the chopped onions into the simmering sauce.

"Okay." Grace took a moment to decide how to handle the situation. She didn't want to do anything to come between her sister and her niece. Alyssa had been shocked when Lex had come out and was probably a little sad that the vision she had for her daughter was never going to be reality. But she'd said all the right things, told Lex she loved her no matter what and that all she wanted was for her daughter to be happy. Likely, whatever prompted this fight had been a misunderstanding. Though if Alyssa was talking wistfully about Lex and Jackson getting married... The idea made Grace wince. That wasn't cool. "Want to tell me what happened?"

Lex closed her eyes and sucked in a deep breath. "I had a job interview today with a new restaurant in town."

Grace nodded, remembering Lex had landed a meeting with the owner and head chef of Premonition Pointe's hottest eatery. "Witches' Garden, right?"

"Yep. They need a front of house manager. Anyway, it went well, but Frankie Moar came in right after me, so I'm not super hopeful."

Frankie Moar was a successful former restaurant owner

who'd sold her place two years ago to a franchise operation. She'd be stiff competition for anyone, much less an applicant fresh out of college. "Don't give up so fast. You never know how people are going to mesh."

"You're right. But that's not what I'm upset about." Lex waved a hand, dismissing that subject. "When I got home, Charlie was there. He wanted to know when Bronwyn was coming over. When I said I wasn't sure, he started talking about what a nice ass she has and how she should show off her rack more."

A sick feeling coiled in Grace's stomach. "He did?"

Lex's pale eyes darkened, and she pressed her lips together in a tight line as she nodded. "It's not the first time he's made inappropriate comments about her. I try to ignore him, but Bron told me he made comments to her about our sex life. Something about how hot it must be. He completely creeped her out, and now she doesn't want to come over when he's there."

"I can't blame her. Does your mom know he's said these things?"

"Yes. I told her, but she just chuckled and said he didn't mean anything by it."

"Holy hell, Lex. I'm sorry." Son of a... What was wrong with her sister? She couldn't possibly be so blind that she didn't recognize harassment, could she?

"It gets worse." Lex sat on one of the stools and buried her face in her hands.

Grace waited patiently, knowing her niece would talk when she was ready. Though it didn't stop her fingers from itching to dial her sister and give her a piece of her mind. She wouldn't talk negatively about Alyssa in front of Lex, but she wouldn't hesitate to speak her mind to her sister.

Charlie lived in Alyssa's house and was being so inappropriate that both Grace and Bronwyn were uncomfortable.

Lex raised her head. "Charlie told me that Mom still cries sometimes over the fact that I've chosen this 'alternative lifestyle' and that if I was a good daughter, I'd stop being so selfish and finally settle down with Jackson like nature intended."

"Charlie said that?" Grace asked incredulously. It wasn't much of a secret that Grace and Charlie didn't get along. For the sake of her sister, Grace tried to remain civil, but after what Lex had just said, pure unadulterated rage churned in her gut. The tumultuous reaction sent her magic straight to her hands, making her palms tingle. It was the natural inclination to hex someone. She pushed off the counter and started to pace the kitchen just to try to use up some of the energy that fueled her need to retaliate.

"Aunt Grace?" Lex said.

"Yeah, sweetie?" The magic was crawling over her arms now. She knew she looked like evil had taken over and as if she was going to lose her shit on someone at any moment.

"I think you might need some salted caramel." Lex smiled gently at her and reached into a nearby jar, producing the piece of caramel that would neutralize Grace's reaction.

"You're right about that." She held out her hand. Lex dropped it into her palm, and Grace popped the sweet into her mouth. After only a few seconds, the visible magic disappeared and Grace started to feel like her normal self again. "Thanks."

Lex gave her aunt a small smile. "Thank you."

"For what?" Grace strode over to the wine rack and selected a bottle of Merlot.

"For getting so worked up you lost control of your magic."

Grace huffed and then pulled the cork. As she poured them both a glass, she asked, "What did your mom say when you spoke to her? You told her about this, too, right?"

"I did but she just brushed me off. Told me Charlie was just being Charlie and to stop being so sensitive." Lex went back to preparing the manicotti. "She's already told me a dozen times how much she wanted Jackson as a son-in-law, and every time she says it, it's like a little piece of me dies." Her eyes welled with tears again. "I don't think I can take staying there one more day. Not with Charlie in the house. If it was just Mom, then I think we could maybe work something out, but she chooses him every single time and I—"

"It's okay, Lex. You can have the guest room. It's all yours."

The tension drained out of Lex's jaw, and her shoulders visibly relaxed. "I can pay rent. I'm still working part time over at Earthly Spirits Deli."

"You're not paying rent," Grace insisted. "I bought this house with my divorce settlement money. I own it free and clear. Okay?"

Lex chewed on her bottom lip. "But, Aunt Grace, I can't just not pay anything."

Grace grinned at her niece, loving that she didn't want to take advantage. But she still wasn't going to accept any money. She'd rather her niece save her cash for when she was ready to get her own place. "I appreciate that, Lex. How about you just pay me in homecooked meals? No need to go out of your way to cook for me if you're not going to be around, but when you are, I'll leave the meal planning and execution up to you. Deal?"

"Deal!" Lex quickly wiped her hands on a dishtowel and then threw her arms around Grace. "You're the best. You know that?"

"I think you're biased, but I'll take it." Grace held on tightly and then kissed her on the temple. "I know you're upset with your mother, and you have every right to your feelings, Lexie Bug, but try to remember that she does love you even if things are a little rough right now."

Lex stiffened and pulled back to stare Grace in the eye. "I know she does. That's part of the reason why this is so hard. Do you have any idea what it feels like to have your own mother dismiss a major part of you?"

Grace knew exactly how that felt. She'd had plenty of issues with her own mother before she'd passed on, but now wasn't the time to get into any of that. "I'm sorry, sweet pea. I know it's hard."

Lex nodded and drained the wine out of her glass.

"Refill?"

"Always." Lex held her glass out while Grace overfilled it. "Thank you."

"Anytime. You know how I like my wine." Grace winked at her and topped off her own glass.

"Not for that. I meant for being the person I can turn to when I need someone." She reached out and squeezed Grace's hand. "Just thank you."

Grace's heart completely melted. "You don't need to thank me, Lex. I love you. There will never be a time when you can't come to me."

Tears glistened in Lex's eyes. She blinked them back and

said, "Okay. Enough. I need to finish this dinner before we're both too sloshed to work the oven."

"I'll take care of the garlic bread," Grace said, heading for the fridge to find the butter. Once she had the bread sliced and buttered with her special garlic butter blend, she slipped out of the kitchen and into her own room. She took a seat on her brand-new queen-size bed, leaned back against the multitude of pillows, and called Alyssa.

"Grace, I don't have time to talk right now. Can I call you tomorrow?" Alyssa said without even a greeting.

"Why? What's going on?"

Alyssa let out an exasperated sigh. "Charlie is having a fit about dinner. I need to get something in the oven before it turns into world war three."

Grace wasn't sure if she wanted to throttle Charlie or her sister. "Why doesn't he make his own dinner?"

"Grace... don't. It's just easier if I do it." There it was, that warning in her sister's tone that was always there when they discussed Charlie.

"Right." Even though Grace knew she should keep her mouth shut, after her talk with Lex, there was no way she'd be biting her tongue. "Because being the one who cooks for him seven days a week, pays the bulk of the bills, and maintains the home is totally easier than fighting about it. You know what would make all of that easier?"

"This again?" Alyssa asked. "You know what? Never mind. I can't do this right now. Lex didn't make dinner, and now I have to throw something together. I've gotta go."

"Lex *is* making dinner," Grace said. "She's just doing it here."

There was silence on the other end of the line.

"Alyssa?"

"Why is she there?"

"To see her aunt?" Grace said incredulously. She was well aware that Alyssa could get weird about her relationship with Lex, but Grace couldn't help that. She wasn't going to push Lex away because Alyssa didn't like that they were close. "That's why I called. To let you know she's here and that I offered her my second bedroom for as long as she wants it."

Alyssa scoffed. "So, Lex is moving in with you now? And what? You called to rub it in?"

"I called so you wouldn't worry. Especially after the fight she had with Charlie today."

"They were fighting again?" Alyssa let out an exasperated sigh. "Figures. Fine. It'll probably be less stressful with Lex there than here. Now, I have to go, or I'll burn the burgers."

"Alyssa?"

"What?"

"Can we talk tomorrow? Maybe get lunch?" Grace asked, suddenly worried about her sister. Alyssa had always made excuses for her live-in boyfriend, but this seemed different. Like she was drowning in that relationship instead of just choosing to stay.

"I can't tomorrow." Charlie bellowed something in the background, making Grace wince. "I'll call you later. I really have to go now." The call ended.

Grace stared at her phone for a minute, contemplating if she should head over to Alyssa's house.

"Grace?" Lex called from the other room. "Dinner's ready."

Sighing, Grace tucked her phone into her pocket and headed out to the kitchen. "Lex?"

"Yeah?" She looked up from where she'd just placed the manicotti dish on the table.

"Is Charlie dangerous?" She hated asking her niece, but what else was she going to do?

Lex pressed her lips together and hesitated for a moment. Then she shrugged one shoulder and shook her head slightly. "No. Not really. I mean, he's a dick and he treats Mom like shit, but he's never gotten physical if that's what you mean."

"It is." She flopped down into her chair and propped her elbows on the table. "I hate that my mind went there, but your mom sounds so... defeated. I just needed to know if I should get in the car and go rescue her."

Lex snorted. "The only person she needs to be rescued from is herself."

"Lex," Grace admonished. "Let's not do that, okay? I know you're upset with her, and you have every reason to be, but she's still my sister and I love her."

"I know. Sorry." Lex averted her eyes and sat stock-still in her seat.

Grace reached over and squeezed her hand. "Thank you for making dinner. It looks and smells amazing."

"Of course." Lex still didn't look at her, but she did reach for the spatula to start serving the manicotti.

"I love you. You know that, right?"

This time Lex did look at her and forced a small smile. "I do. Let's just not talk about Mom, okay?"

"You got it. I did tell her you're moving in for the foreseeable future so that she wouldn't worry when you didn't show up."

"What did she say?" Lex asked.

"Not much. She knows you need your space." It wasn't exactly a lie. Grace was certain her sister would agree that they all needed their space, but that's not what she'd said when Grace had told her Lex was moving in. She'd only spoken about what Charlie might want. Lex didn't need to know that.

Lex rolled her eyes. "I bet she was upset I didn't make dinner."

She was right, but Grace wasn't going to confirm Alyssa had mentioned it. "Who wouldn't be? This manicotti is to die for." Grace made a show of taking a big bite. As soon as the cheesy pasta hit her tongue, her eyes rolled into the back of her head as she let out a moan of pure pleasure. "This is better than sex."

Lex raised one eyebrow. "You sure about that? I think you might be misremembering. Or maybe uncle Bill just wasn't all that good in the bedroom."

Grace let out a bark of laughter. "You know, you could be right on both counts."

"We need to get you a date," Lex said, eyeing Grace with a knowing look. "Someone who can show you a good time in the bedroom."

"Oh, no. I'm not interested in getting involved with another man. No thanks. I just ditched the last one." Grace took a gulp of her wine, flustered and feeling flushed when Owen's face flashed in her mind. She suddenly imagined him in her bedroom, kissing her neck and sliding his hands under her skirt, finding her high waisted panties that doubled as a tummy shaper. She groaned. Mood instantly killed.

Lex laughed. "What the heck was that all about?"

"What?" Grace asked innocently, even though she knew exactly what Lex was asking.

"Come on, Grace. Who put that look on your face just

now?" She gave her aunt a mischievous look. "Have you been browsing Tinder?"

"Tinder? What the heck is that?" Grace asked.

Lex threw her head back and laughed. "It's a hookup app."

Grace's eyebrows rose. "Hookup? You mean like Netflix and chill is actually code for sex?"

"You knew Netflix and chill but not Tinder?" Lex shook her head. "You have weird gaps in your knowledge. We need to fix that before you enter the dating scene."

"I'm not entering the dating scene." She wrinkled her nose, thinking about Owen again. "Except, I think I do kinda have a date tomorrow."

"Oh, so now it comes out. Who is it? That hottie at Bird's Eye Bakery?"

"Carl?" Grace stared at her niece like she'd lost her mind. "Why would I go on a date with Carl? He's like seventy years old."

She laughed, her eyes twinkling with amusement. "He's a silver fox. That's what he is. Like Sam Elliott. You could do worse."

She had a point. Carl was a very good-looking older man. But Grace was only forty-five. If she ever did decide to seriously date someone, she much preferred a man she could grow old with, not someone who was miles ahead of her in the race. "Fine. Carl's definitely good looking. But no. I have a date with my new colleague at Landers Realty."

"You're going out with Kevin Landers?" she asked, her brow furrowed. "Why?"

"Not Kevin. His name is Owen. He recently moved to Premonition Pointe and works at Landers. He asked me out for dinner tomorrow night so we could get to know each other a little bit."

Lex let out a gasp. "Owen Taylor? Tall, dark hair, knows how to wear a suit?"

"Sounds right." Grace's cheeks warmed. "How do you know him?"

"He's been into the deli almost every day since he's been in town," Lex said, referring to Bronwyn's family deli, Earthly Spirits, where she'd been helping out until she found a full-time job. "He's hawt, Grace. Well done."

Grace's entire body heated and sweat broke out on her neck. Son of a witch. Was she having a hot flash just thinking about the man? She grabbed her glass and then took a long sip of water. "Stop. We're meeting as friends."

"Where and what time?" Lex insisted.

"He's picking me up here at seven." Grace averted her eyes, knowing Lex was about to call her out.

"You do realize that's a date, right?" Lex said. "You can call it what you want, but a hot man asked you to dinner and he's going through the trouble of picking you up instead of meeting you there. Face it, Auntie, you need to get your roots done tomorrow and maybe your eyelashes and brows tinted. Want me to go with you?"

Grace turned to look at her niece and nodded. "I could use all the help I can get."

CHAPTER FIVE

"Thank you for meeting me, Mr. Saint," Grace said, rising to greet the older gentleman as he joined her at Bird's Eye, Premonition Pointe's prized bakery.

Mr. Saint was wearing an expensive suit and a scowl on his face. His white hair was styled with product, giving him a youthful appearance despite the pronounced winkles around his eyes. "You have five minutes, and then I have to leave for another meeting."

Five minutes? Grace bit back her own scowl and waved Carl, the manager, over. "Then let's get right to it." Grace flipped open her notebook and waved a hand for the man to sit across from her. "I want to talk about how we can improve your properties in a way that will help us finally move them."

He hadn't sat as she'd suggested, but instead, gripped the back of the chair as he loomed over her. "There is no way I'm pouring even more money into those properties. I've already spent more than is reasonable on them."

Carl appeared holding a silver carafe and a ceramic mug. His royal blue polo shirt complemented his sun-kissed brown skin. He had a dragon tattoo wrapped around his left arm, and Grace was forced to admit that Lex had been right. He was hot for an older man. "Coffee?"

"Yes, please," Grace said, desperation clear in her tone. She'd woken up late and hadn't had time to make any at home. If she didn't get a shot of caffeine soon, she was going to climb over the counter, put her lips to the coffee dispenser, and suck it right out of the commercial pot.

"I don't have time," Saint said, wrinkling his nose at Carl as if the man reeked of a foul scent.

"Muffin? Cupcake? Lemon bar?" Carl asked pleasantly, ignoring Saint's rudeness as he poured Grace a cup of pure heaven.

"Um… coffee cake?" Saint asked.

"Coming right up. Grace? The usual?"

She nodded. "Thanks, Carl."

"Always my pleasure, Ms. Valentine." Carl winked at her and slipped back behind the counter.

Grace poured a bit of cream into her mug and then took a sip of her coffee.

"Four minutes, Ms. Valentine," Saint said, tapping his bare wrist where a watch would normally be.

Grace gritted her teeth. He was being a condescending ass, and after the past three months of dealing with an ex who'd tried to get her to sign a divorce agreement that would've given her less than a quarter of what she was entitled to, she was completely done with men who underestimated her. "I toured your homes yesterday, and here are my suggestions." She slid a report over to him. "The Victorian on Seaside needs the outside painted and some entryway rot taken care of. The cottage overlooking the ocean is gorgeous, but there's something there that needs to be eradicated. You should call in a professional ghost hunting team. And the craftsman—"

"Needs the floors done," he interrupted, narrowing his eyes at her. "I already know all of this. You're wasting my time." He turned to go, paused, and strode up to the counter, no doubt not wanting to leave his coffee cake behind.

Grace jumped out of her chair and ran over to him. "So you've already been advised that your places need work in order for us to move them, but you don't want to put more money into them. I get it. If that's the case, then we should talk about lowering the prices because—"

"Ms. Valentine," Saint ground out. "I don't have time for this. Talk to Kevin Landers. Once you've done that, give me another call."

Carl handed Saint a wax paper bag and a cup of coffee to go. "On the house," Carl said to him. "Hope your day is a pleasant one."

Saint eyed Carl and then chuckled as he shook his head. "I intend it to be." He shoved a tip into the jar, raised his cup and pastry bag in a mock salute, and then took off.

Grace eyed the tip and was surprised to see he'd left twice as much as what his bill would've been. So he wasn't a cheap bastard. At least not when it came to tipping kind bakery managers. But houses that needed work in order to find a buyer? That was apparently an entirely different story. She sighed and slipped a few bills over to the register. "Carl, let me pay for his order."

"Nope." He slid the money back. "No charge today. You look like you could use a break."

"You have no idea." She ran a hand through her hair and

groaned when she remembered she was supposed to meet Lex at the spa. She needed to talk to Kevin, but she wasn't sure she had time to get to the office, find out what information Kevin had kept from her, and get back across town before her noon appointment.

It didn't matter. She had a short period of time to sell those properties. She couldn't afford to put off the chat with Kevin. After sucking down the rest of her coffee and ordering another blueberry scone, she waved at Carl, hurried out to her SUV, and took off down a side street, hoping to avoid the summer traffic on the main drag.

* * *

"LISTEN, Nina, I appreciate that Mr. Landers is working on contracts, but it's important that I speak to him," Grace said, trying desperately to not throttle her boss's assistant. "Can you just let him know I'm here and need to talk about the Saint properties?"

"Sorry, Ms. Valentine," she said with a saccharine smile. "He said he wasn't to be disturbed this morning."

Grace glanced at the wall clock in the office and groaned. If she didn't get in to see him in the next ten minutes, she was either going to have to wait until the next day or skip her appointment.

"Problem?" Owen said, appearing beside her out of nowhere.

His voice sent a shock down Grace's spine, making her startle. "Jeez, Owen. What are you, part cat?"

His dark eyes gleamed. "I did have someone who used to call me tiger, but I'm not sure that's what she meant."

Grace rolled her eyes. "Was that flirting? Because if so, I think your technique might need a little work."

He chuckled. "That was pretty bad, wasn't it? I was actually referring to the hot teenager who used to watch me after school before my mom got home from work. She starred in many of my preteen dreams. That was probably TMI, right?"

"Definitely TMI," Grace confirmed. But his easy smile, combined with his one dimple, just made him that much more charming, and she couldn't help being slightly amused.

"Sorry." He winked at her and then turned to Nina. "Is he ready to see me now?"

"Sure, Owen." Nina smiled brightly at him.

Grace was certain she could see emoji hearts in the young woman's eyes. Although she could hardly blame her. Owen had brought his A game today. He was wearing a blue silk shirt, black slacks, and stylish black boots. The look would've been too polished if it wasn't for his artfully messed up hair. Grace knew it was intentional, but that didn't matter. His look was definitely working for him.

"Go on in." Nina waved at Kevin's door.

"Wait!" Grace demanded. "I thought you said he was too busy to be interrupted."

"He's working on a contract for Owen," Nina said, narrowing her eyes at Grace. "You know, the kind that brings money in."

Grace ignored the condescending woman and turned to Owen. "Could you please tell Kevin—you know what? Never mind. I'll handle it."

"Are you sure?" Owen asked, furrowing his brow. "I can relay a message if you want."

"No thanks. I'd rather talk to him myself." The last thing she wanted to do was enlist Owen to fight her battles. Landers clearly withheld information from her about the Saint properties, and she'd be damned if she'd give him the satisfaction of knowing he got under her skin. "Nina, I need to make an appointment with Mr. Landers. Preferably today."

Owen squeezed her arm gently and then disappeared into the boss's office.

Nina tapped her fingernail against her lips as she checked Landers' schedule. "I don't know about today. He's awfully busy. But Friday morning is free."

It was only Tuesday. Friday was completely unacceptable. Grace shook her head. "I really need about twenty minutes either today or tomorrow morning."

Nina let out a put-upon sigh, and Grace couldn't help but wish an acne breakout on the childish assistant. "I can only give you fifteen minutes at the end of the day, assuming he isn't planning on leaving early."

"I'll be here. What time?"

"Six-fifteen. Again, no guarantees," she said with that sickly-sweet smile.

Grace rolled her eyes. "I'm sure you can call me if anything changes, right, Nina?"

"Of course, Grace." Nina turned her attention back to her computer. "Good luck."

Fuming, Grace left the office and headed across town to the spa.

* * *

"GRACE! THERE YOU ARE," Lex said, meeting her at the door of the day spa and shuffling her to one of the salon chairs.

"Lance is waiting for you." She plopped down in a nearby chair, looking perfect in her skinny jeans, formfitting T-shirt, and light makeup that highlighted her pale blue eyes. Grace remembered the days in her early twenties when it took her ten minutes to get ready instead of an entire afternoon with a handful of beauty experts.

"Sorry." Grace puffed out a breath and pushed her hair out of her eyes. "Traffic. Got caught at the train tracks."

"Finally!" Lance bounced his way over to them, a smile on his full lips. He was a tall, bald, and extremely beautiful black man in his fifties who'd spent his younger years styling drag queens. In addition to being a genius with hair color, his makeup game was off the charts. "I was about to give up on you, gorgeous. But now that you are here, what is it we're doing today?" He turned and studied her too-long locks and frowned. "How long has it been since your last appointment?"

Lance was Grace's longtime hairdresser. She'd already been overdue to get her roots done right about the time her husband blew up their lives, and after that, she hadn't had the money or the will to worry about it. "About four months. Life has been... messy."

He clucked his tongue and ran his fingers through her hair. "Messy?"

"Divorce," Lex confirmed. "Her ex deserves to marry a gold digger and die penniless and alone."

"I see." Lance pursed his lips together and his nostrils flared as he sucked in a sharp breath. "Did the bastard cheat on you?"

Grace nodded. "With our receptionist. It's all just so predictable."

"Men suck," he agreed, his pained expression making her

heart ache. She'd forgotten that Lance's husband had walked out on him just the year before to follow a twenty-something to Hollywood. "The next time he comes in here, it sure would be a shame if someone accidentally mixed his hair dye wrong."

Lex let out a snort and then covered her nose and mouth with her hand as her eyes danced with amusement.

"It would certainly serve him right," Grace said. "But I'd hate for anyone to get into any trouble due to a *mix-up*."

Lance gave her a mischievous grin. "You're not up on the latest gossip around here, are you?"

"Uh, apparently not." Grace glanced around as if whatever he was referring to would jump right out at her. "Catch me up."

Lance spread his arms wide and grinned down at Grace as he said, "You're looking at the new owner of Liminal Space Day Spa."

Grace blinked up at him, shocked. "What about Lily?" she asked, referring to the talented witch who opened the day spa over twenty years ago and had quickly become the most sought-after healing masseuse on the northern California coast. "Where did she go?"

"She's still here, but now she's only working part-time with her established clients a couple days a week. She's spending the rest of her time in her herb garden," Lance said.

"So she's in semi-retirement?" Grace asked.

He nodded.

"Good for her." Grace stood and opened her arms to Lance. "And congratulations on becoming a small business owner. I know you're going to be a huge success."

Lance wrapped his arms around her and squeezed. "Thanks, Grace."

When he pulled back, he eyed her face and frowned. "What?"

He turned to Lex. "Didn't you say she's also going to get her brows and lashes tinted?"

"Yep. My treat," Lex said. "Aunt Grace has a hot date tonight."

"Oh, *really*," Lance said, pumping his eyebrows. "With who? Carl at the bakery?"

"Carl?" Grace whipped around and gaped at Lance. "What is it with you people thinking I'm going to date a man in his seventies?"

"He's hot," Lance said, giving her a look that said she was out of her mind if she didn't agree. "Like Sam Elliott hot."

Lex let out a bark of laughter and then slapped her hand over her mouth.

Lance winked at Grace's niece and the two of them dissolved into laughter.

"Oh, very funny." Grace rolled her eyes, realizing that Lance had already been filled in on the conversation Lex and Grace had the night before. "Laugh it up," she said to Lance. "But just wait until I fix you up on a blind date with someone from the senior home."

"Is he rich? I could go for a sugar daddy for once," Lance teased as he draped a smock around Grace.

"Sure. Why not?" Then she turned her attention to Lex. "And you... Behave or I'll sign you up to volunteer at Puppy Love with that chick who is always making heart eyes at you."

Lex's eyes widened. "She's older than my mom!"

"Yep." Grace snickered. "I bet she could teach you a few things."

"Gross! Stop," Lex cried and covered her face with her

hands as she shook her head. "This is not a conversation I want to have with my aunt."

Grace glanced up at Lance. "And yet, she told me last night I need to get a bazillion because I don't want to get caught with a messy sin cave if things get a little heated."

"Bazillion?" Lance let out a cackle of laughter. "Lex, who is an expert on all things girls..." He paused and winked at her. "She said you need a *bazillion*?"

"I did not say that!" Lex insisted, her face turning a dark shade of maroon as she tried her best to not collapse into hysterics. "I said *Brazilian!*"

"Oh, holy hell. I can't even get the lingo right." Grace groaned. "Forget it. I'm just gonna die of embarrassment right here in the spa."

Lance snickered, ignoring Grace's outburst. "Whatever you kids are calling it, Lex has a point. Don't want him getting lost in the bush."

"That would be tragic," Grace said. Her side ached with the effort to keep from completely losing it and doubling over in laughter. There wasn't much she loved more than embarrassing her niece with sex talk. Considering Lex had a lot of opinions about Grace's love life, or lack of it lately, she felt justified.

"Okay. That's quite enough. Point taken," Lex said, standing and straightening her shoulders. "I'm going to head back for my massage." She eyed Lance. "Do your magic. Her date is a thirty-four-year-old hottie."

"Lex," Grace hissed.

The younger woman finger-waved at her aunt and hurried into the back of the spa.

"A younger man, huh?" Lance asked as he mixed the dye

to touch up her roots. "You'll definitely need that cooter wax then."

That was it. She couldn't hold it in any longer. Laughter burst from her lips and tears rolled down her cheeks as her body shook uncontrollably.

"Laugh all you want, but you know I'm right." He blew her a kiss in the mirror and started to work his magic.

CHAPTER SIX

*W*ith her hair freshly dyed and cut so that it had plenty of movement, Grace already felt like a million bucks as she followed an esthetician named Carrie back to one of the spa's treatment rooms.

"Your hair looks amazing, Ms. Valentine," Carrie said. "Lance outdid himself."

"Thanks. I love it."

"Good. That's what we like to hear. Why don't you lie down and we'll get started on your tinting."

Grace did as she was told and stared up at one of the most beautiful women she'd ever seen. She had long, straight black hair that was pulled up into a sleek ponytail, deep blue eyes, perfect skin, and the whitest smile Grace had ever seen. She was a walking advertisement for the spa services if there ever was one.

"Okay, then. Black for the eyelashes?" Carrie asked.

"Yes, please."

"What about your eyebrows? Usually people go just a

shade darker than their natural brows, but we can go darker if you want."

Grace opted to go just a shade darker. This was the first time she was having her brows done, and she didn't want to end up regretting anything. It didn't take long for Carrie to work her magic, and in no time, she said, "All done. Unless…"

"Unless what?" Grace asked, blinking up at her.

"Your eyebrows could use some shaping, and what do you do about your mustache?"

"Mustache?" Grace asked, automatically bringing her fingertips to her upper lip.

"It's not thick, so not super noticeable. If it was all blond, I wouldn't worry about it. But you do have some dark hair there. Lance said you have a hot date tonight and…" She shrugged. "If you want me to wax it, we have time."

Mustache? Grace knew it would be a problem eventually. As her mother aged, her lady stache had turned into quite the thick garden. But Grace hadn't noticed that hers was that bad. Or had she just not been looking? She sat up. "Can I see a mirror?"

"Sure." Carrie handed her a hand mirror and took a step back to lean against the counter. "Like I said, it's not super noticeable—"

"It is. It definitely is," Grace said, horrified as she turned her head back and forth, wondering when all that hair had sprouted on her face. Had she gone blind? Because the person looking back at her in the mirror appeared to be growing a pelt of fur on her upper lip. "Wax it and the brows, and heck, my chin too if you think it needs it. Wax it all."

"Are you sure? It'll leave you red for a few hours," Carrie warned.

"I'm sure. I'll even take a leg and Brazilian wax if there's time." *Brazilian?* Had she lost her mind?

Carried chuckled. "You must have one hell of a date tonight."

"Let's just say that Grace might be getting her groove back."

"Hmm, well, I wouldn't recommend a Brazilian the day of your date. Things will be sensitive for a bit." Eyeing Grace she said, "I recommend some strategic grooming and a shave for this one. But make another appointment in a week or so and we can get you started with the legs and a Brazilian if you're still up for it."

"Oh, thank the gods," Grace said, breathing out a sigh of relief. "I really, really wasn't looking forward to that."

Laughing, Carrie reminded her to just relax and quickly waxed away all of Grace's excess facial hair. "It'll be red for a few hours but should fade before your date tonight."

"Thanks, Carrie." Grace gave the woman a hug. "I'll be back for the leg wax."

"And the Brazilian?"

"Eh, probably not. That was the nerves talking." Grace glanced down at herself. "I think my sin cave will be just fine with a little of that strategic grooming you mentioned."

Carrie snorted. "You're probably right. Have fun." She winked and held the door open for Grace. "Lots and lots of fun."

Grace chuckled, but as she exited the private room, suddenly nerves took over. What was she doing? She'd just spent most of the day grooming for one date with a guy she barely knew and probably shouldn't be dating.

"Grace?" a very unwelcome but familiar voice called from behind her.

This is not happening, Grace told herself. She squeezed her eyes shut, praying that the woman would just go away. She heard the shuffling of feet and a door opened and closed. Relief rushed through her, and she said a silent prayer of thanks that she didn't have to deal with Shondra Barns. But when Grace opened her eyes, she was staring at the face of the woman who had helped blow up her marriage. Scowling, she turned around, intending to find another way out, but it was very clear the only doors led to private rooms.

Grace turned around and summoned the thickest skin she could muster. "Shondra, what can I do for you?"

The younger woman was wrapped in a plush robe, and her platinum blond hair was tied up into a haphazard bun. Still, she managed to look like she'd just stepped off the pages of Maxim. Or Playboy. Her perfect skin flushed slightly pink as she said, "I just wanted to see how you were doing."

"I'm great. Now, if you'll excuse me, I have somewhere to be." Grace started to move past her, but Shondra grabbed her wrist and held on lightly. Grace glanced down at the connection. "I think you'd better let me go now."

"Grace. Bill and I are worried about you. After everything that happened, you must be having a hard time. We've been wanting to reach out and let you know that we're here for you. All you need to do is let us know what we can do to help. No one wanted you hurt. You have to know that."

Words failed Grace as she stared at the woman she'd once counted on as not only an employee, but a friend as well. Was Shondra really standing in front of her feigning concern? Grace scoffed. "Spare me, Shondra. If you really cared about hurting me, you wouldn't have been boning my husband in his office for the last year while I was doing his laundry and making him dinner. Get the hell out of here with your concern. It's not needed or appreciated."

Shondra jerked back as if she'd been slapped.

Grace smirked and yanked her arm out of Shondra's grasp. "In case there's any confusion, we're not friends. We'll never be friends. And if for some reason I need help with anything in my life, it won't be you and Bill I turn to. In fact, you'd be the last two people I'd ask for help. So do me a favor, and when we run into each other again, just pretend you don't see me and I'll do the same. Got it?"

Shondra's eyes narrowed slightly, a sure sign that Grace had gotten under her skin. Good. The woman had been the catalyst that had destroyed her marriage. And despite how upset and heartbroken Grace had been, the betrayal hadn't broken her. She was moving on, and she really didn't need this woman pretending she cared. Shondra cleared her throat, leaned in, and whispered, "You have a thick black hair growing out of your nose. Should've gotten that waxed, too."

Grace jerked back and unconsciously covered her nose with one hand. "I do not."

"Whatever you say." Shondra gave her a self-satisfied smile and then turned and sashayed toward the women's dressing room.

Rage surged through Grace's blood, and she couldn't stop herself from mumbling, "Joy was right. You do deserve genital warts."

Shondra paused and glanced back at her. "What did you just say?"

"Nothing. Enjoy that massage my ex is paying for," she said with forced pleasantness. "But don't get too used to it. As soon as the honeymoon is over, he's going to put a stop to any spending he deems frivolous."

She raised her chin, looking defiant. "I make my own money."

Grace nodded. "Yep. Working for him. Just wait until after the wedding. Then you'll see. Good luck to you." She turned, and instead of following Shondra into the dressing room to check on the alleged nose hair, she stalked out into the front of the salon to find Lex.

"Aunt Grace, your hair looks amazing," Lex said, rising from one of the massaging recliners. "And look at those eyelashes. They're so long. The tinting was a great choice."

Grace took a step forward and pointed to her nose. "Do I have a black hair growing out of this thing?"

"What?" Lex stared at her aunt as if she'd lost her mind.

"On my nose. Is there a gnarly hair that needs to be removed?"

Lex frowned as she studied Grace's face. "No. I'd have told you earlier if there was."

Grace raised one eyebrow. "You didn't say anything about my mustache."

"What mustache?" She peered harder at her aunt. "Looks like you got half your face waxed."

"Yeah, because according to the esthetician, I had a mustache, caterpillar eyebrows, and chin whiskers." Grace squeezed her eyes shut and shook her head. "I know I'm being dramatic, but that's what happens when you run into your replacement."

"Shondra's here? And you ran into her?" Lex asked in a hushed tone.

Grace grimaced and nodded. "Then she said I'd turned into a hag."

"She said *that*?"

"She may as well have. She's the one who said I had a black hair growing out of my nose."

"It's okay, sweetie," Lance said, sliding up behind her and draping an arm around her shoulders. "It's not like you looked like a wookie or anything. It's Carrie's job to address these things. Trust me. You look fabulous. Now who is this Shondra person? She sounds like a nightmare."

"She is. She's the one who had an affair with my ex and was the catalyst for the divorce," Grace explained.

"She worked with Grace, too," Lex whispered to Lance.

"Oh, that bitch," Lance said. "What a hag. Don't you dare give her one more thought. She doesn't deserve your energy." He squeezed, giving her a slight hug. "Now take that fine ass home and turn yourself into the sexy goddess that lives inside of you. That will be the best revenge you could serve to the likes of Shondra. While she's stuck living your old life with Bill and washing his underwear, you'll be out living life on your terms, answering to no one. Sounds to me like you got the better end of the bargain."

"Hell yeah!" Lex pumped her fist in the air. "You're livin' the dream."

But was she? Sure, it looked great on the outside. She had her own beach cottage, a new job, and a hot date. But the house was on the small side, her job was precarious at best, and her date would more than likely move on to someone Shondra's age as soon as he saw her naked.

Wait? Was she really thinking they were going to get naked together? Was she really going to show him her middle-aged body? Grace groaned and wondered how she could get out of dinner with Owen.

"Oh no you don't." Lex grabbed her by the shoulders and started to steer her toward the exit. "Don't you dare let those doubts creep in. You're going to live a little tonight even if I have to drive you to the restaurant myself."

"But, Lex—"

"No, I mean it. Now come on. I'm not taking no for an answer."

Grace chuckled. She knew her niece meant it, and if she actually did try to cancel with Owen, Lex would never shut up about it. "Okay. Fine. Let's go. But I have to pay my bill first."

"We have your credit card on file," Lance called from behind them. "I'll handle it."

"Make sure I tip you and Carrie," Grace called just before Lex ushered her out of the door.

CHAPTER SEVEN

*G*race pulled her sweater wrap around herself, covering the lowcut dress Lex had picked out for her date. It was what Hope had called her divorce dress. The one that she bought just because it made her feel good. And it had in the store. But now that she was wearing it as she walked into the office to have a meeting with her boss, she was second guessing all of the decisions she'd made in the last few days.

"Wow." Owen let out a low whistle as he looked up from his desk. "Look at you. Hot date?" he asked with a knowing smile.

"Just dinner with a friend," she countered.

"He's one lucky bastard." Owen stood and moved to her side, placing a hand on the small of her back.

"Who said my dinner date was a he?"

"So you admit that it *is* a date," he said, his eyes sparkling with mischief.

She couldn't help it. A laugh bubbled out of her lips.

"Well, I did put these shoes back on. I suppose I should call it an actual date."

He eyed the blue stilettos and nodded. "Those are definitely date-worthy shoes."

That was pretty much what Lex said, too. Only she'd called them sex shoes. Grace couldn't disagree more. The blue stilettos with gold accents were sexy as hell, but more than that, they filled Grace with self-confidence. And that was what she needed for both her meeting and her date.

"I need to see Landers first and then I'll be ready to go," she told Owen before striding back to their boss's office.

"Hello, Nina. Is he ready for me?" Grace asked his assistant and almost did a double take when she spotted a rash of acne covering the woman's chin. Hadn't her face been flawless earlier in the day? Horror rushed through her as she remembered wishing the woman would have a breakout. Was this Grace's fault? Had she cursed her without even realizing it? The memory of the genital warts potion flashed in her mind. Yes, it was possible. Grace concentrated on the woman's face and envisioned her with clear skin again. She didn't know if it would work, but it definitely couldn't hurt.

Nina finally tore her gaze from her computer and eyed Grace from head to toe. "You're awfully dressy for a work meeting."

"I have somewhere to go after this. Is he available?"

Nina picked up her phone and pressed a button. "Grace Valentine is here to see you." She winced at his response and then quietly said, "Yes, sir. She just got here. I'll send her right in." She turned her attention to Grace. "He's waiting for you."

Grace wasn't late, was she? That sounded an awful lot like Landers was annoyed at being delayed. She glanced at the wall clock and breathed a sigh of relief when she noted she was actually ten minutes early. Thanks to Lex's help, she'd gotten ready for her date in record time.

"Grace, finally. Get in here," Landers said as soon as she opened the door.

"I'm sorry you had to wait." Grace closed the door behind her and moved to sit across from him. "If I'd known I'd have been here earlier."

His gaze cut to the office door, and he scowled. "Nina should've told me you were here earlier. I've dealt with that. You won't have that problem again."

"Thank you." Grace eyed her new boss and wondered if she'd misjudged him. Because at that moment he seemed to be respectful of her and her time. Had she been wrong when she'd thought he'd set her up for failure? "I'm here to talk about Mr. Saint's properties."

"I figured that was the case." He sat back and pressed his fingertips together. "I heard you had a meeting with him."

"Yes. This morning. How did you know that?"

The large man placed his hands on his portly belly and gave her a half shrug. "He wanted to know why my newest agent wasn't up to speed on his listings. He chewed me out something good." Landers chuckled softly. "And you know, he had every right to do so. It's my fault we wasted his time. I guess I didn't expect you to get such a jump on things." He gave her a wry smile. "I underestimated you once. It won't happen again."

"Well, I do like to hit the ground running." She gave him a genuine smile, appreciating his candor.

"I understand you have notes on the properties. Can I see them?" he asked, leaning forward.

"Absolutely." Grace pulled the report she'd made for Mr.

Saint out of her messenger bag and handed it over. "The way I see it is that either improvements need to be made or he needs to lower the prices. These properties are stale and—"

"He's already tried all of this," Landers said, squinting at the report.

"Excuse me?" Grace blinked at him. "What does that mean?"

"He had the outside of the Victorian redone six months ago. Within two weeks it was back to looking as if no one had touched it. He had a contractor replace the rotting boards, painted everything, and even had the landscaping redone."

"That's impossible." Grace shook her head. "I mean, sure, if the weather was bad the landscaping could be a problem, but the rest wouldn't deteriorate that fast."

"It would if it's cursed or if the spirits who haunt the place have enough energy to force the accelerated aging." He gave her a tight smile. "The other two properties have the same problem. The one with the scratched floors for example. That flooring has been replaced twice. The second time was right after a cleansing to remove any nefarious spirits. It obviously didn't work."

"And the cottage? I assume he's already hired someone to do a cleansing?"

"Yep. Whatever is there still manages to run everyone off before they even get in the door."

Grace had gotten in the door at least. Still. This wasn't good. It meant the houses didn't need sprucing; they needed exorcisms. No wonder Landers had given them to her. Since she was a witch, she was probably more qualified to handle them than anyone else on staff. But Grace wasn't a ghost hunter. She mostly dealt with restorative potions and minor parlor tricks like lighting candles with her mind. "Why didn't you tell me all of this when you gave me the files?"

His expression turned sheepish. "Honestly, Grace, I guess I was testing you. I hadn't expected you to dive right in without seeking input from me."

Grace's temper flared, but she kept herself in check. Blowing up at her boss wasn't going to help, but she sure as hell didn't appreciate the implication that she needed his help to do her job. After all, she had been in the real estate business for twenty years. "Is that what you expect? For me to run to you with every issue?"

He let out a bark of laughter. "Nope. Not at all. In fact, agents who don't need any handholding are my favorite kind." Landers stood and held his hand out to her. "Welcome to the team, Grace. I really hope you sell at least one of those properties, because I think we could work well together."

Grace sat in her chair, stunned for a brief moment. This wasn't the same guy who'd interviewed her. This guy was a tough-as-nails manager who was also fair and appreciative of his staff. And that was exactly what she wanted in a boss. She pushed herself to her feet and took his hand in hers.

"Do you think you can clean up those properties enough that we can find buyers?" he asked her.

Grace nodded, even though she had no idea. Exorcising ghosts wasn't exactly a skill in her toolbox. But there had to be someone who knew how to do it, and she'd do everything in her power to pick their brains. "Yes. I do. I just need some time."

His lips curved into a pleased smile. "Good. Now get out of here and enjoy your date."

"Um, about that. How do you feel about interoffice dating?"

His lips twitched. "You're not asking me out, are you?"

Grace coughed and her entire body heated... again. She was desperate to shed the sweater wrap, but she really didn't want to flash him her cleavage after that exchange. She forced a chuckle. "No. But I'm having dinner with Owen and wanted to make sure that isn't against company policy or going to affect my job here."

He waved an unconcerned hand. "As long as it doesn't interfere with your work, I don't care what either of you do on your own time."

The tension she'd been carrying in her shoulders eased, and she smiled at him. He wasn't so bad after all. Suddenly she didn't just want the job because it was the only viable one in town. She wanted it because, despite their rocky start, he seemed like a decent man to work for. "Thanks. I'll call Mr. Saint tomorrow with a plan on how to deal with his properties."

"Once you have it worked out, loop me in on the details," he said as he rose from his chair.

"Of course."

Landers followed Grace out of the office.

Nina glanced up at them. She gave Landers a wide smile. "Is that all for the day, boss?"

"No. I just emailed you some contracts I need you to double-check and then send out to the sellers. Let them know I'm out for the night but that if they have questions, they can give me a call. After that, I need you to make a run to the office supply store. There's an email with a list of supplies you missed during your last trip."

"I can go in the morning—" she started.

"You could, but I need you, the supplies, and the bakery

order you're supposed to pick up to be here by eight o'clock. I'm meeting with a new client first thing."

"Oh, okay." Nina bit her lower lip and frantically started texting someone on her phone.

Grace thought it was probable that the woman had plans she needed to delay now that Landers had her working overtime. She also thought he might've been giving her a little payback for scheduling his last meeting so late in the day.

Landers stopped to say something to Owen and then swept out of the office.

"Ready?" Owen asked Grace.

"Ready."

"Good night, Nina," Owen called without glancing back at her.

The woman mumbled something about wearing a condom and hoping Ben Gay wasn't a turn off. Grace just threw her head back and laughed. She was, after all, the one going on a date with the hot real estate agent while Nina would be spending her evening shopping for ink and staples.

CHAPTER EIGHT

"Should we take one car?" Owen asked as they stood between their two vehicles in the parking lot.

"It's probably easier if—" Grace's phone buzzed, cutting her off. "Hold on one sec." She glanced at the screen and frowned when she saw it was Kevin Landers. "Hey, Boss," she said into the phone. "What did you forget?"

"Nothing. Since I'm the agent of record on the listing, I just got a call that a client wants to see the Victorian on Seaside Drive tonight. She'll be there with her agent in a half hour. I figured you'd want to know in case you want to get over there and make sure the house doesn't run them off."

"I'm on it." After she ended the call, she gave Owen an apologetic smile. "I'm sorry. I have to go show one of my houses. Can I get a raincheck on dinner?"

"Which house?" he asked, pursing his lips as if he were contemplating something.

"The Victorian on Seaside," she said as she moved around to the driver's side of her SUV. "Why?"

"Mind if I tag along? I haven't seen it yet. It would be nice to have a reference in case any of my clients might be interested in it." He leaned against his BMW and smiled at her. "Plus, after you're done, we could still grab dinner."

Grace chuckled, knowing he could've stopped by that house at any time. There was a lockbox, and since it was represented by Landers Realty, there was no need for her to be there. "Are you that desperate for a date?" she asked playfully.

"Not desperate, but if you think I'm stupid enough to pass up an evening with a woman as sexy as you, then maybe you aren't quite as bright as I thought you were." He winked at her, making her insides turn to goo.

Why was she reacting so strongly to his cheesy flirting? *Probably because you haven't been properly laid in a couple of years*, her inner voice whispered. And there was no arguing with that logic. While she'd skipped the Brazilian, she certainly had trimmed and shaved and moisturized her entire body. If there was ever a night when she was ready to throw herself at someone, this was it. Her body started to tingle just thinking about it. When she spoke again, her voice came out in a husky whisper. "Yeah, sure."

His dark eyes flashed with pure desire. But as soon as he blinked it was gone, leaving only curiosity. "How do you want to do this? One car or two?"

"I live near the property, so let's take two. That way if we still have time for dinner afterward, we can drop mine off and go together. Does that work?"

His lips curved into a sexy half smile. "Sounds perfect."

Grace climbed into her SUV and immediately cranked the AC. Was it hot in there, or was Owen going to make her spontaneously combust? Probably both. She turned all the vents she could reach so that they were pointed right at her and let out a sigh of relief. Considering the beach town was usually in the high sixties or low seventies in the summer, she should not be sweating this much. But she was learning hormones didn't just torture teenagers. How long had her doctor said this next level of hell would last? Years. She'd said the possibility was years. *Dammit.*

Someone tapped their horn, jerking her out of her pity party. She glanced over to see Owen lifting his hands in the air, obviously asking what was up. Grace waved a hand and pointed at the road, trying to convey that she was ready. Then, without waiting for him to respond, she backed out of the space and headed across town... again.

Owen beat Grace to the house and was parked across the street in his car waiting for her. Grace pulled into the driveway, killed the engine, and did a face check in the rearview mirror. She smoothed her hair, pleased that her makeup was still flawless, but just as she was glancing away, something caught her eye. Was that... a blond hair right in the middle of her forehead? A blond hair that was at least an inch long? She gasped out loud in horror as she frantically searched for the tweezers she kept in her purse.

How had this happened? She'd had half her face waxed. Lex had done her makeup and even inspected her face for a stray hair. Okay, she'd inspected her nose, but still. Was it possible that Shondra had cursed her? Probably. At least the hair was blond, but it was an inch long. How had she missed it? Did she need new glasses? She made a mental note to get her vision checked as soon as possible. Finally, her fingers closed around her tweezers, and she made quick work of the single hair trying to take over her forehead.

Knock, knock.

Grace jerked back in her seat, her fingers tightening

around the tweezers so hard she accidently pinched herself. She let out a yelp and dropped the tweezers between the seat and the console. "Crap!"

"Is everything okay in there?" Owen asked, his face pinched in concern.

"Yep!" She pushed the door open and grabbed her messenger bag. "Sorry about that. Had a grooming emergency."

His lips twitched, but he wisely didn't say anything as he followed her up the overgrown walkway.

"Okay, so this place is a two-story Victorian with a gorgeous deck off the back that overlooks the ocean. If it had been in my budget when I was looking for my place, I would've seriously considered it."

"Even though it's haunted?" Owen asked.

Grace punched in the code on the lockbox. "You heard about that, huh?"

"Everyone's heard about it. Or at least all the real estate agents within a hundred miles. I heard there's a pool going on whether or not you can sell any of these properties."

"What?" Grace jerked upright and spun around on her heels to stare at him. "Other agents are betting if I can move Mr. Saint's properties? Jeez, that news got around fast."

He nodded, looking sheepish.

"Let me guess. You bet against me." She gave him a flat stare and decided she'd have the pint of peanut butter and chocolate ice cream for dinner instead of going out with him. At least that would make her feel good.

"Of course not." He grabbed her hand and held it lightly in his. "I bet you'd sell all three by the end of summer and at least one of them for asking price."

"You did?" She stared at their connection, imagining him

running that hand over her bare hip. She shivered at the thought and had to stop herself from licking her lips. He was just so... delicious.

"I did," he confirmed.

The two of them stood on the front porch staring at each other, and just as Grace started to lean in to kiss him, she heard a car door slam. They both jumped back as if they'd been caught making out in the janitor's closet. Grace let out a nervous chuckle and then peeked around Owen at the tiny woman making her way up the walk. She looked to be in her early thirties and was dressed in classic Chanel and the most beautiful red heels that were accented by red bows tied around her ankles. She was pure elegance and class.

Vince Hill, a Realtor from a neighboring town, followed her. He raised a hand in a cheerful wave. "Grace! Are you the new agent working for Kevin?"

"It appears so." She smiled warmly at him. He'd always been a pleasure to work with. She held out her hand to the client. "Hello, I'm Grace Valentine, and this is my colleague, Owen Taylor. I hope you don't mind him tagging along. He works in my office and hasn't had a chance to see the property yet."

Her grip was firm as she pumped Grace's hand. "It's perfectly fine. I'm Gigi Martin, and I can't wait to get another look at this house."

"Another?" Grace asked. "You've been here before?"

"Oh, yes. I probably shouldn't be telling you this, but I absolutely fell in love with it. So much charm. And the view. Ah! It's everything."

"Well, with that endorsement, now I'm dying to see it." Owen held out his hand to her. "It's nice to meet you, Gigi."

"You too." She smiled and then fluttered her eyelashes as she stared up at him. "Oh, my. You're a pretty one."

Owen sputtered out a laugh. "Thanks."

Grace chuckled when she noticed Owen's cheeks turning pink. "Why don't we go in and take a look around?"

"Yes, please." Gigi took a moment to glance around at the dilapidated porch. "I see the spirits are still trying to run people off."

"Spirits?" Grace asked. She had no doubt the place was haunted, but she didn't know by who. If Gigi knew something she didn't, then she wasn't going to miss an opportunity to get informed.

"Oh, come on, Grace. Everyone knows this place is haunted. But that doesn't bother me." She waved an unconcerned hand. "I've always had a fascination with ghosts. The only real question is will they accept me?"

"That's..." Grace nodded. "Yeah. If you're really interested in a haunted house, I suppose that's the best way to approach things. Let's see what they have to say."

She opened the door for Gigi and Vince. Grace and Owen followed them in.

Owen squeezed her hand briefly. "I'm just going to quietly take a look around while you do your thing. Okay?"

"Okay." She smiled at him and watched as he disappeared up the stairs.

Vince hung back near the entryway of the house. There was a nervous expression on his face, and he kept looking at the front door as if he was ready to bolt at any moment. Grace ignored him and watched as Gigi moved to the sliding glass doors at the back of the house.

She unlocked and then pulled the door open, letting the sea salt-scented air filter through the house. Her honey-colored hair lifted slightly in the breeze as she stood there staring at the dramatic coastline.

Then a strange thing happened. A glowing gold outline of shimmering light seemed to coat her skin, and the walls around her seemed to shift to a brighter shade of white while the wood floors gleamed as if light was shining through the boards. The breeze turned warmer, inviting, and Grace felt the unmistakable tingle of pure white magic filling the home.

Whatever was happening, it was clear the house had fully accepted Gigi. The spirits who had been keeping everyone else away obviously welcomed her.

"This is my happy place," Gigi said with a sigh as she turned around and smiled at Vince and Grace.

A surge of excitement went through Grace. She wasn't one to get worked up about offers. People were often very unpredictable when searching for a home. They could fall in love with a place, promise an offer within the hour, and then change their minds ten minutes later due to something silly like the color of the home. On the other hand, she'd shown more than a handful of houses where the buyer complained about every single detail, including the neighborhood, and then made an offer the next day that was equal or at least close to the asking price. She'd learned quickly to curb her expectations.

But Gigi and the house at 5 Seaside Drive had a clear connection, and Grace knew this house not only wanted her but would scare away anyone else who came poking around. The magic was that strong.

"How soon are you looking to move?" Grace asked, just to get an idea of where Gigi was in the buying process.

"As soon as possible," she said, lightly trailing her fingertips over the white quartz countertops. Her gaze met

Vince's, and some unspoken understanding passed between them.

Grace desperately wanted to ask more but decided to keep her questions to herself. She didn't appreciate when other agents hounded her clients, and she wouldn't do it to theirs. After they left, she'd have a private conversation with Vince to find out if she could expect an offer soon.

Gigi walked back over to the sitting area and started pointing out how she'd arrange her furniture and where her grandmother's side table would go. At first Grace thought she was talking to her and Vince, but Gigi stared into the fireplace and giggled when she said, "Stop. You're making me blush."

Grace's eyebrows shot up. Was she talking to the spirits?

Footsteps sounded on the stairs, and Grace glanced up to see Owen descending down to the main floor. He'd just joined her when the front door banged open and a tall man stormed in. His hair was styled with an excessive amount of gel, and he was wearing an expensive-looking suit with a red silk tie.

"Gigi! What the hell? I told you this place was off the table. Why are you here again?" He spun and glared at Vince. "And why are you taking my wife out to showings alone? I told you I didn't want her looking at homes without me."

"James," Gigi admonished. "Don't berate Vince. He's just doing his job."

"And he's sneaking around behind my back to do it," James said. "Do you two have something going on?"

"Don't be ridiculous." Gigi's eyes were narrowed and her hands curled into fists as the golden shimmer around Gigi vanished, as did the magic sparking in the air. It was replaced with a cold chill that didn't have anything to do with the cool breeze still wafting in from outside. The chill crawled all over Grace's skin, making her want to run from the house and whatever was haunting it.

There was one thing that was clear—the spirits were not happy with James's arrival.

All the hope and excitement about moving the house vanished. The very idea of James purchasing the house was ludicrous. The spirits wanted Gigi, but it was hard to see them ever accepting James.

Grace glanced over at Owen. The grim expression on his face did nothing to soothe her. She cleared her throat. "Gigi, are you all right?"

The woman glanced at her, but it was James who spoke. "Of course she's all right. Gigi, come here. We're going home."

The front door suddenly slammed shut, and an impressive gust of wind blew in from the open sliding glass doors. It was so strong it actually forced James to take a few steps backward, but interestingly enough, no one else was bothered.

"I want to take a look around upstairs first," Gigi said defiantly. "You said I should have the vacation home of my dreams. And this house is the place of my dreams."

"And I told you anyplace but this one." He moved toward her, his arm outstretched as if he was going to grab for her.

Grace was about to step forward and put herself between them because everything about James was setting off her internal alarm bells, but Gigi handled it. She placed her hand out in front of her in a stop motion and said, "That's enough."

James froze, his mouth open in surprise. "What are you doing?"

"Standing my ground." She narrowed her eyes at her husband. Then they flashed with that same golden shimmer for just a moment before they turned blue again. "I will tour this house. If you want me to leave, you'll have to physically drag me out of here."

He let out a low growl. "Gigi, don't make me—"

"I think that's quite enough." This time when Grace moved, she actually did put herself between them. She turned to eye the woman's husband. "I think I'm going to have to ask you to step off the property now, sir."

James blinked at her then glanced back at Vince and Owen, who had both moved to form a small circle around the man. He took a deep breath, craned his head to look over Grace's shoulder, and said, "Gigi, I'll be outside. Don't take all night. We have dinner plans."

"You don't have to wait. I'll meet you at the restaurant in thirty minutes."

James's nostrils flared and his face flushed with anger, but after a moment, he turned on his heel and stalked out. As soon as the man stepped outside, the oppressive energy vanished with him.

Gigi lowered her hand. And as her bravado faded, her entire body started to shake. "Grace, Vince, I'm so sorry. I had no idea he was going to come here. I don't even know how he knew."

Vince cleared his throat. "Uh, sorry. I think that was me. When I returned your call earlier, I hit James's number by mistake and left a message before calling you."

Gigi bit her bottom lip and then nodded. "I see. Well, it's not your fault I had no intention of telling him about seeing the house again until later tonight." She squeezed her eyes shut, and when she opened them, she pasted on a smile and added, "If you don't mind, I'm going to get that look at the upstairs. Then I'll let you nice folks get on with your evening."

"Take your time," Grace said. "It's no problem, really." She had no illusions that James and Gigi were going to buy the house, not after that interaction, but she felt for Gigi. Her connection to the house was palpable.

Gigi nodded once and then disappeared upstairs. Once she was gone, Grace moved to the back door to stare out at the churning ocean.

"Sorry about this, Grace," Vince said from behind her.

"It's not your fault." She gave him a sympathetic smile. "I've had my share of feuding couples."

He let out a sardonic chuckle. "I should've known better. I knew the husband was a hard pass, but when Gigi called..." He shrugged. "You know how unpredictable people can be."

"I do." She patted his arm. "It's really too bad though, isn't it? This house is hers in every way except for the name on the title."

"It is." He sighed and stuffed his hands into his pockets. "This isn't good news for either of us."

"Nope."

Gigi reappeared, looking ethereal as she practically floated down the stairs. Her smile was radiant, and Grace thought she'd never seen another person so at peace. The woman was an enigma. How could she be so Zen after that scene with her husband? Grace would've been spitting nails for the rest of the night. That was one perk of being divorced though. She hadn't had to consider Bill's input when she purchased her cottage. She smiled to herself as she thought about the day she'd moved in. The feeling of having something all her own after years of compromise had been sweeter than she'd ever imagined.

"Grace, it was a pleasure to meet you," Gigi said, extending her hand.

Grace took it with both of hers. "The feeling is mutual. Please let Vince know if you have any other questions about this place. I'd be happy to answer them."

She smiled. "Thanks. There is one thing you can do for me."

"Okay. Name it."

"I really would like to know the identities of the spirits haunting this place. I think it might help convince my husband they aren't evil. To me they feel... protective."

Grace thought she was probably right about that. At the very least, they were protective of her. "I'll see what I can do. I'm not experienced in communicating with spirits, so no guarantees."

"Something tells me you're a quick learner." She winked at Grace and then glided over to Vince. "I have to go. James is waiting."

Vince glanced at Grace and mouthed over Gigi's head that he'd be in touch. Then he placed a hand on Gigi's back and whispered something in her ear that sounded like he was asking if everything was okay with James and if she needed any help.

Good. That guy had warning signs all over him, and it pleased Grace to know that Vince was looking out for Gigi.

Owen moved to the back door to close and lock it. When he returned to Grace's side, he said, "I don't know if I can top the show that just rolled through here, but if you're still up for it, I'd love to take you to dinner."

Grace glanced at the time on her phone. It was already a

quarter to eight, and suddenly she was exhausted after her long day. Not to mention she had an early appointment in the morning with a potential new buyer. "What do you say to takeout? We could go back to my house. There's a really good deli a few blocks from here."

His eyes sparkled as his lips curved into a slow smile. "Sounds perfect."

CHAPTER NINE

"Do you want to walk down to the beach?" Grace asked Owen. They'd just returned to her house with their deli sandwiches, and the summer sun was hanging low in the sky. Her nerves were all over the place as she suggested, "There's a picnic table down there. We could eat while watching the sunset."

"That sounds just about perfect, Grace."

"Give me just one minute to change and lose these shoes." She slipped into her house and emerged a few minutes later wearing her favorite white blouse, jeans, and her flip-flops. She'd also grabbed a bottle of wine and two plastic wine glasses.

Owen clutched the bag of food and then took her free hand in his as he let her guide him toward the path that led to the beach.

"If we're lucky we might even glimpse the seals while they're having their own dinner," she said.

"Really? Do they show up often?"

"Yeah. More often than not. It's one of the reasons I

decided to get a house on this side of town." She glanced over at him, giving him a relaxed smile. "There's just something about watching the sea life that fills me with peace. It's like the natural order of things or something."

"And here I thought it was so you could be as far away from your ex as possible." He gave her a teasing smile and squeezed her hand.

She laughed. "That, too. What about you? Did you move to Premonition Pointe to get away from someone?"

He shrugged one shoulder. "I don't know. Maybe?"

"Maybe?" She shook her head. "I call foul. You know all about my messy divorce. Meanwhile, I know next to nothing about your past. It's only fair that you elaborate. Any failed marriages or long-term relationships I should know about?"

"No marriages," he said immediately. "But I did live with someone for a few years. It didn't work out."

"That was vague." She descended down a path of wooden stairs that would take them right to the beach. Once her feet hit the sand, she said, "Care to share?"

Owen chuckled. "Not really. But the short version is she wanted to get married and I didn't. So we broke up."

Grace took a seat at the picnic table and immediately poured them both a glass of wine. "Commitment issues?" she asked out of pure curiosity. After her divorce, she was done with marriage altogether.

He picked up his wine glass and watched the liquid as he swirled it around. "Not necessarily. I was committed to that relationship. I guess I just didn't see us as forever. She did and told me she'd never have moved in with me if she didn't think we were moving toward something more permanent. Looking back, I probably should've seen that, but I was happy just cohabitating. When it was clear she wasn't, I left."

"Did you love her?" Grace propped her chin on her hand as she watched him.

He raised one eyebrow. "You really want to know this?"

"Only if you want to tell me. I was married for over twenty years and never really did the dating thing much. Bill and I got together my freshman year in college. So I find the dating dynamics of adults fascinating."

"I think I *thought* I loved her. Or at least that I wanted to." He pulled the sandwiches out of the bag and handed the one marked *Turkey* to her. "She was fun, accomplished, and sexy."

"She sounds wonderful. What was the problem?"

"To be honest, I don't really know. When she started talking about marriage, I couldn't see myself in that life. And then it all imploded." He unwrapped his roast beef sandwich and held it up, but he didn't take a bite. Instead, he looked her in the eye and asked, "What does that say about me? Maybe I am a commitment-phobe."

Grace took a bite of her sandwich as she thought about what he'd said. After she washed the bite down with a gulp of wine, she asked, "Do you miss her? Or regret the decision?"

"No. Not really. I think I just miss the companionship." He gazed out at the ocean and pointed to the left near an outcropping of rocks near the shore. "Look. Seals."

Grace squinted until she spotted their heads bobbing in the water. "This is my favorite part of the day."

"I can see why."

After tearing her gaze away from the water, she said, "Based on what you've told me, I don't think you're a commitment-phobe at all. I think you knew that forever wasn't in the cards with her and you were honest about that. I'd say that makes you a decent guy. As long as you didn't make her promises you knew you couldn't or wouldn't keep, then I think this is just a case of a relationship that ran its course. There's nothing wrong with that. It's not like you cheated on her and upended her entire life."

Grace winced when she heard the words come out of her mouth. They sounded so bitter. She didn't want to talk about Bill while she was on a date with this man who was not only incredibly sexy, but smart and attentive, too. He didn't deserve to have her dump her baggage on him. "Sorry." She forced a chuckle. "I got a little heated."

"It must've been rough losing your husband and your career all in one blow," he said, reaching for her hand and lacing his fingers between hers.

"My entire life blew up." She gave him a small smile. "But you know what?"

"What?"

"I'm not sorry it happened. After I left and only had myself to worry about, I realized I have spent my entire life taking care of someone else's needs. He owned the business, right? So I was the support for literally everything. And I went into that willingly because I thought we were partners. It turns out he thought differently. So never again. If I ever do decide to share my life with someone again, things will be different. My career will never be about lifting someone else up again. As far as household duties, those will be shared or else we just won't ever live together."

Owen let out a bark of laughter. "You make it sound like you were living in a fifties sitcom."

Grace wanted to cry because it wasn't far from the truth. Sure, she was a modern witch and had always insisted on being an equal partner when it came to the decision-making, but there was no denying their entire marriage had revolved around Bill's brokerage firm. Grace had done as much or more than him to make it a success, and she'd been tossed aside and treated as if she'd just been office support. Pathetic. "Not exactly, but in some respects it's probably closer than I care to admit." She downed her wine and turned to him. "Make no mistake, Owen. I'm outspoken and strong-willed. I made my own choices when it came to that marriage. Unfortunately, I bet on a person who wasn't one thousand percent in it with me. I won't make that mistake again."

His lips twitched. "I don't think I'd be sitting here right now if you weren't outspoken and strong-willed. Those two qualities are sort of my weakness."

"Is that so?" It was exactly the right thing to say, and Grace didn't even care if it was just a line. She liked Owen, but she knew nothing serious was ever going to happen between them. So what did it matter if she just enjoyed herself?

"It is." His gaze dropped to her lips, and the air between them suddenly became charged.

Grace reached out and placed a hand on his chest, her fingers tingling when she felt his well-defined muscle beneath the button-down shirt. Damn. She'd barely touched him, and she was already fantasizing about ripping his clothes off. The internal flame roared to life, and all Grace could think about was tasting him. "Owen?"

"Yes, Grace?"

"I think you'd better kiss me now."

He let out a short breath just before his hand cupped the back of her head and he pulled her in until his lips brushed over hers.

His lips were soft and warm despite the cooling evening air. Grace leaned into him, the fingers of her right hand curling into his shirt. He tasted of wine and the sea and pure bliss.

Yes, her mind chanted over and over again as he slipped his tongue into her mouth, tasting and teasing and driving her completely mad.

Owen let out a tiny groan, wrapped one arm around her waist, and deepened the kiss. By the time he pulled back, they were both breathless, and Grace felt completely alive for the first time in... forever.

She smiled shyly at him. "Hi."

"Hi." He touched his forehead to hers and stroked his thumb over her cheek. "That was..."

"Nice?" she offered.

Owen chuckled. "Nice doesn't even come close. I was going to say intense."

Grace laughed nervously. "It's been a while since I've been kissed like that."

"Me, too." He pulled back and pressed another soft kiss to her lips. "We're missing the sunset."

Who cared when Owen was touching her like that? "Yeah? Do we care?"

"Nope." Owen tilted her chin up and once again, those magical lips claimed hers.

"Woohoo! Yeah! Get it!" a voice called from across the beach.

Grace jerked back, startled by the sight of a small group of people about thirty yards away. Only a few moments ago, they'd had the beach to themselves.

"Don't stop on our account!" the young man called.

Owen rolled his eyes and got to his feet. "How about I walk you back to your house?"

Grace's stomach fluttered. Would she invite him in? Yes.

There was no question. He just made her feel too good. The voice in the back of her mind whispered, *Slow down, Grace. You don't want to jump into anything with your coworker.*

She quickly squashed the voice. What did it know? She was the new Grace. The one who was embracing her life on her own terms. And that meant if she wanted to invite a sexy man back to her house, then dammit, she would.

Owen cleaned up the remnants of their dinner and then held his hand out to her. She took it, and without another word, they made their way back to Grace's cottage.

CHAPTER TEN

*G*race pulled Owen into her cottage and the instant the door shut, she pressed him up against it, her hands on his chest. As she let her gaze travel over him, she licked her lips.

"Careful, Grace," he said, his voice husky. "If you keep that up, you're going to have a choice to make."

"Really?" She brought her hand up and caressed the small cleft in his chin with her thumb. "What choice would that be?"

His eyes were dark pools of lust as he said, "To either kick me out or let me strip you naked and take you right here against the wall."

Raw desire rippled through Grace, and she had zero confidence that she could stop the runaway train they were on, not that she wanted to. She leaned into him and whispered, "Bedroom."

He kissed her and started walking her backward down the hall. She reached up, already undoing his buttons, while he tugged her blouse out of her pants. His hands were on her bare skin, sending tingles up and down her spine. Was this really happening? If it wasn't, she was having one hell of a realistic dream.

"Which door is it?" he asked between kisses.

"End of the hall." She finished off his last button and was in the middle of shoving his shirt off his shoulders when loud voices echoed from the living room.

"Just stop, okay? I'm not going to call her," Lex said, her voice raised and full of exasperation.

Her outburst was followed by a softer voice, but it was no less insistent. Grace was certain the second person was Bronwyn Bellweather, Lex's girlfriend.

Grace froze and whispered, "That's my niece."

"Niece?" Owen jumped back, stumbling into the wall and tugging his shirt back on.

"Grace? Is that you?" Lex called. "Are you home?"

Since Grace's car was in the garage and they'd neglected to turn on any lights, there hadn't been anything to tip Lex off that she was there. "Yes. I'll be right out."

"Good," she said, her voice sounding closer. "I thought for a moment there might be an—oh!" She rounded the corner into the hallway and came to a dead stop. "Omigod. Sorry, Grace. Bron and I will just get out of your hair." She glanced at Owen, her face flushing red. Then she spun around and hurried back into the living room.

"You don't have to leave," Grace called. "We'll be out in a second."

"It's really not a problem. We can go get ice cream or something."

"There's some in the freezer," Grace countered.

Owen cleared his throat. "Ice cream?"

"Yep. Chocolate peanut butter." Grace chuckled grimly

and slapped her hand over her eyes as she let out a sigh. "I can't believe you just got cock-blocked by a couple of lesbians."

"Seriously?" He laughed. "That's a new one."

Grace hastily tucked in her shirt and waited until Owen put himself back together. Then she guided him back into the living room where Lex was sprawled on the couch and Bronwyn was sitting in the armchair across from her.

"Can we stop talking about this now?" Lex asked, sounding defeated.

Bronwyn brushed her chestnut curls out of her eyes, revealing her concerned expression. "But, babe. She's your mom. You can't just keep ignoring her."

"Who says I can't!" Lex jumped up off the couch, suddenly so angry her face turned red. "She keeps trying to erase you from my life. The worst part is that she's denying a part of me for her own selfish fantasy of what she wants my life to look like. Don't you see how much that hurts me every time she does that? And you want me to just forgive her? No. Forget it. I'm done with that."

Bronwyn stood, too. "How can things get better if you don't give her a chance? When I sat down and talked to my mom—"

"My mom isn't your mom!" Lex buried both hands in her short hair and tugged so hard she winced.

Owen leaned close to Grace's ear and whispered, "It looks like you might have your hands full. I should probably get going."

He was right. There was a full-on meltdown going on in her living room. She didn't want Owen to have to deal with their family drama. "I'm sorry. This isn't how I envisioned the night going," she whispered back and then turned her attention to the two women who were still each trying to argue their perspectives on insensitive mothers. "Hey," Grace said gently. "How about you both take a time out for a sec here. I'm going to walk Owen out, and then maybe we can get that ice cream and discuss this calmly?"

"Whatever." Lex flopped back down on the couch. "No matter what either of you say, I'm not calling my mom."

Grace patted her niece's shoulder as she walked by and said, "You don't have to do anything you don't want to do."

"Sorry, Owen," Lex said as she watched him follow Grace to the door. "I'm not usually this much of a drama queen."

He smiled over his shoulder at her just as Grace opened the front door. "Don't worry. I've had my share of altercations with the parental figures. It's just part of growing up, I guess."

Lex snorted. "If only it were that easy."

"Lex," Bronwyn pleaded. "I'm sure there is a way—"

Grace closed the door on the fight that was picking back up in the living room and walked with Owen to his car parked across the street from her house.

Before opening his car door, Owen slipped his arms around Grace and pulled her in for a soft kiss.

Grace leaned into him, enjoying the hardness of his fit body one last time for the evening. "If we'd met last week, this night would've ended very differently."

"Yeah? What's different about this week?" He ran his fingers along her spine, and even though his touch was through the fabric of her blouse, her skin still tingled.

"Lex just moved in after a fight with my sister's live-in boyfriend. They seem to be having trouble accepting that she's never going to marry a man."

"Homophobes?" he asked, his brows pinching together.

"The boyfriend maybe. But until this week, I never would've described my sister that way. I think she's having trouble accepting that when, or if, Lex starts a family, it's not going to be whatever Alyssa envisioned when Lex was her little girl. She keeps making references to Lex's best friend Jackson and how much she always wanted them to get together. How cute their kids would be and that it's never too late to switch teams."

"That's got to be rough for Lex. Is that what she and her friend are arguing about? Or is that her girlfriend?"

"Girlfriend," Grace confirmed. "Yeah. Bronwyn has a very accepting family. She has trouble understanding how hard it is for Lex to hear her formerly supportive mom suddenly be so insensitive. I don't know, Owen. It just seems like my sister is letting her opinions be influenced by that jackass she's living with. And maybe that isn't giving her enough credit, but ever since he arrived in the picture, she's been different."

"That's tough for both of you," he said, caressing her cheek gently.

"More so for Lex. I'm just irritated." She tilted her head up and closed her eyes, enjoying his touch. When she opened them again, he was staring down at her with an intensity that made her skin burn. "What is it?"

"You're just so lovely," he said. "The last thing I want to do is go home right now. I'd much rather march you right back into your house and into your bedroom, your niece and her girlfriend be damned."

Grace groaned. "Stop, or things are about to get indecent."

He chuckled. "That would be quite the town gossip."

97

She kissed him again and then reluctantly took a step back. "See you tomorrow?"

"Actually, no." He grabbed one of her hands and squeezed lightly. "I'm headed out of town for a cousin's wedding up north. I'll be back on Monday. Can I cash in that raincheck for the dinner date?"

"Sure." Grace was surprised at how disappointed she was that he was leaving for five days. When had she gotten so invested in him? Likely right about the time she'd decided it was a good idea for them to get naked. "Next week then?"

"It's a date. We'll work out the details later." He kissed her on the cheek and slid into his BMW.

Grace watched him go, taking a moment to let the night air cool her heated body. Then she took a deep breath and headed back into the house.

The living room was empty, and Grace followed the sound of clanking dishes into the kitchen. She found Bronwyn fumbling with the coffee grinder while Lex angrily scooped ice cream into three bowls.

Grace moved to Bronwyn's side and showed her how to work the machine. Once they had the decaf coffee brewing, Grace pulled a can of whipped cream out of the refrigerator and squirted the creamy goodness in each of the bowls. When they were all seated at the table with way too many calories in front of them, Grace said, "Anyone want to tell me what's going on?"

Lex shook her head.

Bronwyn sighed and stuffed her mouth full of ice cream.

"Does anyone mind if I talk?" Grace asked.

Lex shrugged one shoulder and Bronwyn nodded her agreement.

"Okay then. Without knowing the specifics of the

argument, I think that relationships are hard enough to navigate and letting parents come between you is a hurdle you don't need."

"We can't just ignore our parents, though," Bronwyn said. "What is Lex going to do, just cut her mother out of her life? Neither of them wants that."

Lex sucked in a sharp breath but didn't say anything.

"It's not what I want either." Grace reached across the table and took Lex's hand and squeezed it. "But, Bron, it's not my decision, and it's not yours either. Lex needs to decide what she needs from her mother. If she needs to talk to Alyssa and get everything off her chest, then so be it. Or if she just needs space for a while to be mad and try to deal with all those feelings of rejection, then we need to give her that space. Feeling as if your parents don't accept who you are can be traumatic."

Bronwyn put her spoon down and leaned back in her chair. After covering her face with her hands, she mumbled something.

"Bron?" Grace asked. "Are you okay?"

She dropped her hands, and her dark eyes were shining with unshed tears. "It's just so hard to see her hurting. I love her so much. I just want to fix it for her."

Lex let out a tiny sob and reached for her girlfriend. "I love you, too," she blurted, clinging to her. "I know you're just trying to help. Don't cry."

"It's just that talking always works with my mom. I figured it could work with yours too."

Both Grace and Lex let out humorless barks of laughter.

Bronwyn glanced between the two of them. "I'm guessing by your reactions that's not at all the case?"

Grace shook her head while Lex said, "Not even close.

My mother lives in her own world view of what she wants. Finding common ground is nearly impossible these days."

As the two women discussed Alyssa and her dysfunctional relationships, Grace picked up her uneaten bowl of ice cream and said, "I'm taking my dessert and heading to bed. You two have a good night, okay?"

"You, too," Bronwyn said.

"Grace?" Lex called just before she turned down the hall.

"Yeah?"

"Thanks for—" She waved a hand between herself and Bronwyn. Grace knew they still had things to work out, but they'd get through it now that they were communicating.

"Anytime. Glad I could help."

"And sorry you didn't get to Netflix and chill. Maybe next time put a sock on the front door as a warning." The two of them giggled.

Grace rolled her eyes. Netflix and chill. Two months ago, Grace had actually thought that phrase meant watching a movie and relaxing. Now she knew it was code for hooking up. "Next time I have the opportunity to get my groove back, I'm going to get the locks changed. No sock needed."

Their giggles turned into full-blown laughter while Grace disappeared down the hallway, wondering what Owen was doing at that moment. He certainly wasn't conducting amateur therapy sessions. Had he still been worked up when he got home? Had he whipped out the porn or jumped into the shower for some personal time? Damn, it was hot imagining him wet in the shower with his hand wrapped around himself as he thought of her.

Her core body temperature ratcheted up, but for the first time in forever, she knew it wasn't a hot flash, just pure desire. She flopped down on her bed, shoved another bite of ice cream in her mouth, and considered texting Owen.

But as soon as she typed out the text, she deleted it. Then she went to take her own shower, determined to wash away the faint scent of desperation.

CHAPTER ELEVEN

"*M*r. Dahl?" Grace asked, striding up to a booth in the Pointe of View Café where a tall, silver-haired man sat in jeans and a tight black T-shirt. Sun shone through the window, illuminating his green eyes, and Grace couldn't help but admire him. She wouldn't say he was sexy, more like alluring. He had an air about him that just made her want to sit down and learn his life story. Instead, she needed to learn his real estate needs so that she could find him the perfect house. "I'm Grace Valentine."

"Please, call me Matt." He stood and held his hand out to her. "It's nice to meet you."

"Same to you. Thank you for letting me help you with your real estate needs."

A waitress appeared and took Grace's order for coffee and a cinnamon roll. She was still feeling indulgent after her date was cut short a few nights ago, and she promised herself she'd get to the gym that evening one way or another.

Grace spent the next hour with Matt Dahl, jotting down notes about the beach property he was looking for. In the process, she learned he was widowed and had two grown sons. The property would need to have enough bedrooms for both of them and their spouses as well as a bedroom or two for any grandkids.

"I have one listing that fits all of that criteria that's on the market now," Grace said, trying not to sound hesitant about the haunted cottage. She and Hope were going to try to smudge the property later that day. Hope had a few tricks up her sleeve. With any luck, when they were done there wouldn't be any creepers waiting to run him off. "But I can't show it until tomorrow."

"That's fine. I'll be in town through the end of next week."

She scribbled a note to herself. "It will also give me some time to go through the local listings and see if I can find anything else that might fit the bill. There might be a few."

"Just as long as it has a spectacular view. Anything less isn't even worth looking at."

"Got it." She took out her business card and handed it to him. "I'll do my best to weed through everything. If you find something online you want to make sure you see, shoot me an email and I'll make us an appointment. Does tomorrow at nine sound okay to start?"

"Meet here for breakfast again? Say eight?" he asked, scanning his gaze over her as if *she* were going to be his breakfast.

Alarm bells went off in Grace's head. "That's kind of you to offer, but I need to run into the office for a meeting first thing," she lied. "I can meet you here for a quick cup of coffee while we go over the listings we'll be touring."

"Okay. I can live with that." He smiled at her, his green eyes twinkling. "It's a date."

"A date?" a very familiar male voice said from behind her.

Bill. Grace stiffened and unconsciously curled her hand into a fist.

"Are you sure that's what you want to do?" He appeared at their table, smiling down at her gently. "It's been a rough few months, and all this dating just seems to be a little much, don't you think?"

"Excuse me?" Grace glared up at her ex and wondered what would happen if she just reached out and junk-punched him.

"It's just a little too fast," he told Matt. "She's been out of the dating pool for over twenty years, and two dates in one week seems a little fast."

Two dates? When and how had he heard about Owen?

Matt cocked an eyebrow at Bill. "Uh, how do you know Grace?"

Bill smiled patiently at the man. "I'm her soon-to-be ex-husband. We had a really good run, but just grew apart. You know how it is."

Grace, who had been shocked beyond words when Bill suddenly decided to inject his opinion on her fledgling dating life, snapped out of her silence and let out a sardonic laugh. "Sure. It's not easy to stay in sync when your husband is boinking the office receptionist."

Matt turned steely eyes on Bill. "Perhaps you should step back and let Ms. Valentine and I finish our business meeting."

"Business meeting?" Bill stared at Grace. "What business?"

Grace gave him a sickly-sweet smile, thoroughly enjoying herself as she said, "Real estate business, Bill. I work for Kevin Landers now."

Bill's pudgy face turned a dark shade of red as he sputtered, "Landers? You work for *Landers?*"

"Sure," she said breezily. "Who else was I going to work for? Surely you didn't expect me to come ask you for a job at On Pointe, did you?"

"Well, why wouldn't you?" he said, appearing completely bewildered.

Grace rose from her seat and grabbed the bill the waitress had left on the table. "Bill, you're an idiot."

"You really are," she heard Matt say as she stalked off to pay for their breakfast. She watched from the counter as the two got into an obviously heated conversation before Bill finally trudged over to the counter.

"That client is a douche, Grace," he said with a sneer. "Bad news. Tell him to get another agent. You don't need that trash."

Grace signed her credit card bill and then turned to stare at him for a long moment.

"What? I'm just looking out for you."

"You are not. You're just pissed I'm moving on," she countered.

He scoffed. "Moving on? It sounds more like you're dating anyone who will have you. Really, Grace? Shondra's brother said you were making out with a guy half your age the other night at the beach. Now you're dating a client? What happened to you?"

Red-hot indignation coursed through her veins. The catcaller who'd seen her and Owen kissing had been Shondra's little brother? That was just freakin' perfect, wasn't it? She poked a finger into Bill's chest as she spoke through clenched teeth. "The moment you decided to sleep with Shondra you lost the right to have any input in my life. Mind your own damned business, Bill. I'll date whoever the hell I want to."

"Grace—" he started.

"I don't want to hear it." She spun on her heel and stormed out.

Matt met her just outside the café.

"I am so sorry," Grace said, mortified that her ex had interrupted their meeting, and worse, made her look like a fool. "That was completely unprofessional. I'll make sure it doesn't happen again."

"Please. No need to say more." He glanced through the window at Bill, who was at the counter ordering something to go. "I guess now's a good time to let you know I interviewed him before settling on Landers Realty."

Grace's eyebrows shot up. "You did?" She hadn't realized they'd met before, but now that she looked back on it, they had seemed more familiar than strangers.

Matt ran a hand through his silver hair and chuckled. "Yes. He was more interested in talking about his... ah, personal life than my real estate needs. I appreciate that you and Landers appear to be one hundred percent professional."

"Thank you," she said, wondering if she'd misinterpreted that look he'd given her earlier. Because right in that moment, he was all business. "We do our best."

"That's what I'm counting on." He gave her a short nod and added, "I'll see you in the morning. I'm looking forward to being impressed."

Grace watched as the man climbed into a Land Rover that was equipped with a surfboard on the top. He waved briefly and then took off toward the beach.

All signs indicated that if she were interested, he just might be the perfect catch. He was attractive in an interesting way, fit enough to surf, was financially secure enough to buy a beach home, and his kids were grown. And even though she'd second guessed herself, she knew she hadn't misconstrued his interest. Not that she'd ever act on it while he was her client, but after... Maybe?

But as she tried to picture herself walking with him on the beach, the only person she saw was Owen. The man who was too young for her and definitely not Mr. Forever.

She let out a bark of laughter and shook her head, trying to dislodge her thoughts. Mr. Forever? That was the last thing she needed.

What she needed was Mr. Right Now. Bill and his judgment could just go to hell.

CHAPTER TWELVE

"I thought Joy was going to meet us," Hope said. She was standing next to Grace in front of the large white cottage. The waves crashed in the distance, and the scent of the sea was thick in the dense fog.

"She's at the courthouse researching property records." The day before when Grace had been brainstorming ways to combat her haunted houses, she'd enlisted both of her coven sisters to help her figure out the best way to cleanse them without inviting new problems. Joy, whose hobbies included genealogy, figured it was best to find out who the ghosts were so they'd have a better idea of how to deal with them. Which was good since Gigi had asked Grace if she could find out the identities of the ghosts at the Victorian house. Hope was more of a take-charge kind of witch, just like Grace.

"What do you think?" Grace asked as she wrapped her sweater around herself tighter. She mentally thanked herself for taking the time to change from the skirt she'd worn that morning to jeans. The air had chilled significantly in the early afternoon, and even though early June was normally all sunshine in their seaside town, the skies had turned gray and drizzle was in the forecast. "Do we just go in with smudge sticks blazing, or should we do a salt circle and call in a goddess?"

Hope, who was dressed similarly in jeans and a sweatshirt, gazed at the cottage with her eyes squinted. She had the most experience with cleansing spaces and had offered to help Grace see what they could do. "It depends on how entrenched the spirit is in the fabric of the house. Can we go in first so I can get a feel for things?"

"Sure." Grace handed her a sachet of cloves. "Put this on."

Hope did so without comment and handed Grace a sage stick. "I got these at that place up north run by the Wiccan elder. They're supposed to be more powerful than the average sage bundles we get around here."

"They're worth a try."

"Let's do this." Hope strode up to the house, and without hesitation, she barged right in.

Grace followed closely behind her, and the moment she stepped over the threshold, icy cold air pricked her skin as if it were tiny little ice needles. "Ouch!" she complained and dropped the sage bundle as she pressed her hands to her cheeks to soothe the ache. She glanced at Hope, who was standing in the middle of the empty room looking contemplative. "Didn't you feel that?"

"Yep. I'm ignoring it." She closed her eyes and started to spin in a very slow circle.

Grace wanted to run back out of the house and demand that the owner find a professional but then realized that she *was* the professional. If she, a witch, couldn't figure out how to deal with the spirits taking over the house, who could? Ghost hunters? The ones she knew were just data collectors.

They didn't do anything but smudge buildings and politely ask spirits to leave. That worked fine most of the time. But some spirits refused to leave, and if they were nefarious, that's when everything went to hell.

Hope started to shimmer with magic.

As soon as the golden light appeared, the house groaned, making the hair stand up on Grace's arms. A shiver ran through her, but she steeled her spine and got to work. She pulled out her camera and started to methodically take pictures of each area of the room.

"That's really strange," Hope said.

Grace continued to take pictures as she asked, "What's strange?"

"As soon as you started to take photographs, the spirits vanished."

"What do you mean, vanished?" She lowered the camera and turned to look at her friend. "Are you saying they're camera shy?"

Hope nodded, her dark curls bouncing around her pink cheeks. "They don't want us to know who they are."

Grace blinked at her. "How do you know that?"

"Just a guess." She dropped the canvas bag she'd been carrying and said, "Let's do this. Maybe now that they have left, we can make it so uncomfortable that they don't want to come back."

"If you say so." Grace walked over to one of the windows that faced the ocean and opened it wide. The thick fog immediately started to seep in through the window. It was both amazing and creepy as all get out. Grace had lived in the small seaside town for over twenty years, and she was still awed by mother nature's natural wonders. "I'm not sure anyone can get out through this stuff."

Hope chuckled. "They can if they want to badly enough."

Grace rejoined her friend, grabbed her sage stick, and held it up with Hope's. Together they conjured a flame to light them both at the same time and chanted, "Purify this home by the sea. Release the ghosts, let them be free. Break the chains that bind, so that the tethers to this place unwind."

Grace broke away from Hope, waving the sage smoke in the air. She had to admit that the house felt much more at peace than it had the day she'd toured it. Could it really have been that easy? Take a few pictures to scare them off and then sage the place? If it was, whomever Mr. Saint had hired must have been the most incompetent—

BOOM!

Grace jerked so hard she stumbled backward into a fireplace mantle, cracking her elbow against the wood. "Ouch. Son of a chicken!"

Hope took off running up the stairs, and with unshed tears stinging Grace's eyes, she followed closely on her heels. Whatever had happened wasn't good, and Grace was likely to be held responsible. A pit formed in the depths of her stomach, and she pressed a palm to her gut, trying to settle the unease.

BOOM!

They both stumbled to a stop as the sound reverberated through the house again.

"Go!" Grace demanded, giving her friend a tiny shove. If the ghosts were destroying the house, they had to stop them somehow.

Hope cursed under her breath and then ran up the rest of the stairs. The two of them raced toward the end of the hall, following the ear-splitting noise and ending up in the master bedroom.

The house went eerily silent.

"Um, Hope?" Grace asked.

"Yeah?"

"I think we're not welcome here."

"You're not wrong about that. We should've summoned a goddess." She let out a breath and held the sage bundle high in the air.

"Can we still do that?" Grace did the same with her sage bundle.

"Maybe, but I doubt anything we do today is going to help. We've already pissed them off."

Dammit. How was Grace going to show Matt the house the next day? The spirits would scare him off in five seconds flat. Not to mention that she wasn't exactly crazy about selling someone a house that was haunted by spirits that might be of the evil variety.

"It's probably better at this point to wait and see what Joy comes up with and try to figure out why the spirits are tied to this place. That might make it easier to form a game plan."

"You're probably right." Grace started to move toward the bedroom door, but then the bathroom light flashed on.

Both Grace and Hope moved into the large en suite bathroom to investigate.

"There," Hope whispered, pointing at the mirror that was fogged over despite the lack of steam or moisture in the room.

Grace focused on the mirror and watched as a message in the most beautiful handwriting she'd ever seen appeared in the condensation on the surface.

Roots run deep. Family is the only thing that matters. We will never give up.

* * *

"Family is the only thing that matters," Grace said, repeating what seemed to be the most important part of the message the spirits had left in the mirror. "Do you suppose they want us to solve a mystery? You know, like they can't move on until justice is served or something?"

Hope flipped the menu over and stared at the cocktails. After they'd left the house, the pair had headed straight for Hallucinations, a beachside bar, to drink a late lunch. "It's a possibility I suppose." She pointed at the concoction at the bottom of the cocktail menu. "Lost Your Bikini. That one sounds like me, doesn't it?"

"Is it a mix of both light and dark rum and something teeth-achingly sweet?" Grace asked, eyeing the totchos. They were a mix of tater tots and nacho toppings and were to die for. So many calories, but after her day, she rationalized that she deserved the indulgence.

"You know me so well." Hope grinned. "I hope it comes in a bucket."

Grace snorted. "I'm sure you can just order more if necessary."

"But that's not as fun," she whined.

After the encounter at the big white cottage, Grace couldn't blame her. In fact, when the waiter arrived, she ordered the same drink and had to stop herself from asking for a double.

"We probably need to hit the gym after this." Hope sighed as she glanced down at her belly.

Grace shook her head. "Forget it. After the day we had, I'm now planning to go home, take a long bath in the spa tub and read a book."

"No you won't. You're much more likely to take a long walk on the beach and spend the rest of the night thinking about what that message means."

"What message?" Joy asked as she slid into the booth next to Hope. Her long blond hair was pulled up into a bun that was secured with a No. 2 pencil.

Grace just looked at her and sighed. "You know, if I rolled in here with my hair like that, a pencil smudge on my cheek, and zero makeup, I'd be a candidate for a production of *Night of the Living Dead*. But this wench? She looks like she belongs on the pages of Maxim selling laptops or something."

Hope snorted. "You're right." She peered at Joy. "How do you do that?"

Joy rolled her eyes. "Stop it. It's just because I'm wearing a pencil skirt and this button-down shirt. I went to the courthouse right after a meeting for the new Arts Market co-op."

"And you decided to dress like a hot schoolteacher for that?" Grace asked. "Why?"

"I'm on the board, vice president, remember?" she said, sounding impatient with their teasing. "I had a meeting with the city council to try to nail down the details for the monthly Art in the Park event. The last thing they needed was another hippy-dippy artist type who says things like, 'It all depends on if Mercury is in Retrograde' or 'Don't worry about the details. They always work themselves out.' Remember when Cynder was in charge? Ads ran days after events. Artists were setting up in two different parks. And she even let that erotica-on-demand writer have a booth next to the bouncy house they set up for the kids. Oh, remember when she—"

"Whoa," Grace said, waving her hands in the air. "Slow

down there, feisty. We were just teasing you. Everyone knows you're going to whip that co-op into shape. No need to defend your outfit, especially when you've got that sexy-librarian thing going on."

Hope nodded and took a long sip of her tropical drink the waiter had delivered during Joy's monologue.

"I'm glad you two think so. Paul wouldn't notice if I was butt-naked except for my flashing tassels on my tatas."

Grace, who'd been sampling her drink, choked and spit out the red liquid. "You have flashing tassels?"

Hope chuckled. "You didn't hear about the tassels?"

"No." Grace peered at Joy. "How come I'm lacking this vital information?"

Joy winced. "Sorry, Grace. It was right after you learned about Bill and Shondra. I didn't want to burden you with my nonsense."

Grace felt the sting of tears hit the backs of her eyes and angrily blinked them back. It wasn't that she was upset that she hadn't been looped in on the story. She didn't need to know every tiny detail of her friends' lives. She was angry that once again, no matter how minor the incident, Bill had robbed her of sharing this with her girlfriends. Who knew how many other things they'd kept from her in an effort to be sensitive? She appreciated them with all her heart, but she hated that anyone had felt it necessary to shield her from their everyday lives.

"Spill it," Grace demanded. "I need to know if I should overnight some before my next date."

"Do it," Hope urged, pumping her eyebrows as if she were in some comedy skit. "No need to hear a story about them before deciding. Besides, the faster you introduce the toys, the sooner you know what you're in for in the bedroom."

"No shit," Joy muttered. "Don't wait twenty-five years to start experimenting. Bad things happen."

"Okay, that's it. Start talking, Joy." Grace propped her elbows on the table and leaned forward. "Did Paul have a stroke when you waltzed in with your girls flashing like strobe lights?"

"That would imply he's paying attention, Grace," Joy said dryly.

"Okay, so no stroke. What happened?"

She sucked in a deep breath and let it out slowly. "You know things in the bedroom have been... lacking a bit the past few years."

"I think the term you're looking for is non-existent," Hope said, patting her arm sympathetically.

"Guh! Don't remind me." Joy grabbed Hope's drink and drank a quarter of it before she continued. "Anyway, in an effort to reignite the spark, I ordered a few things as a surprise for Paul's birthday. We were supposed to go out of town for the weekend, so I thought, what better way to spice things up than to call Pam and get some of those adult toys to try out?"

Grace didn't like where this was going. According to Joy, Paul wasn't the most adventurous man. If he'd rejected her or humiliated her in any way, it was going to take an act of God to stop her from verbally castrating him. "What did you get besides light up tata tassels?"

Her face blushed a bright shade of pink as she stared at the table.

"Joy. Come on. No judgement here," Grace said, eyeing Hope. Of the two of them, she was the one more likely to crack a joke and end up saying something uncalled for. "Right, Hope?"

"Hey, what are you looking at me for?" Hope asked, acting offended. "I'm the one who suggested she go out of her comfort zone a little to see if that would kickstart things."

"She did," Joy confirmed. "I just wish she'd told me that in the wrong hands tata tassels might be mistaken for streamers."

"Um, what?" Grace asked. "Tell me they weren't used as decorations for Paul's birthday party."

"You know how Paul's mother came to town for a few days right before we were supposed to head up north?" Joy asked.

"Oh, no, Joy." Grace sputtered with laughter. "She found them?"

Joy nodded grimly. "I'd ordered some of her favorite coffee online, and while I was out running errands, it showed up along with my other deliveries. Marge took it upon herself to open all of the packages."

Grace said nothing as she cringed for her friend. Marge Lansing was the type of lady who thought wearing shorts in public was scandalous and never missed an opportunity to inform Joy that her necklines were too low and her hemlines too high. If she was involved, Grace knew this story wasn't going to end well.

"Tell her what was in the second package," Hope said, unable to hide her chuckle.

Joy used two fingers to rub her left temple. "You know how I told you that I caught Paul watching porn that one time?"

"Yeah?" Grace wasn't sure where this was going. She didn't know one married woman who hadn't caught her husband watching porn at some point or another.

"I checked his browser history to see what he might like. I

thought... Well, I thought that if I presented him with his fantasy, that might help." Joy's face had gone from tinged pink to bright red.

"That's actually pretty sweet." Grace said. But seeing the horrified look on Joy's face, she added, "I'm guessing it didn't go well?"

"It didn't go anywhere. Because do you know what happens when you order an assortment of butt plugs and your mother-in-law finds them?"

Grace's mouth dropped open, and silence filled the table as the phrase *butt plugs* hung in the air. Finally, Grace cleared her throat. "Um, excuse me, but did you just say—"

"Butt plugs. That's right. I'm so desperate for my husband to notice me again that I ordered those damn things, thinking we'd test them out together. And maybe we'd try... you know."

"But..." Grace shook her head, trying to process what her friend had just said. She didn't have a problem with anyone trying whatever their kinks were, but back door action? In twenty years, she'd never heard her friend talk about anything other than vanilla sex. "Are you sure you want to try that? I thought..." She cleared her throat. "Exit only, remember?"

Hope snickered.

Joy gave Grace a flat stare. "The toys weren't for me, Grace."

"Oh. Oh!" Grace's face flushed hot. "I see. How did that... I mean, did it help?"

"Nope. Remember I said that Marge opened the boxes?"

Grace's eyes felt huge as they nearly popped out of her head. "Paul's mother found them? What did she say?"

"She said they make lovely centerpieces," Joy said with an

exasperated sigh. "They were the glass kind, and Marge used them in the flower arrangements she made for us. Imagine my surprise when I came home and found the dining room table set with three arrangements of silk flowers, each of them with a glass plug right in the center. Meanwhile, the flashing tassels were hung on either side of a *Happy Birthday* streamer. When Paul walked in behind me a few minutes later, he thought he'd walked in on a stripper party."

"Oh my god," Grace wheezed as laughter seized her. Tears started to roll down her cheeks and suddenly it was very hard to breathe.

Hope joined in the hysterics, and the two of them were practically falling out of their chairs when the waiter dropped by with their totchos and basket of wings.

"Can I get the largest margarita you have?" Joy asked him. "And a giant piece of salted caramel cheesecake."

"It's that kind of day?" he asked sympathetically.

"You have no idea."

Grace and Hope only laughed harder.

By the time Grace got herself under control and wiped her eyes, Joy was chuckling along with them.

"You know, in the moment, I was completely horrified. If the floor would've opened up and swallowed me whole, I would've welcomed my demise, but this is a story I'll be telling when I'm rolling around the old folks' home."

"No doubt," Hope agreed, squeezing Joy's hand.

"So, what happened after that?" Grace asked.

"Paul kept his cool long enough to thank his mother for her thoughtfulness and acted as if we didn't have sex toys adorning our dining room table while we had dinner with his mother. Thankfully, it was just the three of us that night. All the kids had other plans. The minute she left, he lost his shit and tossed the centerpieces in the garbage. Then he didn't talk to me for three days."

"Did you ever discuss it after that?" Grace asked, wanting to wrap her friend in a hug.

"Nope. He refused. Even when I tried to explain that I'd just wanted to find something that might spice things up for him, he shut me out and told me everything was fine the way it is."

But Grace knew things obviously weren't fine; otherwise, Joy wouldn't be snooping around his porn history, trying to figure out how to get him back in the saddle, so to speak. She gave Joy a sympathetic smile. "Have you tried talking to a counselor?"

"Paul won't go. He won't do anything." She sighed heavily. "I know he's embarrassed about what happened. So am I. But it's not like I'm not openminded. I just want him to talk to me about whatever it is."

Grace bit the inside of her cheek. She couldn't help but wonder if Paul was seeing someone else. Wasn't that usually why men suddenly lost interest in their wives? Although Bill hadn't lost interest in Grace. Maybe things weren't as black and white as everyone believed. "I'm sorry, honey. I wish I could help."

"I know." She thanked the waiter for the margarita he placed in front of her and said, "Okay, enough about my pathetically lacking sex life. Tell me what happened today. You said something about a message?"

Leave it to Joy to remember what we're really at lunch to discuss, Grace thought. "Right." She launched into the story of what she and Hope had experienced at the house. When she was done, she sat back and crossed her arms. "Any ideas what that might mean?"

Joy pursed her lips. "Nothing past the obvious. I think you could be onto something about needing to solve a mystery, or it could be about passing on a message. I've got the property records from the courthouse now. Tomorrow we can work on digging into the histories of the former owners and see if there was any foul play or anything unusual that might give us some clues."

"Meanwhile, I have to show the house to Matt tomorrow. Any ideas on how to keep the ghost from scaring him off completely?" Grace asked.

She wasn't surprised when neither of them had any answers.

CHAPTER THIRTEEN

*A*rmed with a half dozen properties to show Matt, Grace walked into the café with her head held high and determination in her step. She'd had a moment of clarity the night before when she'd been walking on the beach. There wasn't anything to be gained by not telling Matt about what had happened the day before at the cottage. She knew she had a responsibility to the seller to do everything in her power to move his house, but Matt was also her client. He deserved to know what he was getting into. And while there wasn't anything official that said she or the seller had to disclose unusual paranormal activity, she had a moral obligation to do just that.

Grace couldn't live with herself if she sold someone a property that wasn't right for them, or worse, turned out to be their worst nightmare. "Good morning," she said, slipping into the booth across from him. "Are you ready to find your new beach home?"

"You're awfully confident." Matt pushed a cinnamon roll

over to her and waved at the barista behind the counter. "Can you get Grace something to drink?"

"The usual?" Kari called back, watching Grace.

"Yes, please." Grace waved at her and nodded in appreciation as the barista went to work on her chai tea latte.

"You must come here a lot," Matt said.

"It's better than a stuffy office." She pushed a folder over to him. "These are the houses I set appointments for you to see. They include the two you sent me last night as well as a couple others that show a lot better in person than their pictures indicate. Take a look. If there are any that are an automatic no for whatever reason, just say so and I'll cancel."

Matt didn't even look before he was shaking his head. "I'm up for seeing whatever you think is worth looking at."

"Okay then. Perfect." She smiled at him but couldn't help wondering how the showings were going to go. So far, he'd been pretty vague about what he wanted. The only two requirements were an ocean view and that the place had to be big enough for extended family. That left a lot of room in the middle.

It didn't take long for Grace to finish off her cinnamon roll, and then the two of them climbed in her SUV and headed for the first house on the list. Three hours later, they'd seen five of the houses. Matt had been animated about all of them. He'd been especially pleased that all of them had views, though three were a little further from the beach or the town than he cared for. He'd talked about ideas to update a few of the kitchens, laughed when one had a literal water closet with just a toilet under the stairs, and made jokes about the red and pink floral wallpaper that covered the entire upstairs of one of the homes.

Matt was happily chatting about a trip he had planned

with his two sons later in the year when she pulled up outside the large white cottage. She'd intentionally saved the haunted one for last. Who knew what was going to happen, and she hadn't wanted any negative experiences to taint how he felt about the rest of the showings.

Grace killed the engine but didn't make a move to get out of the vehicle. "There's something you need to know about this property before we go in."

"Okay," Matt said quietly. His entire demeanor had changed. Gone was the chatty guy who'd been excitedly talking about his sons. He'd been replaced by a contemplative man who looked somewhat troubled, with his eyebrows drawn together and his lips slightly pinched as he stared at the large home.

"Matt?" Grace asked. "Is everything all right?"

"Huh?" He whipped his head around, staring at her with a surprised expression as if he'd just realized she was sitting next to him.

"I asked if you're all right," she said, frowning.

"Oh. Yeah. I'm fine." He turned to look at the house again. "It's a pretty one, isn't it?"

His statement should've been a positive one; instead, his tone was flat and almost disinterested.

Grace wasn't sure what was going on with him. Perhaps he was picking up on the vibe of the place. If that was true, then that was just one more reason to level with him. "There's a reason this house has been on the market for so long."

"The price?" he asked, staring out the window again. A muscle in his jaw twitched, and it didn't take much to notice the tension running through him.

"No. Not really. Under other circumstances, I'd say it's a tad underpriced for the market, but..."

"It's haunted, isn't it?" he asked, sitting back and closing his eyes.

"How can you tell?" She couldn't help but wonder if he had some sort of gift that let him see or feel spirits. Most people could see them if the spirits showed themselves. But there were others who always knew, no matter what the spirits did.

"I just know," he said. A few moments passed, and then he added, "I don't need to go inside, Grace. This isn't the house for me."

Disappointment settled deep in her bones. She'd known the minute his demeanor had changed that this property was out of the running, but hope sprung eternal.

"Right." She started the car and took him back to the café. Before she could even manage to put the SUV in park, Matt jumped out.

"Thanks for the showings, Grace," he said. "I have a lot to think about."

"Can I give you a call tomorrow so we can go over your thoughts and decide where we go from here?"

"Yeah. Sure. Have a nice evening." He gently shut her door and then jumped into his Land Rover and sped away so fast his tires squealed.

Grace groaned. After what had started as a promising day, she'd completely screwed up by taking him to see the white cottage. Suddenly, she resented everything about her agreement with Landers. No one in that office had been able to sell those homes. She was a good agent. It was ridiculous that she had to do it as a prerequisite for a permanent job, even though now it was clear he needed more agents. When she'd come in to interview she hadn't realized that Landers Realty was on par to outpace Bill's office. That tidbit was deeply satisfying. Still, they were entirely too busy for just Kevin and Owen to handle. Bastard. What kind of jerk made her jump through hoops when he knew she was more than qualified to do the job? But what choice did she have? None. Not if she wanted to work in Premonition Pointe.

Her phone buzzed in the console beside her. Hope's name flashed on the screen, and a tiny bit of the tension in Grace's shoulders eased.

"Hey? Is it time for lunch? Real food this time?" Grace asked, hoping her friend was done with work for the day. Since Hope was an event planner, as long as she wasn't in the middle of a function, her schedule was fairly flexible.

"Lucas just called me," she said in a hushed tone.

"Lucas King?" Grace asked, her voice rising in shock.

"Yes."

Holy hell on wheels. Lucas King was Hope's one-who-got-away. The one they all thought she was going to follow across the country when he moved to the East Coast. "What did he want?"

There was a rustle on the other end of the line before Hope said, "I don't know. I haven't listened to the message yet."

"Hope!" Grace shook her head. "Hang up right now, listen to it, and call me back."

"I can't. I'm in the middle of dealing with a wedding shower disaster."

"Where are you?" Grace demanded.

"Bird's Eye Bakery. They lost the order I'm supposed to be picking up right now. They—never mind. Miss Francie is here. I've got to go." The line went dead before Grace could say another word.

Grace hit Joy's name in her contact list. The call immediately went to voice mail. "Dammit, Joy. Call me as soon as you get this. It's an emergency. Lucas called Hope, and she's freaking out." As soon as she hung up, Grace sent Joy a text then put the SUV in drive and headed straight for the bakery.

Grace parked right next to Hope's Toyota Highlander and rushed into Bird's Eye Bakery. She spotted her fiery friend at the end of the counter waving her hands in the air and nodding toward the cases full of various treats.

Miss Francie had a pained expression on her face as she nodded and then started to fill various pastry boxes with stock from her cases. Hope frantically typed something into her phone, and when she was done, she leaned against the wall and closed her eyes.

"Crisis averted?" Grace asked, eyeing the vibrant purple silk blouse and black skinny jeans Hope was wearing. She looked incredible with her wild dark curls and her face touched only by the barest of blush and lipstick.

"For now," she said without opening her eyes. "The bridezilla is probably going to flip a table, but at least there will be sugar to appease the guests."

A few minutes later, Grace helped Hope carry the pastry boxes out to her Toyota. Once they had them all stuffed in the back, Grace turned to her and said, "Hand me your phone."

Hope did as she was told without objection. It was just about the only time Grace could recall in recent memory that her friend hadn't argued when given a direct order. Hope wasn't the kind to take directions well. She did what she wanted, when she wanted, and how she wanted, without input from anyone. But not when it came to Lucas King. He was the one person in the world who could unbalance her.

"Do you want me to listen to it or delete it?" Grace asked, holding her finger over the touchscreen.

Hope bit down on her bottom lip. Then she shook her head. "I have no idea."

"Fine. We're listening to it." Grace knew Hope had every reason to be wary of the man. He'd broken her heart not once, but twice. Everyone knew the two were soul mates. They were the type of people who couldn't stay away from each other. Their connection was too strong. And yet, they kept managing to hurt each other. No matter what though, Grace knew her friend loved him, and if she deleted the message, she'd regret it.

"Wait!" Hope cried, holding her hands up.

"What is it?"

"I need to sit down." Hope yanked the back door of her Highlander open and plopped down in the back seat.

Grace suddenly had a horrible thought. What if Lucas was calling to say he was getting married? Or worse, had some terrible illness? Hope would never recover. Grace heard the faint whisper of her mother's voice in the back of her head. *Don't go borrowing trouble, Grace. Stop worrying about things that haven't come to pass.*

"Okay. Do it," Hope demanded, staring at the phone like it might catch on fire.

Grace didn't hesitate. She hit the Play button.

"Hey, gorgeous. It's me. I need the name of a Realtor in Premonition Pointe. Now that Grace's ex is off the list of possible agents, I'm not sure who to call. Do you have a rec for me? Call me back."

Grace and Hope both stared at the phone for a few beats. Then they both spoke at the same time. "How does he know Bill's my ex?" Grace said, just as Hope blurted, "Why does Lucas need a Realtor?"

They spoke over each other again as Hope said, "I have no idea," while Grace said, "Is his mother moving?"

They both chuckled. Then Grace held her hand up and asked, "When's the last time you spoke to him?"

Hope shrugged. "Two and a half years ago? When he was home for Christmas."

"Okay, so it was probably Bell who told him about me and Bill," Grace guessed, referring to Lucas's mother, who owned a house a few blocks from Grace's cottage.

"Maybe." Hope blew out a breath, looking pained. "If Bell is moving…"

There was no need to finish the sentence. They both knew that if Bell left Premonition Pointe then the chances of Hope seeing Lucas again were next to nothing unless she decided to go visit him. And the last time she'd done that it had been a disaster.

"You should call him and find out what's going on," Grace said.

"I don't want to know." Hope chewed on her bottom lip, something she only did when they were talking about Lucas.

"Come on, Hope," Grace urged. "The not knowing is almost always worse than the reality. Maybe he has a buddy who is looking for beach property. We can't know until you ask."

It killed Grace to see her friend so flustered by one phone call. It was so hard to reconcile the vivacious woman who was so put together, so confident when dealing with the opposite sex, turn into a pile of nerves when it came to this one man. But maybe that was why she was so confident with other men. She knew who her person was supposed to be, and there wasn't room for anyone else for anything other than casual dating.

Hope jumped down from her seat and straightened her shoulders. "Enough of this. I have some bakery items to deliver. I can't sit around worrying about Lucas King. If he needs a Realtor, he can call around. I don't know why he needs me to rec—"

"Wait." Grace grabbed her friend's hand. "Before you go brushing him off, try to remember you have a friend who is actively seeking clients." She batted her eyelashes at her friend. "One who desperately needs to make a sale if she's doesn't want to keep drawing from her savings account."

"Right." Hope chewed on her bottom lip one more time and then sent a text. She tapped the phone a few more times before she shoved it into her pocket. "There. I told him to have whoever it is call you."

"You silenced his calls, didn't you?" Grace asked.

"Yep," Hope said as she climbed into the driver's seat. "I don't have the luxury of turning into a fool today."

"Dinner. My house. Tonight at seven," Grace insisted. "We can work on a restorative energy spell."

"Did you already tell Joy?" Hope asked, narrowing her eyes at Grace.

"Yes." Grace slammed Hope's door shut, mouthed *seven*, and then tapped the top of the car twice, indicating it was time for her to go.

Hope nodded once and sped off down the street. Grace pulled out her phone, texted Joy to meet at her house later than evening, and then went to the office and started making phone calls. An hour later, she had the name of a witch who specialized in dealing with troublesome ghosts. It was becoming clear to her that if she was going to sell those houses, it was going to take a lot more work than just hoping a smudge stick would do the job. If that were the case, then she never would've ended up with the listings in the first place.

CHAPTER FOURTEEN

Grace sat at her kitchen bar, sipping a glass of wine and making notes of all the paranormal activity she'd personally witnessed at each of the three houses. The witch she was meeting with the next day wanted a rundown of all the incidents.

By the time she was finished with the Victorian, her hand was cramping. She glanced down at the pencil in her hand and grimaced. When was the last time she'd handwritten anything? Grace had no clue. She eyed her chicken scratch and laughed. If the witch could read her writing, then she truly was magical.

There was a loud knock at the door, followed by someone barging in. "Grace? Are you here?"

"Alyssa?" Grace stood and moved to the doorway between the kitchen and living room. Her sister was standing by the door, pulling her tennis shoes off and muttering something about too much sand.

Grace rolled her eyes. Alyssa was always complaining about something every time she came over. Last week it had been the dog barking next door. The week before that it was the bright pink house two doors down, while apparently this week it was the sand in her landscaping. Not that Grace could do anything about it or wanted to. It was natural. What was she going to do? Lay sod over the sandy earth?

"Where's Lex?" Alyssa demanded. Her dark roots were showing through her dyed blond hair, and there were circles under her eyes as if she hadn't been sleeping well.

Grace shrugged. "I don't know. Work maybe? Or out with Bronwyn. We don't really check in with each other unless one of us is going to be gone all night. Are you feeling okay? You look a little tired."

Her sister blinked. "You stay out all night?"

"No. I mean, not usually." There had been that one night she'd had too much wine and passed out on Hope's couch.

"That's what I thought. My straightlaced sister never does anything wrong," Alyssa said with a little bit of a sneer. "I'm fine by the way. No need to worry about me. And I don't appreciate being told I look like hell."

"Whoa," Grace said, holding her hands up in a surrender motion. "That's not what I meant, and you know it. What's going on? Did I do something to piss you off?"

Alyssa dropped her purse in a chair and placed her hands on her hips. "Yeah. Who said you could offer Lex a place to stay?"

"Um, what?" Hadn't she called and informed her sister the night Lex had moved in? Had she been stewing about the move ever since? Not likely. Alyssa wasn't the type to brood. If she was upset, she made her displeasure known in no uncertain terms. This was probably prompted by Charlie. Pretty much all of the sisters' arguments occurred after Charlie riled up Alyssa.

"You heard me. Are you trying to undermine my relationship with her or something? Just because you never had kids—"

"I'm going to stop you right there," Grace said, suddenly seething. "I think we should both take a breath before one of us says something she'll regret."

"Regret?" Alyssa let out a humorless laugh. "You know what I regret? All that time I let you spend with my daughter. If I'd known you were going to be talking trash about me, you can be damned sure I'd have never left her alone with you."

Grace gaped at her sister. What the actual flaming bag of crap was going on at that moment? She cleared her throat. "Listen, Alyssa, I don't have any idea what you're talking about. Care to explain what you heard and from whom?"

"*Whom.*" Alyssa rolled her eyes. "Listen to you and your college education. Charlie was right. You do think you're better than everyone else."

Ah. Of course. Grace had been right on target with her suspicions. "Is that what this is about? Charlie?"

"No. It's about you and my daughter. Why is she living here and not at home?" Alyssa demanded. "You're not better than me. I'm the one who provided for her, loved her, kept her safe. And now she runs to you? It's bullshit, Grace. She *needs* her mother!"

"You're right, Mom, she does *need* her mother," Lex said from the hallway.

Both Grace and Alyssa startled at Lex's voice. Alyssa turned accusing eyes on Grace. "I thought you said she wasn't here."

Refraining from throttling her sister, Grace said,

"Actually, I told you I didn't *know* where she was, which was the truth. I didn't know she was home."

Alyssa turned her back on her sister and muttered something unflattering about Grace under her breath. Then she turned toward her daughter. "Lexie, baby. I didn't realize you were here."

"Obviously. I was taking a nap. Your arguing woke me up." Lex let her mother give her a hug, but she didn't hug her back.

"Come on, Lexie. You can at least hug your mother hello." Alyssa said, making no effort to acknowledge Lex's statement about waking her up.

"What are you doing here, Mom?" Lex asked, taking a step back from her mother to put some distance between them.

"I came to bring you home. You shouldn't have to be paying rent to your aunt when your room is waiting for you. Charlie and I—"

"No." Lex crossed her arms over her chest. "I'm not coming home."

"But, Lexie—"

"And my name is Lex." There were angry tears in Lex's eyes, and Grace's arms were aching to hold her, to soothe away the pain that was shining in her niece's expression.

How had Alyssa become so clueless? Her daughter was in obvious distress, and Alyssa seemed to be completely oblivious.

"I named you Lexie," Alyssa corrected.

"I'm an adult, Mom," Lex said quietly. "I prefer to be called Lex, and you know it. Just like you know I'm never going to marry Jackson. I'm never going to marry a man. And I'm never going to live up to the perfect picture you have in your head of what my life is supposed to look like. So, no, I'm not coming home. I'm staying here unless Aunt Grace wants me to leave, then I'll sleep on the couch at Bronwyn's parents' house until I can find something permanent."

Alyssa stared at her daughter, her eyes wide and her mouth agape.

"I have to make dinner now," Lex said softly and brushed past her mother.

"Lexie—I mean Lex," Alyssa called after her. "I know you're not going to marry Jackson or any other man."

Her daughter paused and glanced back at her. "Then why do you keep talking about it?"

"I was just joking. Bronwyn has always been welcome at our house. You know that."

"Joking, huh?" Lex asked sadly. "It doesn't feel like joking when Charlie says you still cry over the fact that Jackson will never be your son-in-law."

Alyssa paled, and for once she actually appeared to be chagrined by her actions. "That's just... It's not about you, sweetie."

"Oh, I know, Mom. It's about you. It's always about you. I get it. I'm a huge disappointment. Fine. I can live with that knowledge, but I no longer can live in that environment. So leave Aunt Grace alone. She didn't do anything but give me a room when I needed one. Would you rather me be here or couch surfing?"

"I'd rather you be at home with me and Charlie where we can work through everything," Alyssa said defiantly.

"That's never going to happen," Lex said with a stony expression.

"But why?" Alyssa asked. "There's plenty of space for all three of us."

"You know why, Mom. I've told you more than once. He says inappropriate things and makes me and Bron uncomfortable. I'm happy here for now."

Alyssa's face turned bright red, and Grace knew her sister was only moments away from having a meltdown. She was about to suggest they go take a walk and cool down a little, but before Grace could offer, Alyssa stalked into the kitchen and demanded that her daughter go with her right then and there. She made excuses for Charlie, implying that Bron and Lex were exaggerating and reading too much into his joking.

"That's the problem, Mom," Lex said. "You always pick him over me. And as far as I'm concerned, he's a deal breaker. He makes me uncomfortable, and I'm done putting up with everything just because it's easier on you."

"So you won't move home because of Charlie?" Alyssa asked. "You're on this again?"

"Still," Lex said. "Always. Charlie is a perv, and neither Bron nor I need that in our lives. Go home, Mother."

"Fine!" She threw her hands up in the air and stormed out.

Grace strode over to her niece, wrapped her arms around her, and let her cry.

Lex kept thanking Grace and promising to stay out of her hair and that she'd be gone soon, even as she hiccupped her way through the brief speech.

"Forget it, sweet pea. You're stuck with me. In fact, I like having you here. I insist that you stay as long as you want."

"You're not going to be pressuring me to make up with my mother, are you?" Lex asked.

"Nope," Grace promised. "That's between you and her."

"And Charlie," Lex said dryly. Then she shuddered.

"Hell no," Grace said. "As far as I'm concerned, that jackass can take a long walk off a short pier." She grinned. "My grandpa used to say that."

Lex flung her arms around her aunt and hugged her tightly. "I love you," Lex said, sounding choked up.

"I love you, too, Lex." Grace gave her another hug, and when she let go, she said, "Come on. Let's get dinner going. Hope and Joy are on their way over."

"Uh-oh," Lex said. "Trouble's brewing."

Grace snickered. "No truer words."

CHAPTER FIFTEEN

"*L*ex, babe, you knocked it out of the park with this halibut," Hope said as she used a piece of sourdough bread to sop up her remaining lemon-wine sauce. Grace, Hope, Joy, and Lex were sitting at Grace's table, finishing up the dinner Lex had prepared for them.

When Lex learned that the girls were meeting for dinner, she'd run out and gotten some fresh fish and went to work. With almost no notice, she'd put together one of the best meals Grace had tasted in over a month.

"You know, I never thought I'd say this but these brussels sprouts are amazing. What did you do, spell them to actually taste good?" Before dinner, Grace would've sworn she hated them, but whatever Lex had done to them made Grace do a one-eighty on her previous opinion of the vegetable, and she couldn't get enough.

"It's amazing how shallots, pine nuts, and butter can really liven a dish up," Lex said with a wink. "Glad you like them."

"Everything is fantastic," Joy agreed. "Thank you."

"You're welcome." Lex rose and started to clear the table.

"Oh no. Nope. Sit down," Hope said as she took the plates in Lex's hands. "We've got the dishes. She who cooks does not clean." She turned to Grace. "Neither does the host who supplied us with the booze."

Grace laughed and let her two friends clear the table. She knew better than to argue with them. Instead, she turned to her niece. "How are you doing? You okay after what went down with your mom earlier?"

Lex let out a breath and sat back in her chair. "I guess so? I don't really know to be honest. Cooking helped center me a little."

"Good." Grace reached across the table and squeezed her hand. "Want to talk about whatever else it is you have on your mind?"

Lex frowned. "Like what?"

"Like whatever's making you uneasy." Grace glanced at Lex's phone on the table next to her. "And why you keep checking your phone every few minutes?"

"Do you notice everything?" Lex asked, eyeing her aunt.

"Not everything. But when it comes to you? I'm paying attention. What's up? It's more than just your mom, isn't it?"

Tears filled Lex's eyes, but instead of answering, she unlocked her phone, tapped the screen a few times, and then handed the phone to Grace.

"What's this?" She glanced down at the screen and noted a string of texts from Charlie. They started off benign enough, but quickly devolved into nightmare territory.

Hey, Lex. Give me a call. I have a question.

You're not at work. I tried there. Really, I need you to call me. It's about your mom's cat.

Where are you? Fucking call me already.

Hey, you little bitch. If you don't call me, don't come crying to me if this cat suddenly goes missing.

There was a continuous string of expletives that got more and more abusive, and then the final one: *Since you're ignoring me, I'll just have a chat with your girlfriend. She's always been more fun than you are anyway.*

"I've been trying to get in touch with Bron, but my calls are going straight to voice mail and she hasn't answered my texts," Lex said. A single tear rolled down her face. She angrily wiped it away and added, "I've texted Mom, too, and she isn't answering."

A chill radiated down Grace's spine, and her entire body went rigid. Visions of Charlie tormenting Alyssa's cat flashed in her mind, followed quickly by the bastard laying hands on Bronwyn. There was only one thing to do.

"Hope, Joy, get in here now," she called.

"We're still cleaning up," Hope answered. "Give us a minute."

Grace got to her feet, still clutching Lex's phone, and strode into the kitchen. "It's important. We have a field trip to make." She showed them Lex's phone, and once they read the text, they both dropped what they were doing and headed for the door.

"Aunt Grace, what are you planning?" Lex called, running after them.

"We're paying Charlie a visit; that's all." Grace pulled her black boots on and grabbed her keys. "We have a cat to rescue and a giant ass to kick."

"Don't be going all *Witches of Eastwick* on me!" Lex demanded. "He's likely all talk anyway. I'm probably overreacting."

"What if you aren't?" Joy asked, peering at Lex in that

mom way that made it seem as if she could see straight into someone's soul. "What if something's happened to the cat? Or what if Bronwyn is there and he won't let her go?"

Lex's eyes turned dark blue with emotion. "I'm coming with you."

"Attagirl," Hope said, slinging her arm around the younger woman's shoulders. "Let's go kick some Charlie butt."

"I think you should stay here," Grace said, her protective side coming out in full force. "We don't know how volatile Charlie is right now."

"I'm going," Lex said, holding her ground. "If by some chance Bronwyn is there... I just can't stay home."

Grace nodded, understanding that nothing would keep Lex away if someone she loved was in danger. "Okay. Just stick near one of us at all times, all right?"

"Yes, Aunt Grace." Lex rolled her eyes, but her lips curved up into a tiny smile.

Grace slipped her arm through Lex's and led the way to her SUV. "Everyone in."

"Can we call ourselves the Scooby Gang?" Joy asked from the back seat.

"Or the A-Team?" Hope offered.

"What's the A-Team?" Lex asked.

The other three groaned.

"Never mind," Grace said. "Before your time. I think we should be the Baywatch Babes."

Joy chuckled. "Only if I get to be Pamela Anderson."

"Who?" Lex asked.

"Oh, honey," Hope said sympathetically as she patted her on the shoulder. "Remind me to introduce you to the show later. You'll thank me for it." She turned to Grace. "Baywatch Babes it is. Step on it, girlfriend. We have some ass to kick."

Grace sped down the street and laughed out loud when Hope tapped her iPhone and suddenly "Goodbye Earl" by the Dixie Chicks started to play through the vehicle's speakers. It wasn't long before they all started to sing, "'Cause Earl had to die!"

"Do you think he's home?" Grace asked Lex. They were standing in front of Alyssa and Charlie's small two-bedroom rental. The house was located down a dirt road and was secluded from the neighbors due to the abundance of trees in the area. Grace hated that her sister lived there. If there was ever any foul play, there wouldn't be anyone to see or hear anything. From a safety standpoint, it was a nightmare.

"Yep. See the taillights of the car peeking out of the carport over there?"

Grace squinted, trying to see through the shadows to the carport. Sure enough, there was something parked there. She just couldn't tell what make or model it was. Not that it mattered. She didn't know what Charlie drove anyway. "Yeah. Is that his car?"

"Nope. It's Mom's. Charlie's car was repossessed, so she lets him use it whenever he wants."

"Your mom bought a second car?" Grace asked, surprised. That was something Alyssa normally would've shared with her. "Why didn't she tell me?"

Lex snorted. "Because she overpaid for the old Mustang and is embarrassed to say anything. She says she wants to get it restored, but she doesn't have money for that. So it just sits there unless Charlie is driving it."

"Okay. So we're working under the impression that he's here. Now what?" Hope asked. She was peering at the small house with her head tilted to the side. The structure itself was in need of some TLC. It really could've used some paint and roof work, and the porch looked to have some rot. But the yard was neat and tidy as if the renters took pride in their home. It was the kind of place that looked like decent, hardworking people lived there, but that the landlord wasn't willing to spend any money on maintenance.

"I guess Lex can let us in. We can check on the cat and make sure nothing is amiss." Now that they were standing there, Grace was starting to second-guess her hasty decision to run over there. What exactly were they going to do if Charlie was up to no good? Not that there were any signs of foul play. He'd probably just been drunk when he was texting Lex.

"Let me just do some recon first," Hope said, waving her arms to gather them into a small circle. Joy took her spot to Hope's left, and Grace immediately stepped up to complete the circle.

"Can I join?" Lex asked hesitantly.

"Of course you can," Hope said, moving over to make room. "Have you done any spell work or earth traveling before?"

"No. Mom isn't really big on the witchcraft." Lex glanced away, avoiding eye contact with all three of the witches as she added, "She thinks it's dangerous."

Grace's heart ached for her niece. There was so much Alyssa had kept from her in a misguided attempt to shield her from the dangers of the world. She squeezed Lex's hand

and said, "Alyssa thinks what we do is dangerous because she has an addictive personality. What she should say is that witchcraft addiction is dangerous for *her*. It doesn't mean that you will suffer the same problem."

Lex's eyes widened and then flashed with anger as she scowled. "You mean mom used to practice witchcraft?"

Grace groaned internally. Son of a witchling. She'd thought Alyssa had explained to Lex why she disapproved of using spells. Apparently she'd skipped the whole part about getting addicted to the rush and going on a destructive rampage after Lex's dad left them when Lex was a baby. No matter how badly she wanted to explain what happened back then, Grace knew she couldn't be the one to share those stories with her niece. That was something Alyssa needed to do herself. But she still couldn't lie to her. "Yes, Lex. Your mom used to use her gifts. She has her reasons why she doesn't now, but I think it's better if you hear them from her."

Lex rolled her eyes, clearly unhappy with Grace's answer. "Of course she does. She always has her *reasons*."

"Hey, no," Grace said gently. "I know you're going through some stuff with your mom right now. And I'm right here for you for whatever you need, but on this one, you might want to cut her some slack. She did what she needed to do, and I'm sure it isn't easy for her to talk about."

Lex pressed her lips together in a thin line and gave her aunt a short nod. "Fine. But that doesn't mean I'm happy about being left in the dark... again."

"I know." Grace reached for her and gave her a big hug. "You have every right to be frustrated. The goddess knows I am too about certain things. But she's still our family, right? We'll work through this."

Lex hugged her back, and when Grace let go, there was steel in Lex's eyes. "Let's do this. I'll feel better when I know Bronwyn isn't inside."

Grace really didn't think she was. Bronwyn's car wasn't there, and the odds of her getting into Charlie's car were zero to none unless he'd somehow managed to trick her. An eerie tingle started at the base of her spine, making Grace suck in a sharp breath. She'd felt that tingle a few times in her life before, and in each case, it was right before something awful happened. "Hope?"

"Yeah?" her friend said.

"Do your spell. Find out who is here and where," Grace ordered.

"On it." Hope waved them all back into the circle. "Lex, do me a favor and visualize Charlie. Think of him doing something mundane inside the house. Something that is habitual, like making coffee or sitting in a certain chair. Can you do that?"

"Yeah," Lex said.

"Let me know when you're ready," Hope said.

A few seconds passed, and then Lex nodded. "Got it."

Magic shimmered faintly just inside the circle while Hope whispered into the wind, "Goddesses of Premonition Pointe, reveal what's within the mind. Show us who is present within the walls. Keep us safe; warn us of what lies within."

The magic moved from the circle to Lex, coating her skin and turning her into an ethereal-like being. Grace thought her niece had never looked so beautiful. The glow came from within and nearly brought tears to Grace's eyes. There was no mistaking that she had a special natural talent, and if she had a mentor, there was no telling what she'd be able to do. Considering the magic radiating from her was pure white,

148

Grace guessed she'd be really good at healing the soul. If so, it was a rare talent that shouldn't be hidden away.

"There. I've got it," Hope said. The magic vanished, and the moment was gone. Lex returned to her normal state of being.

"Wow, sweet pea," Grace said to her niece. "That was incredible. How do you feel?"

"Alive," she breathed. "Really freakin' alive. Like I could do anything."

"It's the rush of the magic," Grace said, clutching her hand. "It can be the most wonderful thing in the world if you can control it. If not... Then the consequences can be devastating."

Lex nodded solemnly. "I can see that."

"Charlie is the only one in the house," Hope said quietly.

"Thank the gods," Lex said, clutching her hand to her chest.

Hope gave her a pained look. "The only human anyway. But the cat? She's terrified, so we need to get her."

"Lizzy," Lex gasped out. "What did he do to her?"

"I don't know. She's in the back bedroom, hiding in fear," Hope said.

"That's my old room. She was probably looking for me." Lex gazed at the house. "Where is he?"

"Living room. In a recliner."

"Right. Passed out?" Lex asked.

"That's unclear." Hope frowned. "How do we want to do this? If we sneak in, that's trespassing. If we knock on the door, he might not let us in."

"He'll let me in," Lex said. "I could just go in and get her."

"No," Grace said firmly. "Not after those texts. It's likely he's been drinking, and I don't trust him. Besides, he's not going to just let you take the cat. She's one of his bargaining chips to get under your skin. And if he's been terrifying the cat, who knows what else he's willing to do?"

"True," Lex said. "But he's not going to let you in either. He isn't a fan." She grimaced. "Sorry, Grace."

Grace chuckled. "He's not my favorite either, so we're even. How about I go to the door to distract him? Then you guys can find a way into Lex's old bedroom and get the cat out."

"Not by yourself," Hope said. "Joy? Can you help Lex with the cat while I help Grace keep him distracted?"

"Definitely." Joy slipped her arm through Lex's and said, "Lead on. We have a cat to rescue."

Grace watched the two of them round the house and tried to tamp down her fear. Joy was an experienced witch and a fierce mama bear. She'd never let anything happen to Lex. She turned to Hope. "Let's do this."

CHAPTER SIXTEEN

*G*race strode right up to the door and pressed the doorbell three times. She already knew that her sister had the most annoying door chimes in history and snickered when the clanging just kept going, seeming as if the noise were never going to end.

"What the ever-loving fu—" Charlie's angry voice boomed from within as the door was flung open. He stopped mid-word and let out a growl when he spotted Grace. "What do you want?"

"Is my sister here?" She already knew Alyssa was at work, but she needed to start the conversation somewhere.

"No." He started to slam the door, but Grace flung a hand out, stopping him.

"When will she be home?" Grace asked, peering at him. His eyes were bloodshot, and he reeked of stale beer and cigarettes. She wondered how long it had been since the man had seen a shower. Why was Alyssa still with him?

"How should I know?" His gaze landed on Hope, and his

lips curved up into a creepy smile. "Who's your friend, Grace? She looks like she'd be fun."

Grace's skin started to crawl. She was getting ready to bark out something about keeping his eyeballs to himself, but Hope jumped right in to play along.

She held her hand out. "Hope Anderson. And you are?"

"Someone who wouldn't mind spending a little time with you," he replied.

"Charlie, what the hell? You're living with my sister," Grace said, barely refraining from kneeing him in the balls. She could hardly believe that the man was flirting with Hope right in front of her.

"Your sister won't care. In fact, I bet she'd be thrilled if your friend took care of my needs." He raked his gaze over Hope and then licked his cracked lips. "She's gone frigid in her old age."

Frigid? Grace almost laughed. Alyssa was anything but frigid. More likely, she was disgusted with the do-nothing lowlife she lived with who was more trouble than he was worth.

"As flattering as that is, I actually play for the other team," Hope lied. "Plus, my girlfriend is pretty possessive. I'm sure you know how it is."

It was exactly the right thing to say to a sleaze like Charlie to keep his attention. His eyes nearly bugged out as he actually wiped drool from the corner of his mouth. "Is she as hot as you are?"

"She's way better looking than me. I lucked out in that department," Hope said cheerfully.

"Just like Lex and her hot little piece of ass. What I wouldn't do to get in the middle of the two of them," he said, sounding wistful in the creepiest way possible.

Grace's stomach turned, and a snarl escaped her lips as she said, "That's your girlfriend's daughter you're talking about. Have some respect."

"I'm not related to any of them," he said with a shrug.

Heat crawled all over Grace's body, but she knew it wasn't a hot flash. No, she was ready to burn the man alive with her magic. She was vibrating with the need to let her magic fly, to take him out with one electrifying bolt. The mental image of him twitching on the ground was so satisfying she felt her lips curl up into a hint of a smile.

Charlie's hand shot out and grabbed Grace by the throat. "You keep your mouth shut, you old bitch. Alyssa doesn't need to know about this little chat we've had. Got it?"

Grace didn't hesitate. She let all her pent-up rage loose, sending Charlie flying straight back into the house. He slammed into a wall in the hallway. The man seemed to hang there on the wall for just a moment before he slid to the floor with a moan.

"Damn, Grace," Hope said with awe in her tone. "That was impressive."

"Yeah, well, seems ever since the divorce my magic has been supercharged. Too much anger mixed in with my give-no-fucks attitude, and here we are." She peered in the house at Charlie.

He stirred, and when he opened his eyes and met her gaze, Grace saw nothing but pure insanity. He rose to his feet and began to slowly stalk toward them. Grace stood her ground, ready to do whatever it took to keep him engaged long enough for Lex and Joy to reappear with the cat. But just before Charlie cleared the hallway, Lizzy, the solid white cat, came flying out of nowhere and landed claws first on his face.

"Argh!" Charlie screamed and batted at the cat. She only held on tighter, yowling and hissing as Charlie tried to shake her off.

"Lizzy!" Lex called, running down the hallway after her. When she saw Charlie battling with the cat, Lex let out a low growl just as she grabbed hold of Charlie's arm and yanked as hard as she could.

Suddenly a flash of intense white magic filled the hallway, blinding Grace. When she blinked away the spots, she found Lex clutching her cat and Charlie lying flat out on the ground.

"Go!" Grace ordered Lex. "Take the cat and get in the car. I'll be right there."

"Grace," Hope said quietly from behind her. "Come on. Just leave him."

Grace glanced over her shoulder at her oldest friend. "Take care of Lex. Make sure she and Joy are in the SUV. I'm going to make sure this bastard is still alive."

Hope chewed on her bottom lip then nodded once. "Be quick."

"I'm on it." Grace kneeled down next to Charlie and checked his vitals. His pulse was a little erratic but nothing to be alarmed about, though he did have a large gash over his right eye. She wasn't sure if it was from the cat or Lex's burst of magic, but either way, she needed to stop the bleeding.

After quickly finding the first aid kit under the kitchen sink, Grace did her best to clean up the wound and bandage it, but then she went one step further. She placed her hand over the bandage and imagined the skin knitting itself back together.

Charlie's eyes suddenly popped open, and as if he were

possessed, his hand shot out again, this time clutching her hair.

"Ouch, you bastard," she spat and reached down to grab his crotch. Her fingers tightened around him and twisted as she whispered, "I hope you never get a fully erect penis again, you ugly piece of shit. In fact, I'd be quite satisfied if you walked around frustrated but unable to do anything about it... All. The. Time."

He howled and let go of her, immediately curling in on himself.

Grace scrambled off of him and quickly backed up while he writhed in pain. "Don't ever text Lex again. If you do, I'll go to the cops."

"You don't have anything on me," he ground out, still clutching himself.

"Oh no? You think I'm not aware of the drugs you use or where you get them? Try me, *just one time*, and I'll tip off the police."

Charlie's face went an even paler shade of white, and Grace felt vindicated. Her bluff had worked. She'd only heard rumors that Charlie did favors for the local drug king in the neighboring town in order to feed a growing habit, but she hadn't been sure. Now she was certain of it.

"Do you know what they'll do to you if they find out you turned in one of their own?"

His eyes flashed with pure hatred.

Grace laughed. "But then you aren't one of theirs, are you?" She backed up, stopping right in the threshold of the front door before she added, "They couldn't care less about you, Charlie. Now stay away from my niece. I don't make empty threats."

She ran back to her SUV and jumped in the driver's seat.

"Everyone present and accounted for?" she asked. When she got three confirmations and a reassurance that Lizzy was on board, she peeled out of her sister's driveway.

Fifteen minutes later, Grace uncurled her fingers from the steering wheel and finally felt as if she could breathe again.

"Come on, Warrior Princess," Hope said softly after opening the driver's side door. "Let's get you inside and fix something to settle your nerves."

"Does it involve alcohol?" Grace asked her.

"Definitely."

Once they were inside and Grace had not one but two shots of whiskey in her system, she felt calm enough to walk back out onto her porch, pull out her phone, and call Alyssa.

Her sister answered on the fifth ring. "Grace, I don't have time right now. I only have ten more minutes of my break to scarf down something to eat, and then I have to get back to work."

"We have a situation," Grace said. "It's about Charlie." She swallowed hard, frustrated that her voice shook when she said Charlie's name. The adrenaline had worn off, and the whiskey hadn't done as much to fortify her as she'd hoped.

"Is he okay?" Alyssa asked, her voice going high-pitched. "What happened?"

"He's okay as far as I know," Grace hedged. "But—"

"Oh, thank the gods," Alyssa said, cutting her sister off. "I do not have time for an emergency right now. I'll just give him a call before I have to go back to work."

"He attacked me!" Grace blurted.

Silence.

"Alyssa, are you there?" Had her sister already ended the call?

"Yeah. I'm here," Alyssa said, her tone hesitant.

"Did you hear me? Charlie attacked me. He tried to strangle me tonight."

"Why?"

The question gutted Grace. What did it matter? Did her sister honestly think there was any acceptable reason for her boyfriend to lay his hands on Grace? "Because he's an asshole?"

Alyssa sighed heavily. "Just tell me what happened."

"You didn't even ask me if I'm okay," Grace said as she pressed two fingers to her forehead and massaged the growing ache.

"Obviously you are since you're calling me. Dammit, Grace." Alyssa's tone was quieter and softer now. "Can you please give me the details? I really do have to get back to work soon."

How could she be thinking about work when Grace just told her Charlie had tried to strangle her? Wouldn't a concerned sister ask to leave for a family emergency? Grace would. If Alyssa called and said Bill had attacked her, Grace would've been in the car and headed to her sister without hesitation while simultaneously plotting the demise of the man who'd laid hands on her. Regardless of how Grace felt about the way her sister was handling the news, she knew Alyssa needed the details.

After taking a deep breath and leaning against the porch railing, Grace described the texts Charlie had sent Lex about Bronwyn and the cat. She glossed over the details about their decision to head over to the house. There was no need to explain they'd been more than happy to confront the jackhole. But she did have to tell her that Lex and Joy broke in to save the cat.

"Wait a minute," Alyssa said, sounding annoyed. "Why didn't Lex just go in and get the cat? What is it that you thought Charlie was going to do?"

"Because he was acting so strange. She was freaked out about what he might do. Can't you see that?"

Alyssa huffed out a breath of annoyance. "He wouldn't harm Lex. He wouldn't harm anyone. That's not who he is. Just because—"

"Did you miss the part about how he tried to strangle me?" Grace barked into the phone.

"I'm sure it was a mistake. He was probably startled because people broke into our house."

"Alyssa! You can't mean—"

"Grace, that's enough. I know Charlie. And obviously, there are two sides to this story. You can't call me and expect me to get worked up about some vague texts that sound like he was just trying to get under Lex's skin. As far as attacking you... From where I'm sitting, you were trespassing. What did you expect him to do? Just let y'all break in and do anything you wanted?" She snorted. "Let it go. I'll talk to him and find out why he was poking at Lex. It's likely nothing. Now, I really do have to go."

The call ended, and Grace stood on her porch, staring at the phone. After a moment, she shook it as if that would do anything to get Alyssa back on the line. She braced herself for the bone-deep anger to take over, but instead, all she felt was disappointment. Was her sister so far gone over a guy that she cared more about him than she did about Grace and Lex?

She never would've thought so before, but based on their conversation she wasn't sure what she should think.

The door opened, and Lex stepped out onto the porch.

When she spoke, her voice was full of all the anger Grace hadn't been able to summon. "Mom's more worried about him than us, isn't she?"

Grace raised her hands palms up in an I-don't-know motion. "She might just be in denial."

Lex's lip curled in disgust. "If I ever get like that over a girlfriend, please do us all a favor and put me out of my misery."

There were no words to ease Lex's disappointment in her mother. Instead, Grace wrapped her arms around her niece and held on tightly. "Have you heard from Bronwyn yet?"

Nodding, Lex let out a breath and said, "She's on her way here. Charlie did text her and try to get her to go over there. She said she would've gone if I hadn't blown up her phone looking for her. I guess he told her I was there and that I needed to be *handled*. Whatever that means."

A faint growl escaped Grace's throat. The man was a loose cannon just waiting to detonate. And her sister would be headed back over there when she got off from work. Grace's stomach started to ache. What if Charlie took out his frustration on Alyssa? A shiver of unease skated across Grace's skin. No matter how upset she was at her sister, she still needed to protect her.

Headlights from a car shined in Grace's eyes briefly before the car came to a stop and someone killed the engine. Lex stepped back and wiped at her eyes, squinting in the direction of the vehicle. She sucked in a gasp and then ran down to greet Bronwyn. The two collided into a hug and started whispering to each other.

Grace walked back into the house to give them some privacy and tried her sister one more time. The call went straight to voice mail. She left a message, begging her sister to be careful and reminding her that Grace's door was open if she needed a place to stay or if she just wanted to stop by. Grace wasn't going to let her hurt feelings get in the way of helping her sister when she finally decided Charlie wasn't worth her time.

"Grace?" Joy called from the kitchen.

"Coming." Grace walked through her house, suddenly bone tired. Ever since she'd gone to work for Landers Realty, she'd been running nonstop. Unfortunately, there still wasn't even a nibble on any of the houses she represented. She thought about her bills that were due in a few weeks. She had the money to pay them, but she'd be a hell of a lot more comfortable if she didn't have to touch any more of the money she'd gotten in their divorce agreement. She wanted to be making her own money already.

CHAPTER SEVENTEEN

Grace found Joy and Hope sitting at the table, sipping coffee and nearly cried in relief. "Please tell me there's more coffee in that pot."

"I'll do you one better," Hope said, handing over a hot mug.

"Thanks." Grace took a seat across from her friends and sipped at the rich java. Then she said, "Can you believe Lex? She kicked Charlie's ass. I couldn't be more proud." At the sound of Lex's name, Lizzy the cat appeared at Grace's feet. She reached down and picked up the creature, who was acting perfectly normal as if nothing had happened. "And you, little one. Nice job trying to scratch his eyes out."

"That cat is a hero."

Joy let out a chuckle and nodded. "You got that right. Maybe you should take her on your house showings. She'll scare off any pesky ghosts, I'm sure."

The truth was the cat probably would be a decent deterrent. But Grace had already made the internal commitment to be honest with her potential buyers. It was better for them to know what they were getting into. She shrugged and took a sip of her coffee.

"Now that we have some downtime," Joy said, "I can fill you in on what I found out about the large white cottage on the edge of town."

Grace sat up. "You have info for us?"

She nodded. "Yep. After I got the names of the previous owners, I put my research skills to work, and you're not going to believe what I found."

Grace scooted to the edge of her chair and said, "Spill it."

Joy looked between Grace and Hope, and with her eyes wide, she said, "There are rumors of a suspicious death in the house in the mid-1980s."

"A murder?" Grace asked, choking over a lump that suddenly formed in the back of her throat.

"Maybe," Joy said, her tone ominous. "There was never any proof, but there was speculation in the local paper. A family named Kort lived there. The wife, Jenny, died suddenly. Drug overdose. Heroin. But her family and all her friends swore up and down that she never used drugs and barely even drank alcohol. Then one day she's shooting up enough to overdose? It doesn't make a lot of sense. Although, I suppose she could've just been good at hiding her addiction. Or her loved ones were covering to preserve some sort of family reputation."

"That sounds more likely. Heroin isn't exactly the kind of drug that is easy to hide if you do it regularly," Grace said.

Hope raised one eyebrow. "You sound so... ominous. Is this something you've witnessed before?"

"Unfortunately, yes. Alyssa's birth dad was an addict. We watched him spiral over the course of two years. It was really ugly." Grace's mom had never actually been married. Grace's father died in a car crash before she was born. And then there was a revolving door of men in her mother's life. The worst was Alyssa's dad, and Grace strongly suspected that the reason her sister put up with shitty boyfriends was a direct result of her relationship with her own father. Or lack of one anyway.

Joy frowned. "I never knew that."

"I don't really talk about it." Grace wrapped her hands around her mug. "Anyway, so there was speculation that someone gave the wife a lethal dose?"

"Yep. No arrests were ever made though. If we want to research it, we'd have to get the police records or talk to the detective who worked the case because all the relatives are gone now."

"Moved away?" Grace asked.

She shook her head. "Died. The immediate ones anyway. Looks like there are cousins up in Washington and a couple down south, but no one who ever lived here in Premonition Pointe."

Grace thought of the message the ghost had given them. *Roots run deep. Family is the only thing that matters. We will never give up.*

"It seems clear the ghost is unsettled and wants Jenny Kort's murder solved," Grace speculated. "That would make the most sense as to why the ghost isn't willing to move on."

"*If* Jenny was murdered," Hope interjected. "How are we going to find that out if there's no one to ask about the details?"

"There are police reports we could track down," Joy said. "We could also talk to former neighbors, reporters, even medical professionals. The eighties weren't that long ago. And in this small town? You know how people like to talk."

Grace stifled a groan. Wasn't that the truth. Small towns were the worst for gossip. She was willing to bet she could take a trip to the hair salon and find at least a small handful of people on any given day who had some juicy gossip.

"When can we start this research?" Grace asked. "I'll need to make a list of possible leads."

"Tomorrow?" Joy asked with a shrug.

"No Art Market meetings tomorrow?" Hope asked.

"Nope. My day is completely free," Joy said. "Paul's not even going to be home for dinner. He has a golf game and is planning to eat at the club."

"Okay. Perfect." Grace got up and grabbed her phone. After double-checking the appointment she'd scheduled, she said, "I'm meeting with a witch who specializes in dealing with stubborn hauntings tomorrow morning. After her assessment, I'm available to check things out."

"A witch who specializes in hauntings?" Hope echoed. "Now things are getting serious. What does she do? Break out a Ouija board?"

"Ha, effing, ha," Grace said dryly. But then she shrugged, because in her haste to find help, she hadn't taken the time to find out what methods the ghost whisperer used to cleanse homes. She hoped it wasn't something batshit crazy like blood sacrifices or anything to do with casting curses. Usually Grace was careful about who she worked with, but she'd been so excited to find someone who sounded like they knew what they were talking about that she hadn't hesitated to hire her. "Oh, gods. Please let tomorrow go well. I do not need this to blow up in my face."

"It won't," Joy insisted. "You're too smart for that."

Grace used to think so. Then she'd gone and nearly ripped her younger coworker's clothes off, and not long after that, she'd led a breaking-and-entering mission to rescue a cat. Who knew what might have happened if Grace hadn't had the balls to crush Charlie's with her fist. Things could've gone south very quickly.

"Both of us will be there to back you up," Hope assured her. "Just relax. We're not going to let you do any crazy rituals. We'll just expel an unpleasant ghost so we can all get on with our lives." Hope stood and moved to Joy's side. "Let's go, hot stuff. Grace needs her beauty rest."

"I need a hot shower first," Grace said, "and then some sleep. See you both in the morning?"

"Definitely," Hope said. "I've always wanted to learn some excellent ghost hunting skills. Seems useful."

"Useful, right," Grace mumbled as first Hope and then Joy hugged her goodnight.

"Take care of that precious girl," Joy said, nodding to the front of the house where Lex and Bronwyn had their heads bent together as they whispered to each other.

"I will." Grace walked them to the door and held it open for both of them.

After a long hot shower, just as she was getting ready to head to bed, Grace got a text. There was no name attached to the message, but it read, *Grace, it's Lucas. I'm back in town, staying at my mother's, and I need a house ASAP. Preferably one that Hope adores. But I'd appreciate it if you'd keep that information to yourself.*

Lucas? Hope's Lucas? He was the one in the market for a house? Did that mean he was moving back to town? Hope was going to lose her damned mind when she realized he was back in Premonition Pointe for good.

Well, if he was house hunting, she sure wasn't going to keep him waiting. Except she had an appointment with the ghost-whisperer in the morning. She tapped back for him to meet her at Pointe of View Café the next day for a late lunch so they could get to it. She had a commission to earn.

CHAPTER EIGHTEEN

"*T*his is such an interesting property." Isobel Caligari stood in front of the Victorian, studying the dilapidated porch. "The spirits here are quite entertaining, aren't they?"

"Sure. Entertaining," Grace said from behind the ghost-whisperer and did her best to keep an open mind. The witch had been thirty minutes late and arrived wearing kitten-print pajama pants and a cut-off tank top that showed off a pink sapphire belly button ring. Her hair was tied up into a messy bun, making her look like she'd just rolled out of bed.

"Do you know any history about the previous residents?" Isobel asked.

Grace turned to Joy, who was standing to her left leafing through a folder of paperwork. "Joy? Anything?"

"So far just names of people who owned the property," Joy said. "No news articles or arrest records. Nothing online either. I think this place might have been a second home, so the previous owners weren't based here. It'll take more time to track any details down."

Isobel waved an unconcerned hand. "No problem. Sometimes it's better to not have any preconceived theories." She walked up onto the porch, ran her hand over the peeling paint on the door, and chuckled.

"What's so funny?" Grace asked.

"Just the dedication. It takes a lot of energy to achieve this level of decay over just a few months."

"I'd guess so," Grace mumbled as she followed the witch into the house. Joy and Hope trailed behind her, whispering softly. She wondered what her friends thought of the witch. On the one hand, she seemed completely at ease and full of confidence. The combination made her interesting. On the other, Grace didn't appreciate that the witch had wasted their time. She had a lot to do that day, including meeting with Lucas, her newest client.

"Hmm," Isobel said as she stood in the middle of the room.

Grace opened her mouth to ask what the witch planned to do next, but before she could get the words out, Isobel abruptly sat down cross-legged and pressed her hands together in front of her heart as if she were meditating.

Hope and Joy both moved to stand next to Grace as the three of them waited to see what she'd do next.

Nothing is what she did next. The witch spent what seemed like forever chanting under her breath about listening to the spirits. Only nothing happened. The house was completely silent, and as far as Grace could tell, none of the spirits were making themselves known. Not like they had the day she'd shown the house to Gigi anyway.

"Maybe I should just go continue my research," Joy finally whispered to Grace.

Grace nodded. Who knew how long this would take? And

why should her friend have to stay for the most boring ghost-hunting event ever?

Hope cleared her throat and motioned that she was going to go with Joy.

Grace nodded and whispered back. "Raincheck on tonight? I have a new client this afternoon, and I don't know how long it will take." As soon as she was done with Isobel, she needed to meet Lucas. Since he'd said to not say anything to Hope just yet, she hadn't been sure how she was going to slip away without lying by omission. Grace didn't like keeping things from her two best friends, but she would keep Lucas's secret for the moment, considering he was a client and an old friend.

"No problem," Joy said while Hope nodded her agreement.

Grace watched her two friends leave and then sat back and waited for Isobel to do her thing.

Eventually Isobel got to her feet and then spent the next half hour running her fingers over every surface of the old house. By the time she made her way back into the living area, they'd been there for over an hour.

Grace, irritated that she was paying by the hour for the woman to do next to nothing, crossed her arms and asked, "Did you see anyone?"

Isobel shook her head. "Nope. They aren't showing themselves today. If you want me to come back and try again, I can probably find time later in the week."

"Um, no. I don't think so." Grace was already fishing her keys out of her bag. "Sorry to waste your time, but instead of checking out the other houses, I think it's best if we just call it a day."

Isobel blinked. "Really? You don't even want to know what I learned here?"

Grace raised one eyebrow. "I thought you said the spirits weren't responsive."

"That doesn't mean I didn't get a read on this house." She gave Grace a knowing smile. "I bet you were thinking I was going to have an EMF reader or perform some sort of spell to make the spirits appear, right?"

"Um, maybe?" Grace felt her cheeks go warm with embarrassment. "Is that not how this works?"

"Oh, sure. For the people who can't inherently hear and sense spirits, it's a way of communicating. But that's not how I work." She placed her right palm flat on the front door and closed her eyes. A silver shimmer coated the door, and Isobel nodded as if she were satisfied with whatever she felt. "Did you see that?"

"Sure. You coated the door with magic."

"No." She shook her head. "I didn't do anything except call the magic that is already embedded in the wood. The front door and the entire front porch area of the house are heavily saturated with magic. That's probably not surprising since you can see how fast the conditions are deteriorating. But what's interesting is that the rest of the house has hardly been touched."

"Okay. So what does that mean exactly?" Grace asked, frowning.

"It means that while the spirits here are actively trying to keep people out, they aren't necessarily interested in terrifying anyone. In other words, the spirits aren't dangerous. They're just particular about who they want living here. In order to sell this house, you're likely going to need to find someone they approve of; otherwise they'll continue to make their displeasure known by being a nuisance."

"Gigi," Grace said. She'd loved the house, and the house seemed to love her... right up until her husband arrived.

"Who's Gigi?"

"The perfect buyer for this property. Unfortunately, the house hates her husband. Once he arrived, the spirits were really active and obviously not pleased."

"What did they do?" she asked, her expression full of excited curiosity.

"There was a peacefulness and a rightness while Gigi was here. But when her husband showed up, that energy vanished and the spirits kicked up a lot of forceful wind. Nothing dangerous, just enough disruption for the spirits to make it known they were not pleased."

"Yes. That tracks with what I sensed here," Isobel said.

Grace let out a heavy sigh. "Do you know how long it will take to find someone who the spirits accept? Is there any way that you can get them to leave? We tried smudging but—"

"Smudging won't work even for the most skilled ghost-whisperers," Isobel said, cutting her off. "The spirits here are tied to the home. Their attachment runs deep. It's not all that surprising due to the magical nature of Premonition Pointe. What might work in other towns isn't going to work here."

That made sense. Premonition Pointe had been founded by witches, and magic was woven into the fabric of the town and the older buildings. The Victorian was one of the first homes to be built back around the turn of the twentieth century. She'd suspected all along that ultimately, she'd need to find the right buyer who could deal with the spirits. She'd just hoped there was an easier way. "Right. But what do I do when the house loves the wife, but not the husband?"

Isobel raised her hands in the air, palms up, indicating that she didn't have the first clue. "That sounds like a marriage that might need therapy, not a new house."

Grace couldn't agree more. But instead of gossiping about the couple, she gave the woman an apologetic smile and asked, "Are you still free to look at the next house?"

"Of course." She strode toward the front door, opened it, and stepped outside. As Grace joined her, she said, "Now that I'm all warmed up, it shouldn't take nearly as long."

FAMOUS LAST WORDS. So much for not taking very long. Grace sat on the back deck of the large white cottage and waited for Isobel to do whatever she was doing. They'd arrived forty-five minutes earlier, and so far Isobel hadn't done anything other than sit at the top of the stairs and meditate.

Grace had given up on waiting and went outside to watch the waves churn gently against the sand. There weren't as many people on the beach as she expected. Considering it was a summertime weekend, the shoreline should've been dotted with families playing in the water. She squinted down the shoreline and spotted a much larger crowd about two hundred yards away. Interesting. She knew there was a public access between the house and the crowd. She figured there must be an event going on that she didn't know about that was keeping the tourists occupied.

As she watched, a family of five with two dogs headed toward her end of the shore, but when they got about two houses away, they suddenly turned around and headed straight back to the crowd.

A loud cackle came from the house directly next door. Grace turned to find a woman with long blond hair sitting in a lounge chair and holding a wine glass in one hand and a book in the other. Her wrinkled skin along with her pronounced veins gave away her age, but her wide-legged white slacks and red silk blouse were so stylish that she looked as if she'd just walked off the pages of a magazine.

"Hello there," Grace said, getting the other woman's attention.

The woman jerked up and spilled some of the wine from her glass as she let out a startled gasp. "Oh, my. I had no idea anyone was over there. The house has been empty for so long I just assumed I was alone." She got to her feet and moved to the edge of the deck closest to Grace. "Are you the new owner?"

Grace shook her head. "I'm Grace Valentine, the Realtor."

"It's nice to meet you, Grace. I'm Lara." She held up her glass of wine in a toasting motion. Then she gave Grace a pitying look. "I'm so sorry you've been stuck with that house. Don't get me wrong; it really is fantastic. Under normal circumstances, it should've sold in a bidding war, but instead it just sits here sad and empty."

"Normal circumstances?" Grace blinked at her. "Are you saying this house has unusual ones?" Obviously, Grace knew the answer to that question; she just wanted Lara's take on the spirits that haunted the place.

Lara snorted. "Please. Everyone knows that house is haunted."

"By Jenny Kort?" Grace asked. "The wife who died here? I heard speculation that she might have been murdered."

"Jenny murdered? Goodness no. She had a rare blood disease of some sort. Toward the end she was really thin.

That fueled all kinds of rumors, including drugs. Poor thing. After she died, her husband moved and her sister Emma moved in. Lovely woman, but she never had any children. If I had to guess, I'd say both are still here in some form. They each loved this property in their own way."

"They loved it but don't want anyone else to enjoy it?" Grace frowned. "That's strange, don't you think?"

"Oh no, they aren't the problem. I'm sure they could be dealt with, but it's the curse that's the issue. I just don't think anyone is ever going to buy it. It's too bad, too, because Emma was a fantastic neighbor. I just can't believe that old curse is still working."

"Curse?" Now that was interesting. "What curse?"

"You haven't heard about it?" She chuckled softly. "I thought it was common knowledge. Emma used to talk about it all the time. Or at least she did when we were younger. She said her great, great aunt had cursed the house so that if anyone outside the family tried to buy it or take it away from them, the house would become unlivable. Apparently the family legend is that the patriarch of the family lost their home back east after being spelled into signing a bad business deal. His daughter, Emma's great, great aunt, not only secured that cottage for them but also cursed it so that people who weren't related to them wouldn't want it. It worked, because right up until Emma passed a few years ago, the house had never belonged to anyone outside their family."

"Until now. Mr. Saint isn't a part of their family, is he?"

"Not as far as I know. After Emma died, whoever inherited the house never came here. They just sold it to the first buyer. I'm not even sure Mr. Saint checked it out. He wanted properties to restore and got it at a ridiculously reduced rate." She shook her head. "It's a shame. The place used to have a lot of life to it." The woman started to move toward the back door of her own house.

"Lara?" Grace asked.

"Yes, dear?"

"Why were you laughing when the tourists turned around and went back down the beach?"

A wide smile spread across Lara's face. "That is Emma's work still going strong. She cast a spell to make this part of the beach uninviting to those who don't live here. Genius, that one. It's made our vacation home a true retreat."

"That's not legal, is it?" Grace asked, frowning. She was pretty sure Premonition Pointe had a law on the books that made spells like that forbidden.

"Oh, it is… now. Why do you think the town passed that law in the first place?" She winked and disappeared into her house.

Grace eyed the beach one more time and then chuckled to herself. It really was too bad she'd never gotten to know Emma. The woman sounded like someone she'd have been friends with. Smiling to herself, she walked back into the house to find Isobel still sitting on the stairs. Grace cleared her throat.

Isobel's eyes flew open. Her furrowed brows and turned-down lips were the picture of frustration. "I'm just not getting a read on what's really going on here. All I keep hearing are the words *roots run deep.*"

"Right," Grace said. "I've gotten that message, too. But never mind. The neighbor filled me in on a few things, and now I have a game plan. We can get going now."

Isobel walked slowly down the stairs, her fingertips grazing the wall. "What did you learn?"

"There's a curse on the house. It needs to belong to a member of the original family that owned the property. No one else is ever going to be welcome."

"That's not a curse that can be broken easily," Isobel said, her frown deepening.

"I know. Though it's not impossible if it comes to that." Grace pulled her phone out of her purse and sent Joy a text letting her know they didn't need to find any more information on Jenny Kort. It was time to find out if Emma and Jenny had any remaining relatives. She'd start there.

"Do you want me to work on some counter curses?" Isobel asked.

Considering the woman just spent over an hour listening to the same message without trying anything new, Grace wasn't in a hurry to pay her for any more of her services. "No thanks. I'll take it from here. Will you bill me for your time today?"

"Sure." Isobel sounded disappointed, but her expression remained neutral. "Does that mean you don't want me to take a look at the third house?"

Grace made a show of looking at the time on her phone. "Maybe another day. I didn't realize this would take as long as it did, and I have another appointment I have to get to."

"Right. One never can tell how these investigations are going to go," she said, smiling. "I'm just glad I was able to be of help. Call me if you need anything else."

"Sure," Grace said, but she really didn't mean it. While Isobel had been helpful at the Victorian house, she'd been late and of zero use at the cottage. Grace had a feeling that if she and her coven had just tried to talk to the ghosts, they'd have gotten the same information. When was she going to learn that her coven could handle almost anything if they put their minds to it? They were small but mighty.

A text came back from Joy almost immediately. *I'm on it. Will call tonight with the research.*

Grace grinned, ushered Isobel outside, and locked up. Twenty minutes later, she walked into the Pointe of View Café and nearly gasped out loud when she spotted Lucas King sitting in a booth waiting for her. He was clean-shaven with salt and pepper hair that had been recently cut. And damn, he was built as if he regularly hit the gym. Grace blinked and wondered if Hope was going to lose her mind. Because the man that had just moved back to Premonition Pointe had gone from sexy nerd, to full-blown tattooed hottie.

CHAPTER NINETEEN

*G*race walked over to Lucas, and just as she sat down across from him, her entire body broke out into a sweat as a hot flash took over. Without thinking, she started to fan herself with the folder she was holding. "Damn, is it hot in here, or is it just you?"

Lucas sputtered out a laugh and said, "Excuse me?"

"Um... dammit." Her face flushed so hot she started to wonder if her head was actually going to go up in flames. "I meant is it just me." She pulled her hair off her neck and tied it into a ponytail. "Just one of the joys of getting older. My temperature control button seems to be malfunctioning."

"I can see that." He handed her a napkin and added, "Looks like you could use one of those personal fans they sell on TV."

"Thanks." She took his napkin and dabbed at her neck and cleavage. But what she really wanted to do was grab his glass of ice water and dump the entire thing over her head. It was a damned good thing Grace had zero interest in Hope's ex; otherwise she'd have been a thousand times more embarrassed than she'd ever have thought possible.

Lucas studied her for a moment and then grinned. "It's good to see you, Grace."

She dropped her folder on the table and smiled back. "You, too. You're looking pretty good. Those tattoos are giving you a bad-boy vibe that kinda works for you. Just tell me one thing."

He sat back in the booth and gave her a wary look. "Sure, as long as it isn't about Hope."

Grace snorted. "Oh, those questions are coming, but not yet." She braced her elbows on the table and said, "What I want to know is how you manage to fight off all the admirers. I bet you have women *and* men chasing you down for your number. I mean, you've always been blessed in the looks department, but with the tattoos… sexy, Lucas. Very sexy."

"Shut up, Valentine," he said, laughing.

Grace chuckled. "Just calling it like I see it."

"Sure you are. When did you become such a smartass?"

"Right about the time I stopped giving a shit what anyone thought about me," she said.

He raised his eyebrows. "Was that right about the time you lost two hundred pounds of asshole?"

Grace started to chuckle and then fell into a fit of laughter. Her eyes were watering by the time she got herself together. "Yeah. Right about then." Grinning, she reached across the table and clasped her hand over his. "It's really good to see you, Lucas. Tell me you're home for good."

His smile vanished, and he said, "I'm home for good."

"What is it?" she asked, squeezing his hand. "What's wrong?"

"I'm that transparent?" he asked.

"Yes. You look just like you did when someone stole your favorite Matchbox car back at sleep-away camp when we were eight years old."

His lips twitched into a ghost of a smile. "You would bring that up."

Grace had known Lucas most of her life. They'd met at summer camp and had always been friends, and then later when Grace moved to Premonition Pointe as a young adult, he'd been the one to introduce her to Hope. The only time she'd ever seen him look so serious was after he and Hope had broken up and he'd made the decision to pack up and move across the country. "Come on. Tell me. What's going on?"

He sighed and twisted a napkin as if he needed to keep his hands busy. "It's my mom. She has the beginning stages of dementia."

"Oh, no," Grace said. "I'm so sorry. How bad is it?"

"Not terrible, but bad enough she can't live alone. And please don't say anything to anyone. She's very concerned about being the talk of the town."

"I understand." But Grace didn't know how she was going to keep any of this from Hope. She was one of her best friends and a coven mate. It just felt wrong. "Lucas, what about Hope?"

He pressed his lips together in a thin line. "I need you to let me talk to her first."

"You told me on the phone that you wanted a house that she'd love. It's not hard to work out that you hope she'll be joining you there one day."

Lucas stared Grace in the eye but didn't say anything.

"I assume this means you're ready to work things out?"

Grace knew this wasn't really any of her business, but he'd just asked her to lie by omission. If she was going to go down that road with him, she wanted to make sure it was worth it.

They stared each other down until Lucas finally let out a breath and leaned back against the booth. "Grace, do you think there is any chance that Hope and I could live in the same town and not end up together?"

"No. Not really," she said honestly. "But you've been gone a long time. You've both changed. I'm just not sure you can go back."

"I have no intentions of moving backward, Grace. I'm here to move forward. I'm sure you understand that better than most after this past year."

She gave him a sad smile. "I do. But I'm moving forward on my own."

"So am I. But that doesn't mean I can't try to start over with the only person I…" He glanced away as his face flushed pink. "Anyway. If there's a chance Hope can be a part of my life moving forward, then I'm going to go for it. That's all there is to it."

"Okay then," she said brightly, pleased to hear he still obviously cared for her friend. They were the type of couple who would always be finding their way back to each other. She just prayed that this time they'd stick. Grace pushed the folder across the table toward him. "I put together the homes that are on the market that I think Hope might be most interested in. I didn't know your budget, so I just pulled what I could find. Let me know if there are any you're interested in seeing. Or alternatively, you could give me a list of your must haves and your budget and let me do the vetting."

He shook his head. "No budget. All I care about is that

there are at least three bedrooms and it's a place that Hope would like."

"No budget?" Grace asked, forcing herself to not gape at him. "Business is going good, huh?"

"Something like that." He chuckled and then waved the waitress over to take their orders.

By unspoken mutual agreement, they dropped the topic of Hope and talked about the changes in Premonition Pointe since Lucas had been gone, what areas of town he liked best, and Grace's new life as a single woman.

They were having such a good time chatting that Grace didn't notice Bill until she heard his voice.

"Well, isn't this interesting," he said, his tone full of irritation.

Grace jerked around to stare at her soon-to-be ex-husband. "Bill, what are you doing here?"

"Meeting with a client." He waved at an older woman who was waving at him as she exited the café. "And what about you? Looks like you've moved on to dating someone in the appropriate age range."

"You have some nerve," Grace said, rising to her feet. "How dare you talk about who I'm dating after you went and traded me in for a woman less than half your age."

"I didn't trade you in, Grace. Our marriage was over long before I actually found the balls to leave. You and I both know that."

Grace curled her hands into fists and contemplated decking the bastard. "We had sex two days before you presented me with your separation plan. Don't try to gaslight me. You only left because your side piece gave you an ultimatum."

"Don't call her that, Grace. It's beneath you."

Hatred. Pure hatred ran through her veins. How had Grace been married for twenty years to the gaslighting jackass who was standing at her table? Had he always been such a douche? Had she only seen what she wanted to see, or had he turned into an asshole *after* ditching her for Shondra? She didn't know. And other than feeling like the biggest fool that ever lived, she didn't really care either. "Bill, go away. Go back to Shondra and leave me alone to live my life."

Bill opened his mouth to no doubt say something else completely awful, but Lucas rose and said, "Hey, man. I think you should just do what she asked."

"Who asked you?" Bill narrowed his eyes at Lucas. Then recognition dawned in his squinty gaze. "Lucas King. What did you do? Wait until I was finished with her to come back and stake your claim?"

"Bill!" Grace grabbed his wrist and jerked him toward the exit. "What the hell do you think you're doing?"

"What are *you* doing? Does Hope know you're dating that guy?"

"We're not dating," she spat. "And even if we were, it's none of your business. You. Left. Me. Remember? Your input isn't welcome."

Before he could say another word, Grace spun on her heel and stalked back to her table where Lucas was still waiting and watching.

"Are you all right?" Lucas asked, placing his arm around her shoulders.

She nodded. "Just pissed. What a jackass."

"You've got that right." Lucas slid back into the booth, and Grace followed suit. "It looks to me like he's regretting his choices. Why else would he be so put out by who you date?"

Grace scoffed. "Please. He's a liar. Our marriage might

not have been new and shiny, but we were fine. He's being a dick because he doesn't like seeing me with anyone else. He'd have been content to stay with me and cheat for the rest of his life. Shondra made him choose, and he's not happy about it."

"That's really effed up, Grace." Lucas dropped some bills into the check folder and then handed it to the waitress.

"I know." She rummaged in her wallet and pulled out some money. "Here. I fully planned to pay for that. Client lunch."

He shook his head. "No way. This was me taking an old friend out. Don't give it another thought."

"At least let me pay half," Grace insisted, still shoving the bills at him.

"Nope." He crossed his arms over his chest. "Deal with it, Valentine. You can get the next one."

"Fine." She grinned at him. "It's good to have you home."

"Especially when I buy you lunch," he teased.

"Shut it, King, or I'll tell everyone you used to wet the bed until high school."

He threw his head back and laughed. "That is such a lie."

"Okay, until sixth grade then," she said, chuckling.

"Keep it up. See what happens."

"Grace!" Jackson Dixon, Lex's best friend, rushed over to the table. He was wearing tight ripped jeans and a T-shirt that had *Pointe of View Café* scrawled across the front. "Hey. I was hoping I'd get a chance to say hi before you left."

"Hey, Jackson. What are you doing here?" She eyed him, wondering why he was working at the café when he had a thriving graphic arts business.

"Just some extra cash. You know how it is. Gig economy. It's nice to have multiple cash flows." He shrugged one shoulder. "Plus, it's nice to be around other people a few days a week."

"Right." She gestured to Lucas. "Jackson, this is my old friend, Lucas King. Lucas, this is Jackson Dixon. He's been Lex's best friend since grade school."

Lucas shook his hand. "Nice to meet you."

"You too." Jackson turned his attention back to Grace. "I tried to get over here sooner to run Bill off, but I got held up by a customer. Can you believe Shondra has already cheated on him?"

Shock rendered Grace speechless for a moment. But then she forced herself to swallow and croaked out, "She did? How do you know?"

Jackson glanced over at the kitchen, apparently checking to see if he was needed before sliding into the booth beside her. "Um, I have an acquaintance who works at the women's clinic. We got together one night and had way too much to drink. I'm talking entirely too much tequila, and he started to tell me this story about a woman who came in to get checked for genital warts."

Grace's eyes went wide. "Ohmigod. Your friend discloses private information about the patients at the women's clinic?"

"Oh, no. It's not like that." Jackson shook his head. "He never mentioned any names. He was just telling me this story about a woman who lost her shit after she was diagnosed. She was going on and on about how her fiancé was going to kill her when he found out she'd been with someone else even though he was a cheater himself. Let's just say my hookup gave enough details that it wasn't hard to work it out since I know both of you."

"Your hookup? Did you meet this guy on Grindr?" Grace

asked. She couldn't resist needling him. He was the one who'd mentioned the guy was a hookup after all.

"Um, yeah. But don't worry! I'm safe. No need to lecture me," he insisted.

"I wasn't going to," she said with a laugh. "Although, if you meet up with him again, tell him to keep his trap shut about the patients at the clinic. This town is too small for people to not make connections."

"Oh. Yeah. I won't be seeing him again." Jackson's expression turned dark. "Dude turned out to be a jackass. I should've known when he was going on and on about Shondra. But since she did you dirty, I couldn't resist the gossip."

Grace had to admit she was damn near giddy with the information he'd just supplied. Genital warts. She wanted to laugh, but then she distinctly remembered wishing that Shondra would contract the virus and instantly felt terrible. Had she actually cursed the woman by accident? It wasn't unheard of for thoughts to turn into actual hexes, but until Nina ended up with acne, she'd never thought it had happen to her before.

"You're a good friend, Jackson," she said, patting his hand. "Thanks for that juicy tidbit. You have no idea how happy that makes me to hear Shondra can't keep it in her pants. It's no less than Bill deserves. But now you need to lock it in the vault. Got it?"

"Got it." He flashed his brilliant smile at her and slipped out of the booth. "Tell Lex to call me back or else I'm going to crawl through her bedroom window, climb into her bed, and steal all the covers."

Chuckling, Grace promised to relay his message. "She's had a lot on her plate lately."

Jackson snorted. "I'm sure. And her name is Bronwyn." Wiggling his fingers at her, Jackson hurried over to the kitchen area and tied an apron around his waist.

"He's colorful," Lucas said, still eyeing the recent college graduate. "I like him."

"He's a good kid," Grace agreed.

"What is it he does besides working here?"

"Graphic design artist. Freelance," Grace said, but her mind was on Shondra and the idea that she might have cursed the woman. If she was responsible for the warts, she had to do something about it. There was only one way to find out. She had to offer the woman a counter curse in the form of a potion. She just had to figure out how to get Shondra to drink it without admitting she might've been responsible for her predicament. Because there was no way Grace would ever admit to hexing the woman who slept with her husband.

CHAPTER TWENTY

Saturday evening with Joy and Hope passed quickly. They'd come over as planned, however Joy hadn't been able to do the research she'd promised when she got roped into helping her daughter with an issue at work. Instead, they drank too much wine and laughed too hard when Grace described Isobel's ghost-hunting tactics. By the time they'd left for the night, Grace's heart was full of friendship, but also guilt. Keeping the news of Lucas from them was pure torture. But she'd made a promise, and she intended to keep it.

Grace spent all day on Sunday showing Lucas available houses in Premonition Pointe. There were at least two he seemed interested in but not enough to make an offer. By the time she pulled into the parking lot of Crabby's, the seaside restaurant that specialized in serving steamed shellfish, she was nearly starving.

"My treat. Let's eat before I pass out," Grace said, pushing her SUV door open.

"Um, Grace," Lucas said, grabbing her wrist to stop her. "Hope is over there."

Grace twisted around so fast she wrenched her back, sending a shooting pain straight down her leg. "Ouch!" she cried and pressed one hand to her lower back, trying to support herself enough that she could minimize the pain. "Oh, hell. I don't think I can move."

"What the hell just happened?" Lucas asked as he jumped out of the vehicle and rushed around to her side.

"Threw my back out. Can't walk. Can't get back in the SUV. I'm going to die here," she said dramatically. "Just put me out of my misery."

"Drama queen much?" he mumbled.

"You're not the one frozen in place," she countered.

"Come on. I'll get you in your SUV and get you home." He opened the back door and placed one hand on the small of her back and held out his other arm for her to brace herself. "Ready?"

Grace took a shallow breath, gritting her teeth against the pain as she nodded. "Let's do this."

He slowly guided her the few feet to the back door and then said, "Go on. Climb in and just lie down on the seat."

"How do you propose I do that?" Grace was bent slightly forward, panting from the pain.

"I'll boost you up. You just crawl in."

"This is never going to work," she said even as she reached for something to grab onto. When her hand wrapped around the headrest of the front seat, she squeezed her eyes shut and said, "Now."

Lucas did as he promised and grabbed her by the waist to lift her into the SUV.

A bolt of pain seized her entire back, causing her to let

out a cry that she immediately tried to stifle. She didn't need half of Premonition Pointe talking about how she'd thrown her back out just by getting out of her car.

When her knees hit the back seat and she was finally able to crawl, the pain became somewhat manageable. It wasn't long before she was curled up on her side, wondering exactly how she was going to get out of the SUV when Lucas got her home.

Suddenly he was looming over her, his hand on her back again. "Are you all right? Maybe we should take you to urgent care."

Grace shook her head. "Too late. It would have to be the emergency room. Forget it. This is just a pinched nerve. It will work itself out in a few days. In the meantime, I'll get Joy to fix me some pain potions."

"Are you sure?" Lucas asked.

Grace stared up at his concerned eyes and forced a smile. "I'm sure."

"Grace? Is that you in there?" a very familiar voice called.

Hope. Oh, hell. She was the reason Grace had thrown her back out in the first place. "Yep. It's me."

Suddenly Lucas disappeared from Grace's sightline, and she heard his voice crack a little as he said, "Hope?"

"Lucas?" Hope sounded shocked and then suspicious as she added, "What in the world are you doing here? And what's going on? Why were you with Grace in the backseat of her SUV?"

Grace groaned. *Dammit.* This was exactly why she hadn't wanted to keep anything from her friend.

"Grace threw her back out. I was just helping her into the backseat so I could drive her home."

"So you just happened to be here when Grace hurt

herself, and now you're playing the hero?" The anger in Hope's tone was unmistakable, but Grace didn't necessarily think it was directed at her. There was more going on between Hope and Lucas than she'd realized.

"No," he said with a sigh, and Grace could just imagine him running his hand through his thick hair. It was a gesture she'd noticed earlier in the day when he was thinking. "She was showing me some houses and—"

"Houses?" Hope was clearly surprised. "Why?"

"Because I need to buy one?" Lucas's reply sounded more like a question than a statement. "I did ask you for a recommendation for a Realtor, remember?"

"You didn't say it was for you. I can't believe you're moving back here, and instead of informing me, you went behind my back and had my best friend show you houses. Well, isn't that just perfect."

"Hope, I—"

"Never mind, Lucas," Hope said coldly. "I obviously am not important enough to be in the loop. But I'll take care of Grace from here. You can take off and do... whatever it is you plan to do in Premonition Pointe."

Grace had to stop herself from snorting in amusement because she was pretty sure the only thing Lucas wanted to do in Premonition Pointe was Hope.

"Grace?" Hope said after poking her head into the SUV. "I'm going to take you home now."

"Okay," Grace said, trying not to think about how she was going to crawl out of the vehicle. If Lucas was there, he'd no doubt carry her if he had to. But if it came to that, Hope wouldn't be able to do it. She'd just have to pray they figured it out, or she'd be sleeping in her car that night.

Hope jumped into the SUV, and without another word to Lucas, she cranked the engine and peeled out of the lot.

"Ouch!" Grace yelped as she was tossed against the seat. "Um, Hope, I appreciate you helping me out, but do you think you could be a tiny bit more cautious? I'm dying back here."

"Oh, sorry," she said. "I just…" She shook her head and let out a little growl of frustration. "How long has he been in town?"

"I honestly don't know. We met yesterday for a late lunch to discuss his housing needs and then—"

"So that's why you couldn't join me and Joy to dig into the research on the cottage," Hope said.

"Right. I had a client." Grace wanted to reach out and squeeze her friend's shoulder, but she couldn't. Instead, she said, "I'm sorry I didn't tell you right away. He asked me not to, and I… I just—"

"You were being a decent friend to him. It's okay, Grace." Hope's voice was low when she added, "I'm just not going to be able to get used to having him around. It's too much."

Grace's heart ached for her friends. They had a lot of baggage to work through, and Grace wasn't at all sure things would work out for them. But she sure prayed they would. "Hope?"

"Yeah?" her friend said.

"Lucas didn't have a car at the restaurant. I'm not sure how he's going to get back to his mother's. Want me to call him and make sure he has a ride?"

"Dammit," she muttered. "Yeah. I guess you better."

At least Grace's phone was handy in her front pocket. She pulled it out and dialed Lucas's number.

"Everything all right?" Lucas asked after the first ring.

"So far. We need to know how you're getting home. Uber? Lyft? Calling a friend?"

"If I say no, will Hope come back and get me?" he asked, sounding hopeful.

"Yes." Grace said a silent apology to Hope for throwing her into the deep end with Lucas, but the sooner they got talking the sooner they could get past whatever it was that had kept them apart for the past fifteen years.

"Then no. I need a ride," he said, sounding pleased.

"Okay. Go inside and get something to eat. Hope will be back for you after she gets me to my bed."

Hope groaned from the driver's seat and then whispered, "Thanks a lot, Grace. You couldn't have said we'd send a cab or something?"

Grace ended the call with Lucas and said, "Premonition Pointe doesn't have cabs anymore. He could take an Uber, but all the way to his mom's house would be one expensive trip. And considering he's hired me to be his Realtor, I just feel like he needs to be taken care of."

"Stop. I'll do it," Hope said. "But you owe me."

"Understood."

Forty-five minutes later, when Grace was in her bed with water, leftover pasta, and a bottle of pain killers on her nightstand, Hope reluctantly left to pick up her ex.

CHAPTER TWENTY-ONE

"Grace?" Lex called from the hallway. "Are you decent?"

"Of course I am. I've hardly moved for days," Grace groused. She'd been cooped up in her house for far too long while Lex kept her fed and watered. Even getting up to use the restroom was a challenge because her back still wasn't cooperating. She'd called a healer the day after her injury who'd come by and given her a salve that had worked wonders. She'd been up, showering and even cleaning the kitchen, but she'd overdone it and was right back where she started.

Lex popped her head in the bedroom. "I meant are you decent enough for a visitor?"

"Who is it?" Grace asked as she tried to prop herself up and winced at the sharp pain in her lower back.

"Owen. He says he needs to talk to you about one of your properties."

Grace groaned. He'd been back in town for three days, but she'd put off seeing him due to her injury. Her ego was having a hell of a time getting past the fact she was walking like a ninety-year-old woman. Not to mention the fact that it had been more than challenging to change clothes and take care of basic hygiene such as showering the last couple of days. Grace reached for the mirror sitting on her nightstand. The moment she held it up she let out a gasp. "I look like hell."

"You don't look that bad," Lex said, but her tone was far from convincing.

"Yes. I do. Come over here and help me up." Grace swung her legs over the side of the bed and ignored the sting of tears in her eyes. Why had she been so stupid? This wasn't the first time she'd thrown her back out over nothing. She knew it just took time, but she'd been determined to get the house clean for her date with Owen. Which she'd then had to cancel when she reinjured herself with a sneeze of all things. A freakin' sneeze. She might as well have been ninety instead of forty-five.

Lex stood in front of Grace and held her hands out. Grace grabbed hold and gently eased herself out of the bed. Once she was standing, she was only slightly bent over at the waist. Sadly, that was only a tiny improvement over the day before.

"Need help with your hair?" Lex asked, eyeing the rat's nest.

"No. Just go tell Owen I'll be a few minutes."

"Are you sure?" Lex's skepticism was growing by the second.

"I'm sure. I've got this." She shuffled into her bathroom and closed the door. A second later, she leaned against the counter and took a moment to just breathe. "Get it together, Valentine."

She glanced at the shower, and without hesitation, she opened the taps. Had she showered the day before? She couldn't be sure. There was no time to wash her hair, but she could at least make sure she didn't stink like Ben Gay. A shudder ran through her at the thought of walking out into her living room smelling like someone in a nursing home.

Thank the gods for a walk-in shower, she thought as the hot water rained down on her. If she'd needed to deal with a tub, she'd likely be crumbled on the floor ready to die from embarrassment. Once she washed the stink off, she did her best to dry off, wrapped herself in her favorite silk robe, and slapped on a bit of makeup before tying her hair into a bun on top of her head. It wasn't the most sophisticated look in the world, but she was rocking a bit of a sexy-bedroom vibe. She could live with that.

The sexiness Grace had conjured in the bathroom vanished the minute she started shuffling her way down the hallway. When she finally made it to the living room, she was sweating so much that she was pretty sure she needed another shower.

"Hey there," Owen said, his lips curving into a sexy half smile. "You look…"

"Ridiculous?"

"What?" He shook his head and moved to stand in front of her. His hands landed on her hips as he leaned in and whispered, "I was going to say you look incredible. You're way too sexy to be laid up with a bad back, Grace."

She chuckled. "Smooth talker."

"Is it working?" His eyes glinted and then his gaze moved to her lips.

Her breath caught, and she said a silent thanks that she'd decided to dress only in her silk robe. The truth was she always *felt* sexy when she was wearing the pink cheetah print robe.

"Grace?" he prompted.

"Yes?"

"Is it working?" he asked again.

She pressed a hand to his cheek. "What do you think?"

"I think you have gooseflesh on your arms and judging by the rapid beating of your pulse in your neck, I'd say it's definitely working."

"You're right," she breathed as she leaned in, brushing her lips over his.

He took one step, closing the distance between them. Careful not to jostle her, he gently wrapped one arm around her then parted his lips , and sank into the kiss, making her head spin with his sweet taste.

Grace's eyes fluttered closed as she lost herself in the wonderful sensation of his tongue exploring hers and his large hands sliding around behind her to cup her ass.

"Jesus, Grace," he said huskily when he broke the kiss. "You're not wearing anything under this robe, are you?"

She shrugged. "I just got out of the shower. I didn't want to make you wait too long."

His fingers dug into her backside as he groaned. "You have no idea how much I want to walk you back into your bedroom and tear this robe off of you."

Considering her internal temperature had just gone from normal to scorching, she had some idea. In fact, she was already trying to decide if ignoring her back pain and the slight stubble on her legs that she hadn't been able to shave would be worth it.

He brushed his lips along her neck and then scraped his teeth over her fluttering pulse.

"It's worth it. It's definitely worth it," she said.

He pulled back and studied her, a mischievous gleam in his eyes. "What's worth it, Grace?"

"Uh… dealing with a little backache in exchange for your glorious kisses?" Her face burned with heat.

He chuckled. "Glorious, huh? That's some serious praise."

"I just call it like I see it." She took a tiny step forward and pressed her entire body to his, somehow managing to avoid the shooting pain from seizing her back. Maybe his kisses were just glorious enough to be magical. Whatever worked, right?

"Damn." He let out a breath and then kissed her with so much passion she felt the rush of pleasure all the way to her toes. With her head cloudy with lust, Grace was seconds from inviting him back to her bedroom when he said, "I came by to let you know that Gigi called the office. She wants to take another look at the Victorian."

Grace took a tiny step back, startled that he was talking about work. "Gigi wants to see the house? When?"

"Today. In a half hour," he said.

"Oh, hell." Grace stepped away from him, and in the process took too big of a step and yelped in pain as she froze. "Dammit!"

"Grace," Owen said gently. "I'm going to meet Vince and Gigi for you. Then I'll come back and fill you in on how it went."

"I can't miss the showing. That's my property," she said, but tears had stung the backs of her eyes because she had no idea how she was going to drive or even ride in a car without curling up in the back just to find a comfortable enough spot.

"Yes, it's still your listing. But please, just let me do this favor for you. How about I pick up some dinner on the way back and we can finally have that date you had to postpone?"

"Date?" Had he lost his mind? She was an invalid who couldn't even make it to the couch without breaking into a sweat. "I don't know if you noticed, but I can barely move. What are we going to do on this date?"

That sexy half smile was back when he said, "I think we can figure something out. How about it, Grace? I'll grab some sushi and we can have a quiet night in. It'll be a nice change from the wild wedding weekend."

All she heard was *wild weekend*. Visions of strippers and hot bridesmaids filled her mind.

"Grace?" he asked when she didn't answer him. "Can I bring dinner by afterward?"

"Oh, sure. You said sushi, right?"

"If you're up for that." He frowned. "Are you all right?"

"Yeah." She forced a smile. "I'm just distracted about the Victorian. I hate not being there when clients do their walk-throughs. You know how it is. Want to stay on top of my job."

"Right." He nodded but looked skeptical. "You don't need to worry. You know that, right? I'm not going to try to steer her to another property. That's not my style."

"Huh?" she asked, startled. "That's not... I wasn't thinking that." Holy crow. She was messing this all up. "Listen, Owen. I'm sorry. I'm kind of a mess after being stuck in bed for three days. I really appreciate you showing the house for me and bringing dinner back. I like rainbow rolls and yellow tail sashimi. Pretty much anything, but those are my favorites."

He smiled at her and gently brushed a lock of hair from her eyes that had fallen from her bun. "No need to thank me. I'm happy to help." Then he leaned in and gave her a kiss so tender it nearly brought tears to her eyes. The good kind of tears. He brushed his thumb over her cheekbone and whispered, "Don't you dare get dressed while I'm gone. I really want the opportunity to admire this robe when I get back."

Grace grinned at him. "I think that can be arranged."

After Owen left, Lex appeared in the living room. "Well. That was hot."

"It was, wasn't it?" Grace said with a dreamy sigh.

"I don't think I've ever seen Uncle Bill look at you like that," Lex said. "Was he romantic like that back when you were dating?"

"No. Bill was never romantic. Kind and sweet, yes. But romantic? Never," she said. Then she tilted her head to the side and asked, "You think Owen was romantic? It was kind of him to deal with my listing. And he did kiss the hell out of me, but I can barely move so I don't know if I'd exactly call it romantic."

"He's taking care of you, Aunt Grace. Can't you see that? He didn't have to go show that house. Doesn't it have a lockbox? And then he's coming back and bringing you dinner without any hope of sexy time afterward. If you ask me, the most romantic thing a person can do for another is to show they care without expecting anything in return."

Grace chuckled. "What makes you think there won't be sexy time?"

"Please. You can barely walk. If he thinks he's getting some, you need to dump him yesterday. But I don't think so. He knows you're hurting. When I answered the door and found him standing there, concern was radiating off the man like a cheap cologne. He *likes* you. I think he's a keeper."

"He's too young for me," Grace said automatically, even though she was starting to wonder why it mattered so much.

Lex rolled her eyes. "It's time to get over that. No one cares."

"Trust me, Lex. Some people in this town will have plenty to say about it."

"Who, Bill? The gossips down at the salon? The people who love you will only care that you're happy. If Owen is the one who makes you smile like that, then I'm team Owen. And you should be, too." She winked, grabbed her keys off the table near the door, and said, "I'm off for a little romance of my own. Don't wait up. And don't worry about getting interrupted. See you in the morning."

Grace waved as her niece disappeared out the door and then took a look around her house. It was tidy enough, but it could use a little something extra before Owen returned. It took her much longer than she expected, but an hour later there were a half-dozen candles lit in the living room and a bottle of wine and two glasses sat on the coffee table.

After freshening up again, she got herself a bottle of water and shuffled back into the living room, where she gingerly eased herself down onto the couch. With two pillows supporting her back, she leaned back and sighed in relief. Finally, a position that didn't make her want to kill herself.

She sipped at her water and then closed her eyes for just a moment.

"Grace?" The rough tone of a male voice startled her awake.

"What?" She jerked forward and let out a cry as a thousand knives stabbed her in the lower back. "Oh, hell. That hurt."

"Dammit. I'm sorry," Owen said. "I didn't mean to startle you." He crouched down in front of her and gazed up at her in concern. "Are you all right?"

"Yeah," she said with a small whimper. "It'll be okay. I'm just so tired of this invalid nonsense. I don't like to sit around doing nothing."

"I can see that." His lips twitched with a hint of a smile as he eyed the room. "Very romantic, Grace. Does this mean you don't mind sharing dinner with me after all?"

"Stop fishing for compliments," she teased. "After those kisses, I don't think either of us is fooling anyone."

"You've got that right." He rose up and kissed her gently on the lips before pulling away and dealing with the sushi.

As they ate, Owen filled her in on the showing. "Gigi said she's going to make an offer in the next few days."

"She did?" Grace sat up straighter. "What about her husband?"

Owen shrugged. "He wasn't there. I don't know. She didn't talk about him."

Grace bit down on her bottom lip.

"What is it?"

Sighing, Grace put her plate down on the end table. "The house is haunted. You know that. And I learned that the house is very particular about who it wants to live there. It obviously doesn't like her husband, so I kinda feel like whatever happens, it's going to be a shitshow when the spirits keep acting up. I wouldn't be at all surprised if the deal falls through."

"All deals have the possibility of falling through. But anyway, she said she had to get her finances in order, and you know how that goes."

Grace did. Financing always took longer than buyers

realized. Whether moving money or getting a bank loan, both took time that could torpedo any intentions of a major purchase. "I won't hold my breath, then."

"Good," Owen said, putting his plate down, too. "Because I really like it when I hear your breath quicken, Grace. When I do this…" He dipped his head and gently bit down on her neck.

She sucked in a sharp gasp.

"Yes. That sound. And when I do this…" His tongue danced over her pulse, making her breathing uneven. "Perfect."

"And when I…" He moved to pay attention to her other side, but when he shifted his weight, the couch dipped and the support that had been keeping her in place slipped.

"Holy mother of a black crow!" she practically bellowed as she toppled right off the couch and onto the floor with a thump.

"Whoa, Grace! Are you all right?"

"I'm getting really tired of people asking me that," she said as she slowly pushed herself to an upright position.

Owen's gaze darted to her chest and then lower. His eyes turned molten with pure desire, and Grace's mouth went dry. Or it did until she glanced down and noticed that her robe had come open and she was completely bare to him.

"Ack!" She jerked the robe closed, ready to die right there from pure embarrassment. When she'd envisioned getting naked for a man again, she hadn't thought it would be right after she'd toppled off the couch and was barely able to move. Talk about very unsexy.

Except Owen was looking at her like he wanted to eat her for dessert. And she couldn't lie. It was hot as hell.

"So…" she started.

"So…" He nodded and got to his feet, offering her a hand. "Ready for bed?"

Gulp.

"Yeah, sure. That sounds like a good idea." She let him help her to her feet and then support her lower back as they made their way back to her bedroom.

Once she was beside the bed, she stood there like a fool, waiting for him to do something. Anything.

But he just pulled the covers down and said, "Get in. I'll tuck you in and make sure you have all the pillows you need."

"Tuck me in? I thought… never mind." Her entire body flushed with embarrassment.

"Trust me, Grace, there is nothing I want to do more right now than to crawl into that bed with you. But if I do, things are going to move fast, and I'm not sure I can control myself and be gentle enough that I wouldn't break you for good. You're just too damned sexy. I need you to be whole before we go there."

She stood there like a fool, staring at him. Then she swallowed. "You're saying not tonight because you're too excited?"

"That's right. Now get in that bed before I rip that robe off you," he ordered.

Sizzling heat radiated everywhere. There wasn't a nerve ending in her body that didn't want to be touched by him. But the moment she reached for him, that tightening in her back stopped her and she pressed her palm to her forehead. "I hate that you're right. Our rainchecks are starting to add up."

"Don't worry, Grace. I fully intend to collect." He kissed her on the temple and said, "Go on. Get in. I'll clean up on my way out."

Lex was right. He was the most romantic man she'd ever known. A man who got dinner and cleaned up was a man worth keeping, no matter what his age. Once she was in the bed with her pillows situated correctly, Owen leaned down, brushed his lips over hers, and murmured, "Rest up, Grace. I have plans."

CHAPTER TWENTY-TWO

*G*race woke the next day feeling like a new woman. Her back was stiff, but the shooting pain that caused her to seize every time she moved was gone. After she got up, showered, and was sure she could dress herself without feeling like an invalid, she grabbed her phone and called Owen to invite him out on a proper date.

"Tonight?" Kind of last minute, don't you think?" he asked, his tone full of mirth.

"Kind of, I guess. If you want to put it off until next week, we can—"

"How about tomorrow night at seven? I have a meeting with a new client this evening. I'll pick you up. Dinner, dancing, a moonlit walk on the beach?" he suggested.

"Dinner. No dancing—we don't want to get too crazy—and then we'll see about the beach," she said.

"Deal. Just do me a favor, will you?"

"What's that?" she asked.

"Keep that robe handy. I'm gonna want an opportunity to see you wearing it again."

Grace chuckled. "I think you mean you want an opportunity to take it off me."

He cleared his throat, and when he spoke again, his voice was husky. "That, too."

By the time she ended the call, she was flushed from head to toe and counting down the hours until their date the following evening.

* * *

"Have you heard from Hope?" Grace asked Joy the minute her friend took a seat across from her at the Bird's Eye Bakery. "I called a few times over the last couple of days, but she hasn't called back."

"I talked to her for a few minutes this morning," Joy said as she picked up the menu and buried her face in it. "She said she's slammed with back-to-back events this week. You know how summers are. Beach weddings, bachelorette parties, baby showers, etc."

Grace frowned. "Is there a reason you're hiding behind the menu? It's been the same one for about ten years. I can't imagine you don't already know every item on it."

Joy let the menu drop onto the table. "Fine. She called last night and vented about you not telling her Lucas was in town."

"I was afraid of that." Grace propped her elbows on the table and buried her face in her hands. "I told Lucas she'd be upset with me. And damn him, he's the reason I threw my back out. If I hadn't been trying to hide from Hope this never would've happened."

Joy raised one eyebrow. "You were hiding from Hope?"

"Yes. No." Grace shook her head. "That was the day I took

Lucas house hunting. We were going to grab something to eat at Crabby's and then call it a night. But then Hope showed up, startling me, and I moved too fast in the wrong direction. And well, you know the rest."

"Serves you right." The words weren't said with any heat, and Joy cracked a smile, indicating she was only teasing.

"You know I only did that because he asked me to. I think he wanted to find the right time to talk to her or something." Grace straightened up and stretched her back. It was still a little sore, but she was at least mobile. It had occurred to her that, considering how stiff she'd been the night before, it was possible she'd willed her backache away just like she'd wished those hexes on Shondra and Nina. Because the goddess knew she'd spent an obscene amount of time wishing she'd been well enough that Owen hadn't left before they'd gotten to the good stuff.

"What are you thinking about?" Joy asked, her tone full of suspicion.

"My date last night," Grace said, knowing her cheeks were already flashing pink. "Owen brought me dinner, and things got a little heated."

"Oh, really." Joy's eyes glittered with interest as she leaned in, clearly ready for all the sordid details.

"Don't look at me like that. Nothing happened," Grace insisted. "Or nothing scandalous anyway," she added when Joy's eyebrows rose. "We just made out, and then he helped me get into bed."

"Oh. He 'helped' you, did he?" She used air quotes to emphasize the word *helped*.

Grace rolled her eyes. "Please. I could barely move. That's not exactly sexy. He really did just tuck me in, and then he cleaned up my kitchen before he left."

Joy clasped her hand over her heart as she sucked in a short breath. "He *cleaned*. Are you serious?"

"Yes," Grace laughed.

"Guh. Marry him," Joy said with a sigh.

"Um, maybe I should date him for a bit first, don't you think?"

"Nope. He cleans. Snatch him up before word gets out. Put a ring on it. Sign the contract. Give him the potion. Do whatever it takes. Do you know the last time Paul cleaned?"

Grace shuddered at the potion suggestion and made a note to never wish for a proposal of any kind. Not only did she have zero desire to get married again, she definitely didn't want anyone proposing if it wasn't of their own free will. "No. When?"

"I'm gonna say 1993, right about the time we moved in together. I think he cleaned the bathroom when I had morning sickness." She wrinkled her nose. "I should've known I was doomed when he didn't wipe the base of the toilet down."

"Gross." Grace reached across the table and squeezed her friend's hand. "Are you okay? I know things with Paul have been a little tense."

"Eh. It's fine, I guess. No better, no worse. He's not cheating on me. That's something, right?"

Grace just felt sad for her friend. There was a giant chasm between not cheating and feeling loved and appreciated by your partner. And Joy deserved the best someone had to give. Paul needed to step up, or Grace had a feeling he was going to lose her. But she kept her commentary to herself and said, "I love you."

"I love you, too." Joy glanced down at her menu and said, "Cinnamon rolls?"

"Definitely. We deserve it."

"I'll get them." Joy slipped out of her chair, and within a few minutes, she was back with warm pastries and two lattes. "Eat up. We're gonna need the carbs if we're gonna get through this research." She tapped the large folder she'd brought with her. "I found records of all possible people who might be related to Emma and Jenny. Time to find someone who might want to buy that place."

"You're the best. Thank you."

Twenty minutes later, full of sugar and caffeine, Grace and Joy were busy poring through Joy's detailed research and making a list of who to contact about the house. So far, the closest relatives they'd found were three of Emma's second cousins, all of them on the west coast, and all of them in their early twenties. There were a couple more back east, but they were distant relatives, and from everything they were finding online, they didn't look like they had any ties to the west coast other than a bloodline.

"Look at this, Grace," Joy said. "Didn't you say you had a client named Matt who was looking for a house here recently?"

"Yeah. His wife died, and she'd always said she wanted a place in Premonition Pointe. He was looking for something that would be great for his kids and grandkids. Why?"

Joy handed her a piece of paper. "The parents of two of these twenty-somethings are McKenzie Summers and Matt Dahl. Do those names ring any bells?"

"Matt Dahl! Holy crap. That's my client." Grace stared at the paper and then frowned. "I tried to show him the house, but he wasn't interested. He told me he knew it was haunted, and he didn't even want to go inside."

"You know, I think the house wouldn't have welcomed

him anyway. He's not the one who is related by blood. But his sons are because of their mother's bloodline." Joy looked up at her. "You could try the family-ties angle with him. See if he can get his kids to come take a look. If it's ultimately for them, he might change his mind."

"It's worth a shot." Grace took the paper from Joy just for reference and then called Matt. "Hey, Matt. It's Grace Valentine. How are you doing?"

She listened to him talk for a few minutes about maybe having to wait on buying the beach house. He said his kids had come into town for a few nights, so he'd taken them by a couple of the ones she'd shown him, but none had come close enough to being what they were looking for. "Maybe you can email me as homes come on the market? Keep me in the loop?"

Her heart had started racing when he said his kids were in town. It was the perfect opportunity to make something happen. Her stomach got that tingling feeling it always had before when she knew she was right on the verge of making a deal happen for Bill. But the fact that this deal was all hers made her giddy with anticipation. She just needed to hold it together long enough to see it all work out. "Actually, I was hoping we could look at one more before you go. I think I've found the perfect property. It has everything you're looking for."

"Really? Where? On the beach or off?"

"On. Gorgeous view. Plenty of space. How about we make an appointment and you can bring your kids along? See what they think, since they're here." She only felt mildly guilty that she was misleading him. She'd heard him when he said he wasn't interested in a haunted house. Grace could hardly blame him. But that feeling she had... she just knew this was the right move. If they didn't like it after the second attempt, she'd drop it. Until then, she was going to give it everything she had.

"Well, if it's that good," he said. "Sure. But we can't do it today. We're headed out on an overnight fishing trip. Can we do it tomorrow night? Six-thirty? We'll be back by then and will have had enough time to get cleaned up."

"Six-thirty it is. Meet at the realty office?" she suggested. "I'll drive you over."

"Sounds good. See you tomorrow. And thanks, Grace. I appreciate you working so hard for us."

Okay, now the guilt was sinking in. She pushed the feeling away and said, "It's entirely my pleasure. Have a great fishing trip."

"Thanks."

After she ended the call, she went to put the appointment in her calendar and grimaced. She glanced at Joy. "I had a date planned with Owen tomorrow night at seven, and now I have to cancel it."

"Man, that's sucks. But at least you have the showing with Matt, right? I'm sure he'll understand," she said giving her a sympathetic look. But then her lips curved into a small teasing smile. "There's a silver lining here you're not thinking about."

Grace narrowed her eyes at her. "What's that?"

"By the time you do get together, all that sexual tension will be off the charts."

She wasn't wrong. Still, Grace had really been looking forward to their date. Sighing in disappointment, she tried to give him a call. When it went straight to voice mail, she left a message letting him know they'd need to reschedule due to a work conflict.

She contemplated making the date for later, but she didn't know how long her appointment would take. And besides that, she wasn't in her twenties anymore. Anything after ten and her eyes started watering with fatigue.

Stop it, Grace, she thought. She could survive a few nights until she could get Owen alone again.

CHAPTER TWENTY-THREE

"Grace," Matt called as he walked toward her with two handsome young men. There was no mistaking that the two younger men were Matt's sons. They all had the same green eyes, wide shoulders, and narrow-waisted build. They even all moved the same. Kind of gangly and a little awkward due to their height. It was adorable, and Grace figured she could watch them all day.

"Hi there." She waved and gave them a cheerful smile. "How was the fishing trip? Did you catch a lot of fish?"

"Hunter did. Hayden not so much. He probably needs to stop wearing so much cologne. It scares away the fish." He grinned at his two sons while they both rolled their eyes.

"Deodorant isn't cologne, Dad," the one with a small scar over his left eyebrow said. "Besides, you're probably the one to blame. All that talking you did was sure to scare them off faster than the scent of a personal hygiene product."

"Hayden needs to blame his lack of skill on something," Matt said with a wink at Grace. "It makes him feel less like a failure."

"Oh, here we go," Hayden said with a guffaw. "What's your excuse? Did you just decide to give the fish a few days off?"

"Never mind me, Son," Matt said, draping an arm over Hayden's shoulders. "I've seen my days of successful fishing. You're the one who doesn't have any stats under his belt."

Hunter, the other brother who'd been quiet up until that point, interjected, "The sooner you find a house, Dad, the sooner Hayden can work on making you proud with his fishing skills."

Matt snorted. "I'm not holding my breath."

As entertaining as it was to watch the men needle each other, Grace was getting antsy. She had a house to show... and explain. "Are we ready to go? I can drive us. It's not that far."

"Sure," Matt said, grinning at her. "Work your magic, Grace."

Oh, didn't she wish she could. But her code of ethics required her to keep her magic to herself. It did bode well for her that Matt was in such a good mood. But she was fairly certain as soon as he saw the cottage and realized where she'd taken them, he was going to have questions.

They arrived at the house entirely too quickly, and by the time Grace stopped the SUV in the driveway, she was certain she was going to sweat right through her blouse. Only this time it certainly wasn't a hot flash. She was as nervous as she'd ever been.

"Grace?" Matt asked, sounding confused. "Why are we here?"

She cleared her throat and was about to explain the family connection when Hayden let out a small gasp and then threw the door open and rushed to the front porch. He stood on the top step, clutching the railing and staring wide-eyed at the front door.

"What's he doing?" Matt asked.

"It's Mom," Hunter whispered as he wiped at his eyes. "He's talking to her."

"Mom? That's not possible," Matt said, but his voice trailed off as he watched Hunter stride up to the porch and stand right next to his brother. Both men were smiling through their tears.

Grace sat frozen in the driver's seat. She couldn't see their mother, or any ghost for that matter, and she wondered if Matt could. She doubted it, since Hunter had to tell him who Hayden was talking to. Grace turned to Matt, her eyes brimming with tears, and waited for his reaction. Would she be met with ire or curiosity? Something in between? She really had no idea what to expect. She just didn't know Matt well enough to predict anything.

"How did you know?" Matt asked, still watching his boys.

"That their mom was here?" she asked, her voice hitching a little.

"Yeah." He spun to face her, his brows knit together. "Did you conjure her or something? You and your coven?"

Grace blinked briefly, wondering if they could even do that. She supposed it was possible, but she had no desire to call up ghosts. That was just asking for trouble. "No," she said more forcefully than she intended. She cleared her throat and tried again. "I didn't even know she was here until Hunter said so. We don't conjure anyone other than the goddesses when we're doing our blessings. And they don't exactly show themselves to us if you know what I mean."

He turned to look back at his boys. "No. I don't know. I'm not a witch."

"Oh." Right. "I'm sorry. You can't see her either, can you?"

He shook his head.

"Did your wife have magic?"

"Yeah. So do the boys."

That made more sense. "Okay, I'll tell you what I found out and why I brought you here, but don't you want to go speak to her? At least through your sons. It looks like they're having no trouble communicating with her."

He nodded once and then slipped out of her SUV.

Grace watched as Matt joined his family on the porch. They stood there for a long time, crying, talking, laughing. And then the conversation came to an abrupt stop, and all three men stared at each other in silence. Finally, Matt reached for the front doorknob, but didn't get far since the home was still locked.

Grace got out of the vehicle and asked, "Did you want to see the inside?"

"Yes," Matt said, his voice sounding hoarse. "But unless it's substantially different than the pictures online, I'm pretty sure I'll be making an offer tonight."

Grace's heart soared. Not because she was getting ready to make her first sale and secure her job with Landers Realty, but because there seemed to be a peace that had settled over the Dahl men. She'd managed to give them a moment with the wife and mother of their family. It was a moment that filled her heart and soul.

"I doubt that's going to be an issue, but let's get you guys inside so you can get a peek at the real thing." Grace fiddled with the lockbox until she had the key in hand and then let the men in. Once again, she stayed outside, letting them have the time they needed to process what had just happened.

Normally Grace would never dream of not being present during the first walk-through. Someone needed to be there to ease their fears or validate their concerns. But this was a special circumstance, and she didn't want to interject herself any more than she already had.

Grace sat down on the top step of the porch and made herself comfortable.

It didn't take long for Matt to rejoin her on the porch. He sat down next to her and said, "Thank you."

"You're welcome. But I didn't do much. All I did was get you here." She smiled at him. "I'm glad it worked out."

"I want to know how you knew this was the house for us. When I was here the other day, I felt... Well, let's just say I felt too much. Pain, sorrow, regret. It was very much what I felt in those last days before I lost my wife. It made me never want to come back here."

"Oh, wow," Grace said softly. "I'm sorry, Matt. It sounds like your wife was here that day, too, only you couldn't see her. But you could sense the lingering emotions that were present during her last days. How was it today? Better?" She sure hoped so, because no one would want to live anywhere that had such heavy vibes.

"Much better," he said, smiling. "You're right, she was here, and she gave me shit for running away." He chuckled. "That's just like her. She filled us in on the connection she and the boys have to the place. After hearing about the curse and all about their cousins, Jenny and Emma, those two boys don't want any other place. And that's fine by me. The home is exactly what I asked for." He placed a hand on Grace's arm and squeezed lightly. "You really came through for us. But I'd love to know how you did it."

Grace told him about the ghost-whisperer, the neighbor, and the research Joy had done for her. "I know it sounds creepy and stalkerish, but in order to do my job, I had to find a way to reach out to the remaining family, no matter how distant, to figure out who might be interested. You just happened to be the one I knew already."

He laughed. "Lucky me."

Hayden and Hunter appeared from inside the house, both of them smiling and chattering animatedly about the house, the beach, and spending their summers there with their wives. When they spotted their dad and Grace on the porch, Hayden grinned down at Grace. "You're an angel. Thank you for this. We know dad had already vetoed this place, so thank you again for your tenacity. Seeing Mom again..." He sucked in a steadying breath. "You have no idea what that means to me."

Grace had a vague idea, but her relationship with her own mother had been challenging. She wasn't sure how she'd feel if her mother's ghost just appeared. Overwhelmed? Sure. Grateful? It was hard to say. "I'm just glad I was able to play a small role in all of this. Congratulations on the house. Should we get going so we can start the paperwork?"

A half hour later, Matt and Grace were in the Landers Realty office and she'd just sent the offer to Mr. Saint. Not even two minutes had gone by before her phone rang. "Excuse me," she told Matt as she got up to take the call in one of the private conference rooms.

"Mr. Saint. Hello. Congratulations on the full-price offer. Did you have questions?" she asked him.

"Is this for real, Ms. Valentine? The guy is really offering cash at full price?"

"It's definitely real. The buyer isn't interested in playing games. He wants the house. The house wants him and his family. It turns out they have family ties to the previous owners, so they'll be keeping it in the family, so-to-speak. This one is a no-brainer, Mr. Saint. I can't tell you what to do, but if it were me, I couldn't sign fast enough."

"There's not the potential for a bidding war, is there?" he asked, still suspicious.

Grace barked out a laugh. "Absolutely no bidding war. Just a man who knows what he wants. You're not having second thoughts about selling it are—"

"No. No second thoughts. Tell Mr. Dahl it's a deal. I'm sending the electronic contract as we speak."

"Perfect. And congratulations again."

"I'll believe it after closing. But Grace?" he said, using her first name for the first time.

"Yeah?"

"If this is what I can expect from you as a Realtor, I think we might be able to build something special together. I look forward to working with you."

The line went dead, and Grace pumped her fist and let out a cry of victory. Mr. Saint spent an enormous amount of time buying properties and fixing them up. Some of them he rented out, others he flipped. But either way, he was the type of client Realtors salivated over. This was a huge win.

Grace walked out of the conference room with a happy grin on her face. "Congrats, Matt. You are now under contract."

"Excellent. That was easy," he said.

Sure it was, she thought. Full price on a property that had been vacant for so long that the cobwebs in the ceiling corners were multiplying by twelves.

"How about I take you to dinner to celebrate?" Matt suggested. "You know, since my kids bailed on me. It would be nice to have the company of a smart and beautiful woman."

"You're on," Grace said, hooking her arm through his. "Lead the way, Matt Dahl. I'm starving."

CHAPTER TWENTY-FOUR

*G*race tapped away at her computer at Landers Realty. Mr. Saint had accepted Matt's offer on the cottage, and now that she had everything set in motion for the appraisal, inspections, and coordinating with the title company, she'd moved on to thinking about the Victorian. She knew Gigi wanted that house. But she couldn't just sit back and hope an offer came in. That wasn't her style.

Since the house needed to approve of the buyer, she decided online marketing wasn't the way to go and was working on a series of open houses with the intent to invite as many witches as possible. Since the house was seeped in magic, that seemed to be the most logical course of action. And the sooner the better. The house had already been on the market for far too long.

In an effort to think outside the box, Grace composed an email to a master mailing list of witches in the area, inviting them to tour the magical old home that weekend and asking them to bring anyone who might be interested in purchasing a piece of Premonition Pointe's history. She'd just hit send when Nina appeared, hovering over her desk.

"Mr. Landers wants to see you in his office," the assistant said.

Grace glanced up at her and was pleased to see the acne was fading. If she had hexed the younger woman, it was good to know her hex wasn't permanent.

"What are you staring at?" Nina demanded and then touched her fingers to the fading breakout on her chin. "I usually have really clear skin."

"I was just thinking that you looked nice today," Grace said, trying to make peace with the woman. Petty office politics had never been her thing and accidental hexes aside, she really did value a positive work environment.

"Um, thanks." Nina dropped her hand and gestured to Landers' office. "He's waiting for you."

"Thanks." Grace closed her laptop and went to meet with her boss.

"Congratulations, Valentine," Kevin Landers said, meeting her just outside his door. "It looks like you definitely have the chops to work at Landers Realty, and anyone who can sell one of the haunted properties at full asking price is on her way to being a star."

He moved to Nina's desk and picked up one of the full champagne glasses that had been prepared. "Nina, pass these around, will you?"

"Sure, boss." Nina strode over on her impossibly high heels and made sure everyone in the office had a glass, including Owen, who had snuck in when Grace hadn't been paying attention. Grace smiled at him, but then frowned when he averted his gaze. What was that about? Normally Owen was flirty at all times. But it seemed like he was irritated with her. Or maybe she was just reading too much into it. It was possible he just wanted to keep the office professional and if that was the case, she certainly didn't blame him. In fact, she was one hundred percent on board.

Nina shoved a glass of champagne into Grace's hand and whispered, "He never does this, you know. Never. You must've really impressed him."

Grace blinked. Had Nina just complimented her? She had. Maybe Nina was ready to drop the office bullshit, too. "Thanks, Nina. I appreciate it."

She nodded and moved on until everyone had their own glass.

Landers raised his glass in the air and said, "A toast to our newest and brightest agent. It's not only impressive that Grace managed to get a house under contract within her first two weeks here, but it's also one of the houses this agency has struggled with since the beginning. No one who has taken it on has even come close to finding a buyer, including myself. So cheers to Grace. I think we have a star on our hands."

Her fellow agents all cheered and then downed their champagne. Grace just stood there gaping at her boss.

Landers chuckled. "What is it, Grace? Did you think I wasn't capable of acknowledging good work?"

"I..." She shook her head, stunned. "Sure. But not mine. You did, after all, make my employment conditional on selling one of those houses, knowing full well they are some of the most difficult on the market. And you did it because I used to work with Bill. It's not exactly the best look for you."

He pursed his lips thoughtfully and nodded. "You're right. I did do that. Maybe it wasn't my finest hour, but you did run the office of my biggest rival for two decades, Grace. I needed an easy way to let you go if you turned out to be like Bill."

"What do you mean 'like Bill?'" she asked. "What does that even mean?"

Landers eyed her for a moment before he shrugged and said, "Your ex poaches clients and isn't above coloring the truth significantly if he thinks it will get him the sale. That's not how we work here. I needed to make sure you didn't have those same tendencies."

Grace wanted to deny his accusations about Bill but couldn't. He was on the nose about her ex. Those were two things they'd argued over plenty of times, with Bill always insisting that she was making a big deal out of nothing. And he did his best to hide his actions from her, so she had no idea just how many times he'd crossed the ethical lines, only that she was in no way surprised that he did. "That's fair," Grace said. "I hope I've proven to you that I'm not him and that just because his ethics are lacking that doesn't mean mine are, no matter how many years I worked there."

"So far, Grace," Landers said, "you've exceeded my every expectation. Consider your conditions of employment lifted even if for some reason this sale doesn't go through. You're the type of agent a firm needs to keep on staff. I hope you like it here well enough to not go out on your own, because you're one I'd rather have on my team instead of the other way around."

She couldn't keep herself from beaming. "Thank you. That means a lot."

He gave her another small salute with his glass and said, "Now get back to work. We all have properties to move."

Grace and Nina both chuckled, but the rest of the staff had already gone back to doing their own work. It was just as well. Grace didn't need them eavesdropping on her conversation with the boss. She nodded to Nina and then crossed the room to talk to Owen.

"Hey," she said. "Looks like you're going to have to put up with me for good now."

"Looks like it," he said, but he didn't look up from his computer.

What was happening here? This was more than just not flirting at the office. This was starting to feel an awful lot like the cold shoulder. "Are you all right?"

"Sure." This time he did glance up at her. "Congratulations on the sale of the cottage. Looks like you'll now have an opportunity to see more of Matt Dahl once the sale goes through."

Grace frowned. She was about to ask what he meant by that when Nina called, "Grace? Vince Hill is on the phone. He says Gigi Martin is ready to make an offer on the Victorian, but she wants to see the house one last time before Vince turns in the paperwork."

"What? You're kidding!" Grace glanced at Owen. "Can I call you later? Maybe we can get dinner."

"Sure, Grace." This time he sounded more like himself. "Good luck with the house."

She smiled at him and then hurried to get Vince's call.

* * *

"Hi, Vince," Grace said, striding up the steps onto the porch of the large Victorian. She was surprised he'd beat her there since he was from a neighboring town. "You made good time."

"Gigi was in a hurry," he said, taking her hand in both of

his. His crooked smile and brown eyes were warm as he smiled at her. "Hopefully we can get this done tonight."

"I'm all for that." Grace glanced at the open front door. "Is Gigi inside?"

"Yeah. I hope you don't mind. We used the lockbox."

"Not at all. Should we go in or give her some more time?" Grace didn't want to rush Gigi. But she wanted to be around to answer questions should any come up.

"We can go in. I think this was more of a ritual thing." He winked at her and added, "You know how witches are."

Grace chuckled. It was no secret that Grace was a witch, as were many of the permanent residents of Premonition Pointe. Her kind naturally flocked to the magical town.

They found Gigi standing at the back door, staring out at the churning ocean. And to Grace's surprise, there were also two transparent ghosts in the shape of women flanking her on both sides.

She blinked. Yep. Still there.

""When you weren't able to find out who the spirits were who lived here, I did a little digging of my own," Gigi said absently. "They couldn't let just anyone buy this place." She turned to face Grace and Vince. "They needed a witch who was willing to share their space, not someone who wanted to displace them."

The two ghosts nodded their agreement and moved just a little closer to her.

"After the smudgings, they got kind of upset," Gigi explained. "That's when the Hannigan sisters combined their powers to accelerate the decay out front." The woman chuckled softly. "I can't say I blame them. They lived here first after all."

Grace let out a small gasp of surprise. "The Hannigan sisters? That's who's here?"

The forms of the two ghosts solidified briefly, showing Grace two lovely young women dressed in high-waisted dresses with untamed curls that would have been completely out of the norm for women of their social class. But witches never really did follow the rules. The one on the right smiled at Grace, while the one on the left smirked.

"It's nice to meet you both," Grace said, meaning it. "I apologize for the smudgings. Dealing with occupied homes is new for me. But I'm beginning to understand that finding the right buyer is far superior to forcing friendly spirits out of their homes." Bill had been afraid of ghosts and had actively turned down clients trying to sell haunted real estate, so it wasn't something she'd run into before. "I know better now."

The two ghosts faded back into the ether, leaving Gigi looking angelic with the light glowing around her.

"I'm ready to sign the paperwork, Vince," Gigi said, moving toward the counter where there was a folder waiting. The glowing light moved with her, and it was then that Grace realized the light was actually coming from Gigi and not the sun outside.

"I don't think I've ever seen a witch look so radiant," Grace said.

Gigi glanced up at Grace and said, "You know, I could say the same about you."

Grace glanced down to see a tiny sheen of golden magic clinging to her skin. She let out a small gasp. "Where is that coming from?"

"It's a gift from the Hannigan sisters. It means they like you."

Warmth blossomed in Grace's chest, and she had the thought that maybe she'd found her calling. That dealing with haunted properties could be her specialty. Real estate had always come easy for her, but matching challenging properties with the right buyers made her feel useful in a way she hadn't before. For the first time since her divorce, she started to feel settled. No matter what happened in her personal life, she had a career she loved, wonderful friends, and a niece she adored. Life was only going to get better.

Grace watched as Gigi pulled a fancy ballpoint pen out of her bag and opened the folder with the contract. After scanning it, she put her pen to the paper and signed.

"Gigi!" James Martin stormed into the house and stalked toward his wife. "What are you doing here?" Before she could answer, he glanced down at the paperwork and let out a low growl as he grabbed it and tore it up.

"James!" Gigi tore the paper out of his hands. "What do you think *you're* doing? This doesn't have anything to do with you."

"I'm your husband," he bellowed. "I told you no. We aren't getting this house."

All of the good feelings that had filled Grace a moment earlier vanished. She'd thought James was going to be a problem. Real estate transactions never went smoothly when spouses weren't on the same page. She cleared her throat, intending to offer a cooling off period, but before she could get the words out, James grabbed Gigi by the arm and started to drag her across the house.

"Whoa, man," Vince said, rushing over to them. "What are you—"

James's fist flew and landed on the side of Vince's head, sending him crashing to the ground.

Grace stared at Vince in horror as blood ran from a cut on his cheek. She rushed to his side, using the hem of his shirt to staunch the bleeding. "Vince?" she said softly. "You okay?"

The other Realtor opened his eyes and winced. "Jesus. What the hell just happened?"

"Gigi's husband just clocked you."

He groaned and rolled to his side.

"That's what you'll get too if you don't mind your own business," James warned Grace as he grabbed Gigi with both hands and hauled her off her feet.

"Oh my god! Let go of me," Gigi demanded at the same time that Grace cried, "Hey! Get your hands off her." Grace didn't give one flying pig if he was Gigi's husband. No man had the right to lay hands on a woman.

James threw Gigi over his shoulder in a fireman's carry and started to run out of the house.

Magic sprang to Grace's fingertips. Before she could think too hard about it, she rushed after the couple and grabbed James's arm. Her magic shot into him like a bolt of lightning, causing him to immediately let go.

Gigi fell from his shoulder, and Grace was sure she was going down, but something—or someone—caught her and settled her on her feet.

"You bitch!" James turned his ire on Grace as he reached for her, his eyes red and wild with anger. "No one interferes with me and my wife. No one. Got it?"

Fear and sheer determination coiled in her gut, and before she even knew what she was doing, Grace launched herself at him, her hands outstretched. But before she could grasp onto him, the spirits of the house picked him up and threw him across the room. Grace stumbled and fell to one knee while the man hit the wall, hung there for a few seconds and then slid to the floor. He fell in a heap, knocked out cold.

Silence filled the space, and all Grace heard was the rush of blood in her ears. Had she really gone after Gigi's husband? What had she been planning to do, scratch his eyes out? Hex him with an STD? Cause an acne breakout all over his body? She had no idea, but one thing was for sure; she wasn't going to stand around and let him abuse his wife. Not on her watch.

"Thank you, ladies," Gigi said, sounding a lot less shaken than Grace felt.

Grace got to her feet and cleared her throat. "Are you all right?" she asked Gigi.

"Yeah," she said softly. "Thanks for that. I was just so stunned my fight or flight reflex got stuck and turned me into a deer in the headlights."

"You're welcome, but I think it's the Hannigan sisters you should be thanking," Grace said, annoyed that her voice was shaking.

The two ghosts appeared briefly and then vanished again. Likely they'd used up most of their energy and were running on fumes.

Grace fished her phone out of her pocket and called 911. Once the first responders were on their way, she slipped her hand into Gigi's. "Come on. Let's get Vince and get out of here before he wakes up."

Gigi glanced at Vince and winced. He was sitting upright now, holding his head in his hands. "Vince, are you okay to stand up?"

"I think so." The pair of them helped the other Realtor to

his feet, and then the three of them left the house to wait outside.

Gigi sat next to Vince on the porch steps. No one said anything for a few moments. Then Gigi turned to Vince and said, "I'm gonna need you to print that contract again."

He blinked at her. "Are you sure? What about James? If he's going to make trouble for you, it might be in your best interest to wait a bit."

As much as Grace wanted Gigi to have the house, she had to agree with Vince. If Gigi ended up pressing charges against her husband or filing for divorce, a new real estate purchase was just a complication she didn't need.

"He doesn't have any say in this," Gigi said, her expression made of steel. "My family trust is purchasing this place. James doesn't have any rights to that money or any of its holdings. I want this house, Vince. It doesn't matter what he wants. Besides, after that nightmare in there, once our family lawyer gets ahold of him, what property I purchase will be the least of his worries."

"All right," Vince said quietly. "I can email you the electronic forms if you want."

"Now that the jackass ruined my signing ritual, I think that's fine. I don't want to wait."

So while they sat on the porch and waited for the police to arrive, Vince pulled out his phone and send her e-docs to sign. A few minutes later, Grace had the offer in her inbox.

CHAPTER TWENTY-FIVE

"*L*ex?" Grace called from the kitchen. She stared at the turnovers her niece had prepared for her and frowned. They hadn't been baked yet, and Grace didn't have the first clue what temperature to use or how long they needed to be in the oven. "What am I supposed to do with these pastries?"

"I left the instructions on the note on the fridge," she called back.

"Right." Grace walked over to the refrigerator and scanned the directions. Twenty-five minutes at four hundred degrees. She could handle that. "What about the glaze?"

Footsteps sounded on the tiled kitchen floor, announcing Lex's arrival. "No glaze, remember? I already brushed them with egg and sprinkled the powdered sugar on them, so you won't have to worry about that. Just put them in the oven when you sit down to eat, and they should be done right about the time you're finished with dinner."

Grace eyed her gorgeous niece. Her short hair was styled with some sort of product to tame her curls just enough that they were artful instead of unruly. The purple eye makeup made her blue eyes seem almost sapphire. And she was wearing ripped skinny jeans with a feminine floral blouse that was just the right amount of juxtaposition to be interesting. "You look fantastic."

"Thanks. Bronwyn is taking me to a poetry reading and then to a late dinner with some of her college friends. I wasn't really sure what to wear, so I went with some version of modern bohemian. Am I pulling it off?"

Grace laughed. "Hell if I know. But if I was a young lesbian, I'd date you. If we weren't related, obviously."

Lex cackled. "Stop. Let's not go there."

"Fine." Grace pulled two plates out of the cabinet. "I already have enough to worry about trying to navigate my own situation."

"What's to navigate? Owen's coming over. You'll eat, talk, laugh, and then rip each other's clothes off and finally do something about that sexual tension that threatens to suffocate everyone who's in the same room with you. And if you're lucky, he'll give you multiple orgasms. Sounds like a win to me."

Butterflies took up residence in Grace's stomach. Would it be that easy? Owen had been distant in the three days since the incident with Gigi and the Victorian. She'd been so shaken up after the altercation that she'd forgotten to call Owen that night, and it was obvious he was hurt by it. She'd explained and he'd said he understood, but he'd been keeping his distance a little, and she figured their fling that hadn't ever gotten off the ground was probably getting ready to come to an end.

She'd decided to try one more time, but even she wasn't sure moving forward was the right thing to do. If he was going to get upset because of scheduling issues, then it wasn't a relationship she was interested in, even if he was so hot that she kept dreaming about him running his hands and tongue all over her. Grace shivered just thinking about him.

"See, Aunt Grace? That's a good sign. You're getting all worked up just thinking about him," Lex teased.

"Ugh. Am I that obvious?"

"Yep." Lex cackled. "Sorry. You might want to work on your poker face if you don't want everyone to know what you're thinking."

Grace never had been good at keeping a straight face. She figured at forty-five that wasn't going to change much. She glanced at the clock and then shooed her niece out of the house. "Owen will be here any minute, and if you don't get going, you're going to be late. Thanks for the help with dinner."

"No problem. I have to pay rent somehow." She kissed Grace on the cheek and rushed out the door.

Not even five minutes later, Owen arrived.

"Hey," she said almost shyly as she opened the door. He stood on her porch, freshly shaven, his hair neatly trimmed, and had a faint, enticing spicy scent. Her mouth watered just looking at him. "You look great."

"So do you," he said as he walked in and gave her a light kiss on her cheek. "These are for you."

She took the small bouquet of sunflowers he'd been holding behind his back and beamed. "How did you know these are my favorite flower?"

He shrugged one shoulder. "I have my ways."

Maybe this date was going to go a lot better than she'd feared. Smiling to herself, she led him into the kitchen where she put the flowers into a vase and then placed them on her already set table. "They look perfect there."

"*You* look perfect," he said as he leaned against the bar.

Her cheeks heated and she knew she was blushing, but she didn't care. She liked this guy and wanted him to know it. "Wine?"

"Sure."

Grace poured them both a glass and got busy plating the crab-stuffed halibut Lex had made for them. Once she was done, she popped the turnovers into the oven and then beckoned for Owen to join her at the table.

"Dig in," she said.

"This looks amazing, Grace. I didn't know you could cook like this," he said and then took a bite. His eyes rolled to the back of his head as he moaned in pleasure.

The sound did all kinds of things to her lady parts. She just sat there watching him until he focused on her again.

"It tastes as amazing as it looks," he said.

She grinned at him. "Thanks, but my niece made it. I was just the sous chef who was mostly in the way."

"Can I adopt her?" He took another bite, and the look on his face made her want to drag him to her bedroom right that second.

"She's twenty-two," Grace said, digging into her own fish. It was just as fantastic as he said it was, and she wondered if she could entice Lex to live with her indefinitely.

"Bummer." They talked and flirted their way through dinner, and eventually they moved to the living room where they sat next to each other on the couch.

"I missed this," Grace said.

"Missed what?" Owen took a sip of his wine.

"This." She waved a hand between the two of them. "We didn't really talk much this week. I missed it."

"Oh." His smile vanished, and he gazed at her as if he were trying to work something out.

She put her wine glass down on the coffee table and asked, "What's going on in that brain of yours?"

He sighed. "I'm just trying to figure out what exactly it is you missed. Me, the flirting, or the attention?"

Grace sat back, stunned at his question and a little offended. "Before I answer, can I ask where that came from?"

"Dammit. I didn't want to do this tonight." He ran a hand through his hair and glanced around the room before meeting her gaze again. "The other night when there was the altercation with that client's husband, you forgot to call me. Worse, when something bad happened, you didn't even *think* to call me. Who did you call that night, Grace?"

She frowned as she recalled what she did after she'd gotten home from making her report with the police and checking in on Vince after he was released from the care of the EMT. She'd gotten herself a cup of tea and curled up in bed. She had to admit, her first instinct was to call Bill. They had been married for twenty years after all. But she'd refrained and called her girlfriend instead. "I only called Joy."

"But not the guy you were dating? Did it even occur to you that I'd hear about the incident and be worried?" he asked.

Actually, it hadn't. Not that night. Calling him had completely slipped her mind. And in the morning, when she realized she'd be the talk of the town and the office, she hadn't called him then either. She'd waited for him to call her.

When she didn't answer him, he sighed. "I sometimes get

the vibe that you like being out with a younger guy more than you actually like being out with me."

Okay, Grace might have been a little thoughtless when it came to communicating with him, but she was just offended by his comment. She stood up just to put some distance between them and said, "So you don't think I like you for you? That I was just in this for a fling with a younger guy. Is that it?"

"The thought crossed my mind, yeah." His expression was guarded as he watched her pace her living room.

"So, what? You came over here tonight to have dinner with me, thinking that even if I wasn't all that into you that, at the very least, you'd get laid?" Her words sounded harsh to her own ears, but there was no taking them back now.

Anger flashed through his gorgeous dark eyes as he got to his feet. "Is that really what you think of me? If so, maybe you should just stick to dating your client Matt Dahl. He seems like the type of guy that you probably should be dating anyway."

"What the..." Grace trailed off and just stared at him for a moment before she shook her head. "What is it with you and this thing about Matt? I'm not dating him. I've never been dating him."

"Then why did I see you at Crabby's with him that night you canceled on me?" he asked, staring her down with an intensity she hadn't seen from him before.

"You were at Crabby's?" she asked, completely taken aback by his comment. She hadn't seen him. If she had, she would've invited him to join them. If it was an actual date, she'd never have done that.

"Grace," he said, shaking his head. "If you want to date someone else you think is more appropriate, just tell me."

"I..." She trailed off because she didn't know what to say. The truth was she did have thoughts that she should be dating someone closer to her own age. But there was also the fact that she was really attracted to Owen. Was that all she wanted from him? How should she know? She hadn't dated anyone in over twenty years. "I guess I thought we were just getting to know each other and having a little fun."

"I think I should go." He strode to the door and paused. "It's probably better if we just remain friends and coworkers. I was never looking for just a casual hookup. As uncool as it might sound, and despite the fact that I wasn't ready to marry my last serious girlfriend, I'm a relationship guy. And I think I'm just not the person you're looking for. Goodnight, Grace."

Grace just stood there in her living room as he gently shut the door behind him. It wasn't until she heard his car pull away from the curb that she realized she'd never explained her dinner with Matt. It hadn't been a date. It had been a Realtor taking her client out for food after signing paperwork. But surely Owen would know that, right? Didn't he ever take his clients out?

Her head started to ache. With her heart heavy, she wandered back into her kitchen to look for some ibuprofen and groaned when the rancid scent of burnt pastry hit her nose.

"Dammit!" She'd forgotten to set the timer for the turnovers. After she pulled the ruined dessert from the oven, she tossed them in the trash and felt the first tear spill down her cheek as she retreated to her bedroom.

Her chest ached with sadness and disappointment as she stripped out of her clothes and climbed into bed. The fresh sheets were crisp and cool and only made her more depressed. When she'd changed them earlier that day, she'd thought Owen would be joining her. Instead, he'd left because her communication skills sucked, and he'd picked up on enough of her insecurities that he'd felt like she wasn't taking him seriously.

Was she taking him seriously? No. Not really. But she was recently divorced. She hadn't been looking for anything resembling a relationship, let alone anything serious. Maybe he was right to leave. If so, then why was she so sad?

Grace rolled over and stared at the clock. It was only eight-thirty. She grabbed her phone and was about to send a text to Owen to apologize and ask if they could talk, but the screen flashed with a text from Alyssa.

Alyssa: *I need a ride ASAP. It's urgent. Can you come get me?*

Grace: *Where are you?*

Alyssa: *Urgent care.*

CHAPTER TWENTY-SIX

*A*lyssa sat in the passenger seat of Grace's SUV, cradling her arm. As near as Grace could tell by the few words her sister had spoken, she and Charlie had gotten into a physical fight, and she'd come away with a black eye and a sprained elbow. The doctor at the urgent care had put her arm in a sling and told her it would be about three weeks until it healed.

"Did you make a report?" Grace finally asked.

"No." Alyssa's voice was flat, void of any emotion as she stared out the window.

"Do you want to?"

Alyssa turned slowly toward Grace. "You're actually asking me what I want to do? Not telling me?"

Grace stifled a sigh. "Of course I'm asking you. You've been through hell tonight, Lyssa. I don't want to make you do anything you aren't comfortable doing."

Alyssa didn't say anything until they pulled into Grace's driveway and Grace killed the engine. Finally, she whispered, "Thanks."

Grace's heart shattered into a thousand pieces when she heard the vulnerability in her sister's voice. Yes, they had their share of disagreements, but Grace loved her sister fiercely, and it was taking all of her willpower to not drive over to Alyssa's house and strangle the bastard who'd hurt her.

"Come on. Let's get you inside." Grace released her seatbelt, jumped out of the vehicle, and was opening her sister's door before Alyssa could even release her own belt. "I've got it." She reached across her sister, undid the belt, and then helped her to her feet.

Alyssa winced as she made her way up the walk and was breathing hard by the time Grace got her settled on the couch. Kneeling down in front of her sister, Grace asked, "What is it you need from me right now? Should I call the cops? Get you tea? Find something for you to punch? Anything. You name it, and I'll make it happen."

Tears filled Alyssa's eyes and fell unchecked down her cheeks.

Grace gently wiped them away while murmuring soothing words about how everything was going to be okay now and that Grace was there no matter what.

Finally, Alyssa choked out, "I need Lex."

"You got it." Grace had held off on calling her niece until she knew what to expect. Alyssa's initial text just said she was at urgent care. It wasn't until she got there that Grace realized her sister had been assaulted by Charlie. Honestly, if she'd called Lex right then, it would've been bad. Really bad. Because Grace had been full of hateful rage. She still was if she was honest, but she'd had to calm down for her sister. "I'll call her now."

Alyssa rubbed at her red eyes and sniffed, trying to get

herself under control. "Don't tell her what happened over the phone. I don't want her upset while driving."

"I have to tell her something," Grace said.

"Just tell her... I don't know. Anything other than Charlie tried to break my arm."

"Got it." Grace disappeared into her room and dialed Lex's number.

"Aunt Grace? What's wrong?" Lex asked.

She should've known Lex would realize something wasn't right. Grace never called her at ten o'clock at night. "Can you come home? It's your mom. She had an accident and—"

"What happened?" There was a rustling on the other end of the line, indicating that Lex was up and moving.

"She has a sprained elbow and a black eye, but she's gonna be okay. She just needs to see you."

"It was Charlie, wasn't it?" Lex barked into the phone. "I knew that guy was going to go after her one day."

Grace sighed. There was no use lying. "Yes. It was Charlie. But Lex, please be careful driving home and do not, under any circumstances, stop by your mom's house. Do not engage Charlie in any way, got it?"

Lex let out a low growl and relayed the information to Bronwyn. After a short lecture from Bronwyn, she said, "Fine. But if he crosses my path—"

"Grace?" Bronwyn's voice came over the line.

"Yeah, I'm here," Grace said.

"I've got this. I'll bring Lex home and make sure she stays out of trouble."

"Thank you." Grace ended the call and headed back out to check on her sister.

* * *

"MOM?" Lex called the moment she stepped into the house.

"I'm right here, baby," Alyssa said, her voice cracking with emotion.

Lex ran to her mother and buried her head in her lap as she held on, clutching her tightly. "That bastard. I hope you ripped his dick off for this."

To Grace's surprise, Alyssa barked out a laugh. "No need for that, baby doll. Your aunt took care of that for me."

"What?" Grace's eyes went wide in surprise. "Why do you say that?"

"Sit down, Grace," her sister ordered.

And because Grace was dying to know what her sister had to say, she did as she was told.

"You, too, Bronwyn," Alyssa said.

Grace glanced up to find Bronwyn standing by the front door, clearly not sure what to do.

Bronwyn cleared her throat. "I think maybe I should go and let you three talk."

"No," Alyssa said mildly. "This is family business, and you're Lex's family. So please, take a seat unless..." She glanced down at Lex. "I don't mean to overstep. Do you want Bron to stay?"

"Yes," Lex said, staring at her girlfriend with pleading eyes.

"All right," Bronwyn said softly and moved around the couch to take a chair next to Grace.

"The fight with Charlie broke out because he was talking shit about you, Grace," Alyssa said. "I told him to stop ranting about my sister, and that's when he lost it."

Grace wasn't surprised to hear that Charlie wasn't her biggest fan. She just didn't know what she'd done that had set him off that night. It wasn't like she'd seen or spoken to him since the night they'd catnapped the cat. "Why was he mad?"

"Because you cursed his penis, and now he can't get a full erection." Alyssa gave her sister a wry smile. "Thanks for that, by the way. I've never been happier to hear that news in my life."

"What?" Lex and Bronwyn said at the same time as both their heads swiveled in her direction.

"Um, it was kind of an accident," Grace said.

"What does that mean?" Lex asked, frowning.

"I..." Grace cleared her throat. It was really strange to be talking about her sister's boyfriend's penis with her sister and her niece. *Awkward.* "You know that night we went to get the cat?"

"Yeah?" Lex said warily.

"Well, I had a little chat with him and told him I wished he had erectile issues for the rest of his life. I thought it was just talk, but I recently learned that when my ire is up, my wishes have been turning into actual curses. Total accident."

"Who else have you cursed?" Alyssa asked.

"Bill and Shondra, oh, and Nina at work. But that curse wore off. I'm not sure about Bill and Shondra's."

"Good lord, what did you curse them with?" Alyssa asked.

"Erectile disfunction—"

"That seems to be a favorite of yours," Bronwyn said.

Grace chuckled. "Yeah, when it comes to assholes, sure. Shondra was unlucky and ended up with genital warts."

All three of them gasped.

"Aunt Grace," Lex said, sounding scandalized. "That's terrible."

"I know. Like I said, I had no idea my wishes were coming true. But then Nina got acne after I wished it on her, and

Jackson told me he heard a rumor about Shondra cheating and that due to her genital warts there was no denying it. My anger management issues were a little out of control, and my uncharitable thoughts turned into actual curses."

Alyssa snorted her amusement. "I'm not sure what Nina did, but the other three certainly deserved what they got."

Grace grimaced. "I don't care about Charlie, but I need to make a neutralizing potion for Bill and Shondra. They were assholes to me, but that doesn't mean I'm comfortable stooping to their level."

"You didn't really if it was just an accident," Bronwyn reasoned.

"Sure, but now that I know…" Grace lifted her hands palms up. "I need to reverse any lingering effects."

"It's the right thing to do," Alyssa agreed. "But don't you dare do anything about Charlie. That bastard deserves to rot."

"What happened tonight, Mom?" Lex asked, moving to sit next to Alyssa on the couch.

"Oh, baby." Alyssa closed her eyes, and when she opened them, there was real pain in her expression. "I'm so sorry. I owe you such a huge apology."

"Mom, I—"

"Shh, now. I've been a terrible mother this past year. The things I've said to you about Jackson, my dismissive comments about you and Bronwyn. I know I've hurt you. When Charlie parroted my words back to me tonight, I heard them. Really heard how that talk about Jackson must've felt to you, and I just…" Her words got caught on a sob. "You deserve so much better. You and Bronwyn both do. I'm so sorry." Alyssa reached over and hugged her daughter with her one good arm. "Can you forgive me?"

"I... um, think so," Lex said as she met Bronwyn's eyes. Bronwyn nodded and gave her girlfriend a reassuring smile.

"Okay." Alyssa pulled back and dabbed at her eyes again. "I'm sorry. I'll do better."

Grace was skeptical that her sister wouldn't hurt Lex again with thoughtless comments, but it was a start. And that's what mattered.

"Mom, you still haven't really told us what happened tonight," Lex said, and Grace was grateful she knew how to keep Alyssa on track.

"Oh. Charlie was drinking again." Alyssa wrinkled her nose in disgust. "I'd had it. The man hasn't worked in I don't know how long, so I told him to get his ass out. That's when he blew up and started talking shit about Grace and then you. When I told him to knock it off, he said why and started shouting at me all the things I'd said to you as if I was just as bad as he was. But the worst was when he started talking about how he should've moved on to you and Bronwyn already, that I was too old and boring, and that it was too bad the hot piece of ass had already moved out."

Grace's stomach turned. Charlie was such bad news she couldn't understand why her sister hadn't thrown him out earlier. She imagined he was usually better behaved around his cash cow and kept most of his sick comments to himself. But she was glad Alyssa had finally had enough.

"It was then that I hauled off and decked him," Alyssa said, her voice strong and full of ire. "No one talks about my daughter like that. No one."

"That's why you don't want to talk to the police," Grace said, understanding that Alyssa had assaulted him first.

"That's right. And if you don't mind, can I stay here for a while until I can find a new place? The lease is up on that house at the end of the month. If I just move out, Charlie will have to move somewhere else or face getting evicted, and it won't be my problem anymore."

"Of course you can," Grace said. "The couch is free, or if you want, you can share my bed. Lord knows, no one else is."

"Is that what you were waiting for?" Lex asked Alyssa. "For the lease to expire?"

Alyssa nodded. "I knew months ago I was done. I just didn't know how to leave safely. Baby, I'm sorry I put you in that situation. And I know I dismissed a lot of your concerns. I was wrong. I had my reasons, but I was wrong."

Grace gestured for Bronwyn to follow her into the kitchen. It was time to let mother and daughter have a little privacy.

"I think I'm going to go," Bronwyn said softly once they were out of earshot of Lex and Alyssa.

"You don't have to," Grace said. "I know Lex wants you here."

"I know. But they need time, and I'm just a distraction. I don't want to be in the middle of that. Tell Lex to text me later when she's ready. I'll be up."

"I will." Grace gave the other woman a hug and then watched her slip out the back door. Then before she lost her nerve, she grabbed her phone and made a call to the police tip line to let them know who they might want to start watching if they wanted to crack down on the drug problems in Premonition Pointe.

CHAPTER TWENTY-SEVEN

*G*race spent the next three days close to home, fussing over Alyssa and making sure her sister had everything she needed to heal after her altercation with Charlie. Lex had taken time off work, too, and she cooked all of her mom's favorite meals. The three of them spent the days playing cards, taking short walks on the beach, and talking about how to move forward. The conversations weren't easy for anyone, especially Lex and Alyssa. The two had a lot of trust to rebuild. But Grace was confident that with some work they could get there.

For the first time since Grace's split with Bill, she started to feel like she had a real family again. Alyssa's ordeal with Charlie made Grace furious every time she thought about that man laying hands on her. But she couldn't regret the outcome. She had her sister back, and for that she was grateful.

On Tuesday afternoon, Grace made her way up the walk of the cute turquoise blue cottage that was just a few streets off the beach. She took a deep breath and knocked. It had been almost two weeks since she'd heard from Hope, and it was time to put this situation with Lucas behind them.

The door swung open, and Hope stood there wearing pajama pants, a stained T-shirt, and big fuzzy puppy slippers. She rolled her eyes at Grace and said, "I figured I'd be seeing you sooner rather than later."

"I would've warned you, but there seems to be something wrong with your phone," Grace said as she swept past the woman who looked like she hadn't showered in days.

"There's nothing wrong with my phone," Hope admitted as she followed Grace into her small vintage kitchen. "I just wasn't answering it."

"I know." Grace grabbed the tea kettle and filled it. "When's the last time you had a decent meal?"

Hope shrugged. "I dunno. I had pizza for breakfast."

Grace raised an eyebrow. "That's not… never mind. When's the last time you were dressed and out of the house?"

"Yesterday." Hope sat at her breakfast table. "There was a breakfast banquet I had scheduled. Trust me, I haven't been wallowing for a week or anything. I really have been working hard. When I got home yesterday, I crashed and haven't been able to convince myself to do anything today. I was thinking one day of swimming in my own filth would be just fine… then you showed up."

Grace chuckled. "Fair enough. Still, if you hadn't been ignoring me, you could've avoided this invasion."

"I know." Hope gave her a smile.

Grace laughed. There was no doubt that Hope knew Grace would stop and check on her. By not answering the phone, she hadn't had to swallow whatever anger she was still holding onto in order to ask Grace to come by. "So, spill it. What's going on with you and Lucas?"

"Nothing."

Grace prepped two tea mugs and set them on the table. "Then why are you wallowing in your pajamas?"

"Because I'm angry he's back. My life was perfect. I was happy. Carefree. Now all I do is think about how he left fifteen years ago. And I hate it. I'm independent, dammit. Ask anyone. I date guys who need to figure out how to move on after devastating breakups and loss. I teach them how to love again and then send them off to find the next love of their life. And now here I am, wallowing about some guy I haven't talked to in ages. It sucks."

"Love is hard," Grace said.

"Is that all you have to say? Love is hard? My life isn't a meme, Grace."

Grace laughed as she poured the hot water into the teacups. When she was done, she sat across from her friend and said, "Sorry. Why don't you tell me what happened back then? Maybe I can be more helpful."

"There's not much to tell," she said with a sigh. "The short version is that he expected me to give up my job, my house, and my coven to follow him across the country to a temporary job that could barely pay the gas bill much less rent." She paused and gave Grace a no-freakin'-way look. "I told him no way. I wasn't giving up my whole life to follow *his* dreams. So he left. And we broke up. End of story."

"Now he's back and he wants… what?" Grace asked.

She shrugged. "To go back to where we were fifteen years ago, I guess. But I'm not that girl, and he's not that guy. If that's what he's after, he's crazy."

"I think he's here to take care of his mom," Grace hedged.

"Oh, sure. He is. But he also wants something from me, and he's not going to get it."

"Okay," Grace said, knowing better than to try to argue any different point of view. "Then it's a no. It is what it is."

Hope slumped back into her chair. "I hate you sometimes."

Grace laughed. "Why?"

"Because you didn't give me any warning. If I'd known he was coming or was here already, I could've prepared. Instead, I just looked like a pissed-off ex who couldn't get it together."

"*Were* you a pissed-off ex who couldn't get it together?" Grace picked up her tea and took a sip.

"Yeah." She ran her fingers through her hair and closed her eyes. After a few moments, she said, "Do you know what it was I wanted back then?"

"Nope. I knew you were working hard to build your art business." Back in those days, Hope had a gallery where she sold paintings and custom portraits of people's pets along with other artists' work. But then she got tired of being tied to a shop, so she sold it and started her party planning business, which was thriving just like the art gallery had been. She was a brilliant businessperson. Grace had no doubt she could do just about anything she put her mind to.

"I wanted a house with enough room for a giant garden, chickens, and maybe goats so I could make my own goat cheese." She chuckled. "That, along with my gallery and spending my nights with Lucas, all seemed like heaven. But then he wanted me to give up everything I'd worked for and I just... Nope. I watched my mom do that for a man. Forget it. I had dreams, too."

"The house sounds lovely, Hope. I can see you doing that," Grace said.

"Yeah. I'd still like to do that, but no room here for goats, or chickens for that matter." She laughed. "Besides, that would be a lot of extra work for just me."

Grace nodded, but in her mind, she was already thinking of how Hope just might get her house with enough room for her animals one day.

"Do you think I can just ignore him, and he'll go away?" Hope asked, bringing the conversation back to Lucas.

"Probably not, but you can try." She reached across the table and squeezed her friend's hand. "You do know that you were right back then to not just pick up and go, don't you?"

"Of course I do," she said, almost defiantly.

"Good. Because if you were second guessing yourself, I wanted you to know I agree with you. If Lucas really expected you to leave everything behind for his dreams while he ignored yours, then he was being a selfish jackhole. Nothing was wrong with him following his dreams, but pressuring you to give up yours was."

Hope stared at her mug for a few beats, and when she looked up there were fresh tears standing in her eyes. "Thanks, Grace. I think I did need to hear that."

THE SUN WAS SETTING when Grace finally pulled into her own driveway. By the time she'd left Hope's, her friend had showered and changed out of her pajamas, eaten a bowl of pasta, and was back to sounding like her sassy, confident self. Grace still didn't think there was any way Hope and Lucas wouldn't end up in some sort of relationship, but that was for them to work out. All she had left to do was find Lucas a house, and now she knew just the one. She took a second to send him the link. A few seconds later, her phone buzzed with an incoming call. She fully expected to see Lucas's name, but instead it was Matt Dahl's name that flashed on the screen.

"Hi Matt. Is everything okay with the house? Closing is tomorrow, isn't it?" With the cash offer, everything had gone really quickly, and as long as there weren't any last-minute disasters, they were good to go as far as she was concerned.

"Yep. Tomorrow. That's not what I'm calling about, though."

"No? What can I do for you?" she asked.

"Actually, I was hoping you might join me for dinner tonight. My sons left town, and I really enjoyed your company that night we went to Crabby's. So, if you're free… how about it?"

Grace sat frozen in her SUV, not really sure how to respond. She hadn't spoken to Owen much since the night their date had gone horribly wrong. Just a few polite hellos at the office. But she still sought him out, looked for his dimple when he was smiling, and had on more than one occasion reached for her phone to text him before thinking better of it. If she did that, she needed to have answers about what she wanted, and she just wasn't sure.

At least she hadn't been. But hearing Matt ask her out on a real date, she felt nothing but dread. It was clear to her now that, given the choice, she'd much rather be with Owen. The man might be ten years younger than her, but he was sweet, attentive, and just made her feel good when she was around him. All he'd asked for was a chance, and she'd never given him one. Not really.

"Grace?" Matt prompted.

"I'm here." *Damn.* It really was too bad she wasn't interested in Matt. She should be. Or at least she used to *think* she should be. He was her age, handsome, successful. But there was no spark. And she deserved a spark, dammit. "Thanks for the offer, Matt, but I think there's somewhere else I need to be."

"You're seeing someone?" he asked.

"Not officially," she hedged. Not at all, really. But she was hoping to change that. "But there is someone else."

"I understand. It was worth a shot. Have a nice night, Grace."

"Thanks. You too."

Knowing what she needed to do, Grace jumped out of her SUV and ran into her house. Fifteen minutes later, she'd fixed her makeup, changed her clothes, and put on her fancy blue witch stilettos. Owen had mentioned them once, hadn't he? Either way, they made her feel sexy, and at that moment she needed that confidence.

Grace climbed back into her vehicle and drove the twelve blocks to Owen's house. She hadn't been inside before, but she had seen the picture of it up in the office as a recent sale and recognized it immediately. It was a beautiful two story, set two streets off the ocean with gorgeous views of the water. She remembered seeing it on the market when she purchased her house, but it had been out of budget.

She parked in front and was relieved to see his BMW in the driveway. Now she just had to pray that he was home alone. If he had a date, she'd be mortified. Pushing those negative thoughts out of her head, she made her way up to the porch and rang the doorbell. It took a few moments, but suddenly, there he was in his dark jeans and a tight T-shirt that stretched across his well-defined chest.

Holy hell. He was sexy as hell when he was dressed down.

Grace licked her lips before finally raising her gaze to meet his eyes.

"Good evening," he said with a knowing chuckle.

"Dammit," she muttered and laughed at herself. "You look far too good in that T-shirt."

"Should I take it off?" he teased as he opened the door wider and waved her in.

"That's… probably not the best idea if you want to hear what I came here to say," she said honestly. Because seriously, she was about five seconds from throwing herself at him.

"Okay. Shirt stays on then." He led her into the living room and paused at the stairs. "Do you want to go up where we have a view of the water while we talk?"

"Yes. That sounds perfect." She followed him up the wooden staircase and into a sitting area that was furnished with a comfortable white couch and two matching chairs, each of them positioned for optimal viewing of the Pacific Ocean. "This is incredible, Owen."

"It really is, isn't it?" He walked over to a small wet bar off to the side. "Do you want something to drink?"

"Um, just water, I guess."

He grabbed two mini bottles of water and then led her over to the couch. Once they were seated, he turned to her and said, "So, what are you doing here, Grace?"

That was certainly direct, wasn't it? She opened her mouth, closed it, and then shook her head and chuckled. "I didn't think through what I wanted to say."

Owen just nodded and waited her out.

Finally, she blurted, "I don't want to date Matt. Or anyone like Matt. I want to date you."

His eyes widened at her outburst, but then a smile crept over his lips. "Why?"

"Why?" she echoed. "Why not? You're smart, sexy as hell, sweet, charming, a damn fine kisser, and you don't play games. Besides all that, I just like you. You're kind and helpful, and you seem to genuinely like people. Who wouldn't want to date you?"

"Someone who thinks they're too old for me?" he asked, not letting her off the hook so easily.

Grace blew out a breath. "Okay, listen. The age thing... I admit I was having some issues with it. They weren't rational, but they were there. That has everything to do with me thinking about what I *should* be doing and not recognizing what I *want* to be doing, if that makes sense."

He nodded. "I think so."

"And I'm sorry if I made it sound like I was only seeing you for a little fun. I wasn't. That's not who I am either. I was just... flailing a little bit after jumping back into the dating pool."

"What about Matt? Does he know you don't want to date him?" he asked, holding her gaze.

"Oh, for crying out loud! I was never dating Matt. That dinner was me taking a client out after he made an offer. I should have told you that right away, but I was so caught off guard by the conversation I didn't manage to get it out. But besides that, he did call me today and ask me out. I said no because there's someone else I'd rather be with."

"You did?" He reached out and took her hand in his.

"Yeah, I did." Her skin tingled where his fingers were caressing her palm.

"I hope that someone is me. Otherwise, this is going to get awkward really fast," he said in a husky tone.

"It's you, Owen. Definitely."

"Good." He scooted closer, and in the next moment his

lips were on her neck while he buried his other hand in her hair. "You taste so good, Grace."

"I bet it's cinnamon roll glaze," she said absently, practically drunk from the feel of his soft lips on her skin.

He pulled back and chuckled. "Cinnamon roll glaze? What do you do? Use it as a fragrance?"

She snickered. "No, but I will if it keeps you kissing my neck like that."

"You can count on it." He leaned back in and nibbled on her ear. "So, what happened? Did you get into a food fight with your niece or something?"

"Close. My sister threw it at me. She's been staying with us while she looks for a new place."

"Uh-huh," he muttered absently. "It's good you came over here then."

"Why's that?" she breathed.

"Because in about five minutes I'm going to have you completely naked except for those sexy-as-hell shoes, and we don't need an audience when I make you scream my name."

"Oh," she said, already nearly combusting from the heat beneath her skin though he'd barely even touched her. "Okay. Good."

"Okay. Good," he repeated. And then he picked her up and carried her to his bedroom where he made good on his promise. Twice.

CHAPTER TWENTY-EIGHT

*H*ope Anderson sat at the round table near the front of the banquet hall and watched as Grace whispered something into Owen's ear. They were at a luncheon for Landers Realty where Grace was being honored for selling the most houses in the entire region over the summer season. It was a big enough deal that her boss had given a speech, and Grace had been awarded a sizable bonus and a vacation to the Caribbean. Not to mention she was now the top Realtor for any sort of haunted or cursed properties. And as it turned out, Premonition Pointe had a lot more than anyone had realized. Now that someone was able to move them, a lot more were coming on the market, all under Grace's care.

Owen smiled at Grace and whispered something back that made her giggle. The woman actually *giggled*. It was enough to make a lesser person want to vomit.

But Hope was actually thrilled for her friend. Owen was a great guy, and they'd been going strong for the last couple of months. It made her heart full to see Grace thriving after Bill had done her so wrong. In Hope's opinion, Grace never should've spiked Bill and Shondra's coffees with an anti-hex potion last month during the annual beach gala. If it were up to Hope, she'd have just let them deal with their new ailments. When she'd voiced this opinion to Grace, she'd waved her off and said she was cleaning up her karma and moving forward.

Gah. Her friend's heart was much bigger than Bill had ever deserved.

So when Shondra left him two weeks earlier, all Hope could do was laugh. Served him right. Now he had no wife and no one to run his office. Life was going to suck for the man who'd always been taken care of by the women in his life.

"I heard Bill already has himself a new girlfriend," Joy said as if she were reading Hope's mind.

"Really? Who?" Hope asked.

"Some coed who's taking a semester off from college," Grace interjected. "Anyone want to bet he marries her next month and installs her in his office immediately? Now that we're finally legally divorced, there's nothing stopping him."

"Nope. No bet from me. Sounds exactly like something he would do," Hope said.

"Ditto," Joy said.

Owen just laughed. "What a jackass."

"You have no idea." Grace leaned in and gave him another kiss.

Both Hope and Joy looked away. Hope turned to Joy. "How are things with Paul? Any progress in the bedroom?"

Joy sighed. "Nope. Now he's not even talking about it. I swear, one of these days I'm just going to break out the vibrator right in front of him."

Everyone at the table turned to look at her. Joy's cheeks turned pink. "Sorry. TMI, right?"

"Maybe just a little," Grace said.

"Nope," Hope and Owen said at the same time. Then they all laughed.

"I just can't seem to get him interested, and I don't know what else to do," Joy said, staring into her margarita glass.

"Sounds like your only option is couples therapy," Owen said. "Or, the vibrator thing might work."

Joy groaned and downed her drink while everyone else chuckled.

"I'm sorry, Joy," Hope said. "I know our troubles are vastly different, but I commiserate. I haven't had anyone stay over in months." Not since Lucas had waltzed back into town, actually, but she wasn't going to verbalize that.

"What happened to that hottie from down south? He hasn't been up to surf recently?" Joy asked.

"Oh, he has. But I think he has a girlfriend now," she lied. Benji would no sooner tie himself to one person than Hope would. Their arrangement used to work for them until her ex showed up and messed with her head. "It's fine. It's not like I don't know how to take care of myself."

Joy raised her hand for a high five, and Hope slapped it in solidarity.

The group continued to fill each other in on the town gossip. Charlie had been arrested during a drug buy and was currently spending five years in prison. Alyssa was still living with Grace, pretending to look for a place to live. But Grace knew she was really holding off to save money for a down payment on something. It was fine, since Grace was spending most nights at Owen's and Lex stayed over at Bronwyn's new apartment a lot.

Matt Dahl and his sons moved into the white cottage, and Matt was currently fighting off all the single women over thirty. The women of Premonition Pointe all seemed to think he was a catch. All of them except Grace, of course. Gigi Martin filed for divorce, moved into the Victorian, and was now having lunch with Grace, Hope, and Joy once a week. If things kept working out, they were considering asking her to join their coven.

And then there was Lucas. They didn't talk about him. No one did around Hope because she always shut them down. She was aware that he'd purchased a house somewhere in town, but she hadn't bothered to find out where. She was also aware that he was taking care of his mother. Honestly, she admired him for that. If she had to do it, she wasn't sure she or her mother would survive.

Hope's phone buzzed, and when she took a peek, she groaned. It was her mother. Of course it was. Why was it that every time she thought of her mother she heard from her? But Hope knew the answer to that question. They lived in Premonition Pointe. Clairvoyance was an everyday thing.

Hope read the text and felt a moment of panic. *I'm at your house. Going to stay for a few weeks. Where's the extra key?*

She quickly typed back a response, steering her toward the sunflower pot to the right of the door and then adding, *You could've given me some notice. I would've put fresh sheets on the guest bed.*

It was last minute. Sorry, Bunny. I didn't have a choice.

What did that mean? She considered texting again but dropped it. If she was here, she wasn't going anywhere for the foreseeable future. The only thing to do was stay out late and party it up with her friends. Too bad it was only two in the afternoon.

While Hope was busy angsting about her mom's sudden appearance, the rest of her friends had gotten up from the table and were waiting on her. "Is it time to go already?" she asked.

"I thought you were bored out of your mind?" Grace asked with a laugh. "Now you want to stay?"

"No, I just... never mind." Hope rose to her feet and followed her friends outside. Once they were next to Grace's car, Hope pulled her into a hug and said, "I'm proud of you, you rock star Realtor. Good job."

"Thanks, Hope. I love you for coming. I know it was dull," Grace said.

"Nah. Joy and I entertained ourselves, didn't we, Joy?"

Joy snickered. "Yep."

"What did you two do?" Grace demanded.

"Nothing much," Hope said. "We did give out the number of a phone sex operator to everyone who hit on us though. So that should be fun for her. A bunch of new clients. We deserve a kickback, I think."

Owen threw his head back and laughed. "Did I ever mention how much I love your friends?" he asked Grace.

Grace smiled at him. "Glad they entertain you. Now take me back to your place. We have more celebrating to do."

Hope watched them go, and for the first time in forever, she felt a pang of sadness. It wasn't jealousy. It was just an ache for the intimacy they shared. She sighed and walked Joy to her car before heading to her own. Just as she was opening the door, she got a text from her newest client, Against the Grain Interiors.

She'd been contracted to coordinate an open house once a month for the next six months, a grand opening party, and at least two showcases. The contract was shaping up to be one of the largest on her books this year. The only strange thing was that she hadn't met LK in person yet. She thought that was kind of weird, but all the locations and dates checked out. It also helped that the large deposit check had cleared without an issue.

Need to go over some details. Do you have time to meet in person today or tomorrow?

There it was again, that clairvoyance. Hope smiled to herself. *Sure. Today is good. Text me an address, and I'll be right over.*

A moment later, an address popped up on the screen. Hope didn't waste any time. It was either meet with her client or go home to find out why her mother was in town. The client won, hands down.

Hope punched the address in her GPS, and when she got to the home, she let out a gasp. It was the craftsman Grace had finally sold a few weeks earlier. She smiled when she spotted the chicken coop that was already set up and the two golden labs that were running free in the yard. The place was perfect. Just the kind of home she'd always wanted. Now she was dying to meet the owner.

Feeling lighter than she had all day, she strolled up to the front door and knocked.

The door opened almost immediately, revealing none other than Lucas King in all his tattooed glory.

LK.

She gaped at him. "Lucas? What the hell?" Without waiting for an answer, she spun on her heel and started to head back to her car.

"Wait!" He bounded out of his house and moved to stand in front of her, blocking her from getting back in her vehicle.

"I really do need someone to tackle all of my events. This wasn't a ploy to get you out here."

"No? Then why didn't you just tell me who you were?" she asked, sounding bitter to her own ears.

"You know why," he said softly. "You wouldn't have returned my calls, and I'd have been stuck finding someone inferior from fifty miles away."

He was right about that. She was the best damned party planner on the coast. She sighed. "I don't appreciate being lied to."

"I didn't lie... exactly," he said. "I just omitted."

"Same thing," she insisted.

"Maybe. But please, Hope, can't we put us aside for a while and work together? I really need someone I trust to do this. I just don't have the time between my woodworking and my mother. It's been... a lot."

She'd heard about his mom, and her heart was breaking for him. She'd always loved Bell King. The woman was beautiful inside and out. What she hadn't known was that Lucas was now a woodworker. Impressive if his business was as successful as he had made it sound during their emails for the event planning. Judging by his budget, she had to believe he wasn't pulling her chain.

"I don't know if that's such a good idea," she hedged.

"Hope Anderson? Is that you?" a woman called from the porch.

Hope spun and smiled at Lucas's mom. She was so cute in her capri pants and T-shirt that said *Witches rule the world.* "How are you doing, Mrs. K?"

Bell frowned, glanced around, and then disappeared back into the house.

"What—"

"It's the dementia," Lucas explained. "One minute she's fine, and the next, she's not. I have to go check on her."

"Okay."

He paused and then said, "You're not bailing on me, are you? Like I said, I really need the help."

Knowing in her heart that she could never say no to helping him, especially knowing what he was facing with his mother, she said a silent prayer for strength and shook her head. "No. I'll stay."

Those last two words hung in the air, and she knew in that moment both of them were wondering what would've happened if he'd uttered those words fifteen years ago.

Lucas's expression softened, and he said, "Thank you." Then he took her by the hand and led her into the house she'd always envisioned the two of them living in.

DEANNA'S BOOK LIST

Witches of Keating Hollow:
Soul of the Witch
Heart of the Witch
Spirit of the Witch
Dreams of the Witch
Courage of the Witch
Love of the Witch
Power of the Witch
Essence of the Witch
Muse of the Witch

Witches of Christmas Grove:
A Witch For Mr. Holiday
A Witch For Mr. Christmas

Premonition Pointe Novels:
Witching For Grace
Witching For Hope
Witching For Joy

Jade Calhoun Novels:
Haunted on Bourbon Street
Witches of Bourbon Street
Demons of Bourbon Street
Angels of Bourbon Street
Shadows of Bourbon Street
Incubus of Bourbon Street
Bewitched on Bourbon Street
Hexed on Bourbon Street
Dragons of Bourbon Street

Pyper Rayne Novels:
Spirits, Stilettos, and a Silver Bustier
Spirits, Rock Stars, and a Midnight Chocolate Bar
Spirits, Beignets, and a Bayou Biker Gang
Spirits, Diamonds, and a Drive-thru Daiquiri Stand
Spirits, Spells, and Wedding Bells

Ida May Chronicles:
Witched To Death
Witch, Please
Stop Your Witchin'

Crescent City Fae Novels:
Influential Magic
Irresistible Magic
Intoxicating Magic

Last Witch Standing:
Bewitched by Moonlight
Soulless at Sunset
Bloodlust By Midnight

Bitten At Daybreak

Witch Island Brides:
The Wolf's New Year Bride
The Vampire's Last Dance
The Warlock's Enchanted Kiss
The Shifter's First Bite

Destiny Novels:
Defining Destiny
Accepting Fate

Wolves of the Rising Sun:
Jace
Aiden
Luc
Craved
Silas
Darien
Wren

Black Bear Outlaws:
Cyrus
Chase
Cole

Bayou Springs Alien Mail Order Brides:
Zeke
Gunn
Echo

ABOUT THE AUTHOR

New York Times and USA Today bestselling author, Deanna Chase, is a native Californian, transplanted to the slower paced lifestyle of southeastern Louisiana. When she isn't writing, she is often goofing off with her husband in New Orleans or playing with her two shih tzu dogs. For more information and updates on newest releases visit her website at deannachase.com.

Made in the USA
Monee, IL
17 March 2022

93026629R00163